THE EXHAM-ON-SEA MURDER MYSTERIES VOL 1

FRANCES EVESHAM

Boldwood

First published in Great Britain in 2020 by Boldwood Books Ltd.

Copyright © Frances Evesham, 2020

Cover Design by Nick Castle Design

Cover Photography: Shutterstock

A CIP catalogue record for this book is available from the British Library.

Paperback ISBN: 978-1-80483-224-0

Boldwood Books Ltd.

23 Bowerdean Street, London, SW6 3TN

www.boldwoodbooks.com

For my fellow residents in Burnham on Sea, Somerset.

MURDER AT THE LIGHTHOUSE

AN EXHAM-ON-SEA MYSTERY

1

UNDER THE LIGHTHOUSE

The autumn high tide discarded Susie Bennett under the light-house, on the beach she'd avoided for twenty years.

A fierce autumn wind whipped across Exham beach, driving sand rain in Libby Forest's face. It tore at her hood as she trudged across the expanse of deserted beach. The locals knew better than to brave this morning's weather. Libby shivered. Newly arrived in Exham on Sea, she'd underestimated the strength of the storm. She tugged her hood closer, as the wind snapped strands of wet brown hair across her face.

No wonder Marina, one of the handful of people who'd welcomed her to the town, had jumped at her offer to walk Shipley, the Springer Spaniel. Excited by the storm, Shipley pulled at the lead, dragging Libby towards the lighthouse.

She'd never seen a building like it. White-painted, perched on the sand on nine wooden legs, the lighthouse looked hardly strong enough to withstand a breeze, never mind this gale.

The dog ran around Libby, wrapping the lead round her legs. She stepped out of the tangle and hesitated. The dog pulled harder and her arms ached. Marina had forgotten to mention the animal's lack of training.

Could Libby let him run off some of his energy? She didn't want to lose Marina's pet. It seemed hard enough to be accepted in a town like this, where everyone seemed to know other people's business, and Marina was chairman of music club and the history society. Her opinion counted in Exham.

'I'll chance it,' she told the dog. 'You're pulling my arms out of their sockets.'

Free from his lead, the animal raced in excited circles, twirling and spinning, ears alternately flat against his head or standing at right angles, like aeroplane wings.

As Libby squinted into the wind, Shipley skidded to a halt, right by the lighthouse. She ran to catch up, and he barked, whiskers quivering, head pointing.

'What's that?' Libby gasped as she reached his side. 'Looks like an old sack. Still, we'd better take a closer look.' The tide had receded, almost out of sight, leaving a layer of mud surrounding the lighthouse. It stuck to Libby's boots, dragging her down, sucking at her feet as she picked her way to the shapeless bundle, testing every step.

'It's a person. A drunk, I suppose,' Libby said. 'We'd better wake him. He'll freeze, in this weather.'

The drunk lay awkwardly, half supported by one of the lighthouse legs.

Libby braced herself for a mouthful of abuse from the drunk, and shook one of the leather-jacketed arms.

The drunk slid noiselessly to the sand. The spaniel nosed it, whining. 'Quiet, Shipley.' Libby squatted beside the body, brushed sopping wet hair from an icy cheek, and searched the neck for a pulse. 'It's not a man, it's a woman.'

Shipley howled into the gale. Rain beat down on Libby,

sliding into her hood and slipping down her neck, but she hardly noticed. Her stomach felt hollow.

She staggered up, legs trembling. 'It's a woman, and she's dead.'

She scanned the beach, but they were alone. Libby shivered. 'We'd better tell the police.' She tugged a mobile phone from an inside pocket and fumbled, jabbing 999, calling the emergency services.

'Hello, do you need fire, police or ambulance?'

This was only the second corpse Libby had seen, and an image of the first floated into her head. She'd seen her dead husband, Trevor, laid out at the hospital. The memory triggered a painful mix of horror and guilty relief that he was dead and she was free at last.

She wiped her hand across her wet face. This was no time to think about Trevor. She looked closely at the body. Who could it be? A local? No one Libby recognised, but then, she hardly knew anyone here apart from Marina, a few members of the history society and Frank Brown, the owner of Brown the Bread, the bakery where she worked part-time.

Slim and tiny, about Libby's age, the dead woman wore skin-tight jeans. A brown ankle boot encased one foot, but the other was bare, the expensive footwear long gone. The woman's lips were fuller than nature intended. Cosmetic work in the recent past? Drenched hair half concealed a small, neat face with a turned up nose. A line of darker hair, along a parting on the side of the head, suggested highlights; a proper salon job, not a do-it-yourself.

Libby peered into the puddles under the lighthouse, looking for a handbag, hoping for clues, but the sea had left nothing behind.

I shouldn't touch the body again. Libby knew the rules:

everyone did. *Don't disturb the scene.* She should wait for the police to arrive, but something about the woman's arm, tucked at such an awkward angle into a jacket pocket, nagged at Libby. It wouldn't do any harm just to give it another small nudge, surely?

She twitched the sleeve and the arm jerked. Libby, startled, jumped back and almost tripped over Shipley. 'Just rigor mortis,' she muttered. She pulled again, harder. The stiff hand popped out of the pocket, rigid, fingers pointing to the bleak, wide Somerset sky. A chunk of plastic tumbled from the jacket.

Libby whispered, 'Sorry,' as though the dead woman could still hear. Shipley nudged the woman's face, and Libby pulled him back, clipping the lead to his collar.

The sudden, shocking wail of police sirens brought an officer, younger than her own son, running down the beach. Libby held out one hand, as if to protect the body. 'Be careful.'

The young plainclothes officer raised an eyebrow above intense blue eyes and waved an ID card under Libby's nose. 'Detective Sergeant Ramshore. Step over there and leave it to us now, please, madam. We need to clear the scene. The constable, here, will ask you a few questions.'

A female, uniformed police officer led Libby and Shipley along the beach, up a short flight of steps to a seat on the promenade, its roof providing some shelter from the wind and rain. As she answered the officer's gentle questions, Libby gazed through relentless rain, past the tiny pier with its deserted kiosk, to the brightly coloured houses and shops of the town.

The dead stranger still lay, forlorn, on the beach, a small plastic ring with a pink stone tumbled beside her on the sand.

2

COFFEE AND CAKE

'There's no reason to cancel the meeting.' Marina folded her arms, enclosed in the purple sleeves of a wafty silk caftan, across an ample chest. She settled comfortably in her chair and beamed at Libby. 'Folk will arrive in a moment.'

The local history society meeting was due to begin. Libby had dashed home from the beach to Hope Cottage, her new home. She shut Shipley in the hall while she located Fuzzy, her marmalade cat, safe in the airing cupboard, and changed, grabbing the first skirt and jumper she found.

Retrieving the cake she'd baked yesterday, juggling the tin as Shipley pulled on the lead, she hurried past the empty children's play park to return the dog to his owner and deliver refreshments, as promised, for the meeting.

'I'm sorry we took so long,' she'd gasped as Marina opened the door.

'Did you?' The other woman had raised an unconcerned eyebrow. She hadn't been worried about her pet, then.

Marina had taken the lead, winced as Shipley shook water all over her hall carpet, and shooed the dog into a room at the back of the house, closing the door firmly. Libby hoped his bowl was full – Shipley deserved a good feed.

She wished, now, she'd taken more trouble with her appearance. In her hurry, she hadn't bothered to dry her hair properly and it hung in a tangle of brown round her face. She tugged at the hem of her sweater as she told Marina about the dead woman on the beach.

Marina shrugged. 'I expect the woman was on drugs. There's no need for you to worry. The police said they'd keep you informed, so they'll let you know.'

'Yes, but...' Libby wasn't confident Detective Sergeant Ramshore would bother.

'Now, listen to me.' Marina was not the newly retired deputy head of the local primary school for nothing. She understood command. 'You need a distraction, Libby. Come into the kitchen. We'll slice up your cake and forget about this down-and-out.'

'She didn't look like a down-an-out,' Libby mused, waving a knife. 'Her jacket was leather – expensive, I think, but not new.' She remembered the dark roots to the woman's hair but kept that to herself. She felt oddly protective towards the unknown woman.

She was grateful to Marina. The woman had been kind, taking Libby under her wing, and persuading her to join the society. Somehow, and Libby was unsure how Marina had achieved it, she'd talked the newcomer into providing cake for the history society meetings.

'Everyone's sure to love it, dear. People are already talking about your cakes. Frank Brown has never had so many customers, and we're all looking forward to seeing your book.'

'Hmm. If I ever finish it.'

Marina had waved away such nonsense. Writing a book about celebration cakes, full of photographs, must be the easiest way possible to make a living. 'Anyway, you can practice your cakes on us.'

As a result, Libby supplied at least one elaborate confection for each meeting. She had to stand on her own feet now her husband was dead and she needed all the publicity she could get.

Marina sampled a slice of today's contribution, a pineapple and coconut upside-down cake with a cream cheese frosting. 'Delicious. Your best yet.' The doorbell rang. 'There you are.' She beamed. 'It's too late to cancel now. Angela's here.'

Soon, Marina's grand drawing room was full.

'Quite a turn out,' Angela Miles murmured in Libby's ear. 'Almost everyone's braved the rain today. They've heard about your adventure. News travels fast in Exham.'

Libby had only met Angela once before, at a previous society meeting, but she instinctively liked her. While Marina overpowered with her confidence and easy assumption that she knew best, Angela was calm, with a dry sense of humour.

'Good heavens,' she said now. 'Samantha Watson's gracing us with her presence.'

Libby had not met Samantha, but Marina had described her. 'Our resident intellectual. She's a solicitor, and she tells me she can complete the Telegraph crossword in half an hour.' Marina had snorted. 'She also claims to answer most of the questions from University Challenge. If you believe that, you'll believe anything.'

Samantha sashayed into the room. As Marina introduced her to Libby, she let her eyes roam over Libby's unkempt hair and everyday clothes.

'Pleased to meet you,' she murmured, lowered herself into a chair and crossed one long leg over the other. Her sheer tights hissed as she smoothed a tight pencil skirt over shapely knees.

'We don't often see her at these meetings,' Angela murmured. 'Her time's too valuable.'

Libby bit back a laugh as Angela continued, 'She doesn't come to many social occasions with the likes of us.'

'One of my clients cancelled an appointment, so I've just popped in for a minute.' Samantha explained, raising a hand, as though granting the society a favour. 'Such a shame, by the way, another tragedy on the beach.' She glanced at Libby. 'I hear you found the body.'

Marina said. 'A visitor stuck in the mud, I suppose, when the tide came in. How foolish. When will they learn not to go walking over the riverbed?'

Angela explained to Libby, 'You can only see it when the tide goes out. The coast guard often rescue people. They put red flags on the beach, but strangers don't take enough notice. It looks calm, but the sand turns treacherous and it can suck you in.'

Libby shuddered.

'Ships have been caught out, as well. The town's had three lighthouses over the years, to keep them from running aground.'

'Three?'

'The low lighthouse where you found the body, the Round Tower on the esplanade – that's not in use any more, and neither is the High Lighthouse near the sand dunes.'

'Good grief. I thought I was coming to such a safe, quiet little town.'

Angela smiled. 'I don't think any coast is truly safe, do you? When the gales blow in the autumn, you can't ignore the force of nature. I lost a summerhouse last year.'

Marina joined in, 'And my fence blew down. Luckily, I was insured.'

Samantha allowed Marina to place a slice of cake on her plate. She cut it neatly into tiny squares and popped them, one after another, into a lipsticked mouth, a little pink tongue flicking out to chase stray crumbs.

'Quite nice,' she pronounced.

Marina's pent up excitement overflowed. 'Such a shock, finding a body. It gave me palpitations just hearing about it. You must be in *pieces*, Libby dear.' Her voice sunk to a dramatic whisper. 'Imagine, a dead body, lying there all night, out on the beach, in such dreadful weather.'

Samantha cleared her throat to focus attention back on herself. She had a glint in her eyes. 'I spoke to Detective Chief Inspector Arnold on the telephone a while ago.'

Angela murmured, 'So that's why she's come.' She leaned closer. 'Samantha hears all DCI Arnold's secrets.' She whispered, 'Pillow talk.'

'You mean, they're an item?' Libby murmured. 'I'm sure Marina told me she was married to that builder, Ned.'

Angela nodded. 'She was – but I think she finds a senior police officer more to her taste these days. She's something of a social climber – that's why she married Ned in the first place. His family used to own Mangotsfield Hall, the Victorian stately home. One of Ned's ancestors was the earl, but the title died out years ago and the family sold up. You don't often see Ned and Samantha together, nowadays.'

'I rang him the other day. I'm hoping he'll sort out my bathroom in Hope Cottage,' Libby said.

'Hope Cottage,' Marina had overhead. 'Such a dear little place, tucked away in that funny little lane.'

Samantha coughed, raising her voice above the chatter, an edge to her voice. 'Detective Chief Inspector Arnold told me the woman is Susie Bennett.'

A shocked silence followed. A glow lit Samantha's face. She had her audience's full attention now.

Marina's jaw hung open. 'Susie Bennett?'

Samantha beamed; smug mouth curved in a complacent smile. 'That's right, Susie Bennett, the folk singer – or rock singer, was it?' She shrugged elegant, cashmere clad shoulders. 'The Susie Bennett who used to go to school with some of us.' She let her eyes rest on Libby, who was never at school with 'us'. 'The Detective Chief Inspector thinks she committed suicide.'

Seriously? He's already decided? In three hours? Libby pressed her lips together and kept her thoughts to herself.

Everyone in the room seemed to have known the dead woman. Marina gasped. 'Oh good gracious me. Susie Bennett! She hasn't been back for years. Whatever was she doing here?'

Angela set down her cup of tea. 'Libby, Susie is Exham on Sea's most famous export. She went to America and sold millions of records, back in the eighties. She was in a band called Angel's Kiss. I remember, because my name's Angela. Actually, Angel's Kiss was a cocktail, I believe.'

Marina interrupted. 'I remember one of their albums. It came with a drinking straw attached to the cover. That lovely song, 'What's In a Name,' was one of the tracks. Susie played the guitar and sang, and there was Guy with a violin and another boy – what was his name, now? Oh yes, James. He was on keyboards.'

Samantha fiddled with her pearl necklace. 'I don't want to be unkind, but Susie, or Suzanne, as she was in those days, was rather — how can I put it — strange. You know, she had a big voice, big blue eyes, and a great deal of blonde hair, but there was no brain there at all.' She waved, dismissing Susie as a failure. 'She left school with absolutely no qualifications.'

'We were all madly jealous of her, to be honest,' Angela admitted. 'Off we went to University or started work as trainees at Barclays Bank or Marks and Spencer, while she made records. She married a fabulously wealthy record producer, but the marriage didn't last long. I don't know about the rest of you, but I haven't seen or heard of her for years.' She sighed. 'We were rather unkind to her, I'm afraid.'

When the teapot was drained and the cake plate empty, the meeting broke up. 'Next time,' Marina said, 'we really must talk about history.'

Finally, only George Edwards, the sole male member of the society, remained. He wrapped the last slice of cake in a paper napkin to take home and, breaking his silence, begged Libby to write down the recipe for his wife, who was at home nursing a cold and laryngitis. 'She'll be sorry she missed everything.'

Libby collected the empty cake tin and left. Angela walked by her side, heading for her car. 'I wonder what Suzie was doing in Exham, after all these years.'

ROBERT'S DISCOVERY

Recessed spotlights picked out the details of Libby's beautifully equipped kitchen as she made coffee, using the state-of-the-art, instant hot water dispenser, installed last week. She pulled out mixing bowls, sieves and scales, and settled down to a trial run of the perfect, elaborate, light-as-air cake she was developing. If it turned out as beautifully as she expected, it would make a wonderful cover picture for the follow up to her recent book, 'Baking at the Beach.'

It was this room that had persuaded Libby to buy Hope Cottage. Facing south, always either sunny or cosy, perfect for a baking fanatic. Without a qualm, she'd sold her husband's treasured trainset, lavishing every last penny it fetched on her workplace.

Their son, Robert, had been horrified. 'You can't sell that, Mum. It was Dad's pride and joy.' It had filled a room in the London townhouse.

'I know, but I'm moving to Somerset, to a cottage. There won't be room for everything – me, my professional kitchen, and a trainset. I have to earn my own living now your father's gone.'

Robert had sighed. 'He didn't leave you that badly off, did he? You never said...'

Libby smiled. Robert was such a worrier, and he'd adored his father – she could never tell him the whole truth about the man. She'd never told anyone how Trevor had treated her, criticising her clothes, telling her she was fat, constantly making excuses to prevent her friends coming to the house. It had taken all her strength to keep his bullying from Robert and Ali.

She sometimes thought Ali, her daughter, suspected the truth. Ali had been keen to leave home for Bristol University, six months before Trevor died, and she'd not returned home during those months, although she'd telephoned Libby every week.

Now, at least, the money from Trevor's railway had been put to good use. From the KitchenAid mixer on the granite counter, to the gleaming rows of heavy bottomed pans that hung on the wall near the range cooker, Libby adored every inch of the room.

She'd once confided to Trevor the dream of setting up her own chocolate shop. Trevor had taken off his glasses and glared, his nose less than an inch away from her face.

'Don't be so stupid.' Libby had flinched as saliva hit her face. 'Throwing good money after bad. Besides, I expect to find you at home when I come back after a hard day.' He sneered, replaced the spectacles right on the end of his nose, poured a tumbler of whisky and settled down to read the newspaper's business section. Libby's new kitchen would have been enough to make him choke on his drink.

What a pity the bathroom didn't reach the standard of her kitchen. The orange made her feel sick every time she saw them. In a day or two, Ned, the builder, was coming to get rid of the horrid, 1970s bathroom.

The phone rang as she shaved fractions of an inch from the sponge cake. Robert was excited. 'Mum, I've got news.' Libby's heart leapt. He was getting engaged at last. There would be a wedding. She'd need a new dress, and a hat...

'Are you listening? I've discovered a new great, great, great aunt, and what's more, she lived in Somerset.' Libby sighed and cast a despairing glance at the meringue mixture she'd whipped to exactly the right consistency, as it collapsed, ruined.

When he was a studious, serious teenager, Robert preferred history to football and Latin to art. Libby had little interest in the Forest relations, Trevor's ancestors, but Robert worshipped his father. He never saw Trevor's dark side.

Now, Libby tried to be interested. 'Do tell me about it, darling.'

'You know Dad always said his family were landowners?'

'Mm-hm.' Did he? Libby swallowed a mouthful from a second cup of coffee. She added a slug of whisky to settle her nerves and licked her lips.

'Well, I've found someone called Matilda Forest, who was a maid at a stately home.' Libby almost wished Trevor were here now. An ancestor in service – how he'd hate that. So much for landowners.

Robert was still talking. 'And the house is in Somerset, near you. A place called Mangotsfield Hall. It's open to the public. Maybe we can all visit? Sarah's keen and we can come down in a couple of weeks.'

Sarah was Robert's girlfriend, and her parents lived in the West Country. That had helped, when Libby insisted on selling the family home and moving to Somerset. 'At least, Sarah and I can come and see you and her parents at the same time,' Robert had admitted.

Her interest sparked by the mention of Mangotsfield Hall, Libby asked. 'What did you find out about this Matilda?'

'Well, she had to leave the Hall because she was pregnant –

the family wouldn't have her in the house. She didn't go far, just to Wraxall. The baby kept her surname, but, get this, Mum, his Christian names were Stephen Arthur, and those were the names of the earl who lived in the house.'

Libby chuckled. 'Are you telling me your father's ancestor was what they used to call, 'No better than she should be,' after hanky-panky with his lordship?'

'Honestly, Mum, Dad would be mortified.' Even Robert laughed at the thought.

'So, he would,' she agreed.

Libby said, 'By the way, I had an adventure, yesterday.'

'You did?'

'No need to sound so surprised. I'm not that old, yet.'

'Sorry.'

'But I found a body on the beach.'

He sounded puzzled. 'What sort of a body?'

Libby took a breath, enjoying the moment. 'A dead one.'

'What?' His reaction was everything Libby had hoped for.

By the time Robert rang off, keen to pass on such interesting gossip to Sarah when she came home from work, he'd squeezed every detail from his mother.

The phone rang again. Still smiling, Libby picked it up. 'Hello, darling, what did you forget?'

The deep voice on the other end of the phone brought her back to reality with a thud. 'Is that Mrs Forest? It's Detective Sergeant Joe Ramshore here.'

Libby let the silence draw on for a moment. She really didn't want to talk about the body under the lighthouse again. She was exhausted from answering Robert's questions. She let out her breath in a long sigh. 'Yes, it's me.'

'Well, I'm ringing to thank you for your help today.' Joe Ramshore was the young detective from the beach. The one with blue eyes and a superior expression. 'We wanted to let you know we've identified the lady you found.'

'Susie Bennett?'

'Oh. You've heard, then.' He sounded put out. 'We think we know what happened, Mrs Forest. I thought you'd like to know that the deceased—' He coughed. 'I mean, Susie Bennett, seems to have been alone when she died. I didn't want you to worry. It was all an unfortunate accident, or at the worse, intentional.'

'Intentional?' Samantha had said it was suicide. Libby shivered. Setting out to drown yourself in the autumn gales was a strange way to take your own life. Why not swallow a few pills, or jump off Clifton Suspension Bridge?

The detective was still talking. 'Well, I'm afraid she had an awful lot to drink. We think she-er-vomited and choked. The forensic examiner found traces. We couldn't see them on her clothes – the rain had washed them away. No one else involved. It must have happened the night before you found her, though it's hard to tell the time of death, what with the cold water, and so on.'

'Oh.' What an anti-climax: to die like that, so foolishly. 'What about the ring?'

'The ring?' He sounded puzzled. 'Oh, yes, that bit of plastic on the sand. It was just a toy ring, nothing valuable. I expect it was in one of her pockets.'

'But—' Libby broke off. No need to confess to moving the body. She compromised. 'I just wondered why she'd have a plastic ring in her pocket.'

'Oh, I see. Well, we don't know.' The police officer's tone was measured, pedantic. 'She wouldn't have been wearing it, would she? It's a child's ring.'

Libby rolled her eyes. She could work that out without his help. 'Yes, but—'

'We had a look at it, but there wasn't anything we could use: no fingerprints or anything, I mean. The weather saw to that.'

Libby insisted. 'I meant, did Susie Bennett have a family?'

'Ah, I see what you're thinking. You're wondering if she has young children.'

Libby, exasperated, crossed her eyes and waggled her head. Good thing the police officer couldn't see her. 'Yes.'

'I can put your mind at rest on that, Mrs Forest. We don't know of any family. Of course, we're getting records over from the US, because her husband was American.'

'Yes, yes I heard that. You know, from people in the town.'

'Well, it's a small place. I'll let you know when the inquest comes up. The coroner will want to ask you some questions. Nothing you need worry about. It's not like going to a criminal court.'

'No, well, thank you. Oh,' Libby exclaimed.

Yes?'

'I wondered how she got there. Did you find a car, or anything?'

The police officer sighed. 'No, but there are buses, Mrs Forest. Exham's not that remote, you know. She was a local lady, prob-ably came back to the place she grew up, if she wanted to end her life. That's not unusual, you know.'

His voice was warmer now. 'Try to put it out of your mind, Mrs Forest. I know it's upsetting, but these things do happen, I'm afraid.'

Libby put the phone down. Too restless to go back to the spoiled meringue, she climbed the stairs to the bathroom. A hot bath might relax her.

She tried to unwind by reading a magazine, but her mind drifted away to the image of Susie Bennett, drenched and cold, slipping sideways under the lighthouse, in dreadful slow motion.

The scene played over and over in her head, like a YouTube video on a never ending loop.

It didn't ring true. Surely, no one would choose such a place, on a stormy night, to drink alone.

It was no good. She stepped out of the bath. How could she leave it at that? The police might be satisfied there was no foul play, but Libby wasn't. If they weren't going to try to discover the truth, she would find out for herself. Was Susie's death really an accident, a deliberate suicide, or something much worse?

4

The early morning sun peeped, pink and coy, over the horizon, as though the past two days of storms and wind belonged to another era. Libby walked Shipley along the beach in the opposite direction from the lighthouse. She wasn't ready to repeat yesterday's disastrous trip.

She'd tossed and turned all night, unable to forget Susie's face, the pink plastic ring, or the nagging suspicion that Susie might be a victim. She hoped the walk would clear her mind.

A dozen fishermen, with all the time in the world, leaned against the sea wall, rods extended into an ebbing tide. They nodded, mumbling a greeting as Libby passed and George Edwards wrapped a fish in newspaper, holding it out to Libby. 'For breakfast.'

She took the package, stowing it safely in her backpack, hoping it wouldn't leave too pungent a smell.

'How's your wife?' She asked, wondering if she'd ever meet the woman.

'On the mend. The voice is back, more's the pity. By the way,' he called Libby back. 'She loved the cake. Let me have a copy of your book, will you? Do for her Christmas present.' *Poor Mrs Edwards, was that going to be her only gift?*

When Libby arrived home, Fuzzy left the airing cupboard to follow her mistress into the kitchen, meowing pitifully.

'Are you hungry, then?' Libby picked her up, nuzzling the soft fur. Fuzzy allowed this display of affection for a count of three, then squirmed, squeaked and wriggled away. For some reason, she'd never taken to Libby, always preferring Trevor. Trying to please, Libby opened a can of salmon.

Full, content and purring, Fuzzy left the house via the cat flap in the back door. She'd work off breakfast chasing the mice, frogs and birds that had made the neglected garden their home long before Libby moved in.

'A wildlife garden,' Libby explained, when Ali phoned. 'No need to weed the borders.' Her daughter, like Robert, had been nonplussed by Libby's crazy move from London to a quiet seaside town.

Libby downed a second mug of tea, shrugged on a bright red trench coat guaranteed to brighten her mood, and climbed into her tiny, eleven year old Citroen, to drive to work at the bakery.

Reversing out of the drive could be a challenge. The road she lived on wasn't exactly busy, for most traffic used the parallel main road, but it was ever-changing. Mums and Dads walked their children around the corner of the road each day, heading for the nearby primary school. Teenagers, ears plugged with headphones, materialised suddenly from behind parked vans, mouths open in amazement at finding cars on the road.

It was too early for young people, today. They'd still be struggling awake. Libby switched on the ignition and reversed the car, hands light on the wheel, head turned to peer through the rear window.

A flurry of barking exploded nearby, like breakfast time at the boarding kennels. Libby jumped, foot jerking on the accelerator. The vehicle lurched. She jammed on the brake, but it was too late. The rear of the car crumpled with a sickening crunch as it hit the lamp post opposite her house.

Libby threw the door open, to find her exit blocked by a dog. It reached almost to her shoulder as it struggled on its lead, howling like a wolf. 'Be quiet, Bear.' The grey haired man on the other end of the lead yanked the dog back to let Libby out of the car. 'Sit down.'

The dog subsided, panting, saliva dribbling from its tongue. Libby slammed the door. 'That animal should be locked up.'

The man bent over the rear of the Citroen. 'I'm afraid there's a dent.'

'Of course there is. Your dog's a menace.'

He straightened up, towering several inches above Libby. 'He's not mine,' he said. 'I hope you're not hurt?'

Libby pointed. 'Just look what you've done to my car.'

'Forgive me, but you were driving. All Bear did was bark at that cat.'

Libby followed the pointing finger. Her shoulders slumped. Fuzzy crouched on top of the fence, fur fluffed out, laser beam eyes trained on Bear. The dog, tantalised by a tormentor so close, yet out of range, howled again.

If a cat could be said to smirk, that's what Fuzzy did. Libby groaned. 'Oh. That's my cat,' she blurted. 'Well, my husband's. Late husband.' The back of her neck was hot. She tried to smile. 'I'm afraid Fuzzy's nothing but trouble.'

'Fuzzy?' The man grinned.

'Her fur goes fuzzy in the rain.'

'Well, I'm afraid there's not much we can do about the car. Your insurance will cover it.' The stranger smiled, waved and went on his way. Bear barked once more, in a forlorn attempt to entice Fuzzy down from the fence.

Libby rubbed at the dent. The paint was intact, and it was only a tiny bump. A garage would knock it out in minutes. She straightened up. That man could have apologised a bit more, though. Who was he? Where had he come from? She hadn't seen him before but he looked familiar, nevertheless.

She glared at Fuzzy. 'Last salmon you'll get from me.'

5

THE BAKERY

Frank Brown brought a tray of bread, steaming and fragrant, through from the kitchen at the back into the shop just as Libby arrived. 'Morning,' he grunted. 'What's the latest on Susie Bennett, then?' He scooped up a pile of baking trays, already on the way back to the kitchen. 'They say her last album will be back in the charts, now she's dead. Too late for her, but it makes you wonder who'll get all those royalties.'

Libby had never heard him talk so much. His communication was usually limited to 'yes', 'no', and, 'those loaves need to come out of the oven', but under the gruff exterior he had a kind heart. Marina had told her Frank was a staunch supporter of the Rotary club and its charitable work.

The shop's work experience teenager leaned on the counter, twirling a stud on her lip. Libby secretly called her Mandy the Goth. 'My Dad went to school with her.'

Libby laughed. 'So did half the town, I gather.'

'I heard you found her. Was it gruesome? Was there much blood?' The girl's eyes, black with layers of kohl and mascara,

were enormous in the white-painted face. Two silver rings decorated one nostril above purple lips.

'Mandy.' Frank put his head round the door. 'Get on with
those sandwiches before the rush starts. Wash your hands and
put some gloves on.'

Mandy sighed, rolled her eyes, hitched up a long, black lace
skirt and went back to scraping egg mayonnaise into baguettes.

'Dad said she was always asking for it,' she muttered under
her breath, glancing towards the kitchens. 'Sexy but stupid, he
said.'

The bakery did a roaring trade. Almost everyone in town
dropped in, keen to look at the person who found the body.
Frank beamed. 'That's the most sandwiches we've sold since
Jeremy Clarkson came down to drive off the pier.'

By eleven o'clock, Libby's feet ached. Her head throbbed from
the effort of repeating, 'I just happened to find her', and, 'The
police say there's nothing suspicious'. When the queue no longer
snaked out of the door and around the corner, but had shrunk to
one or two stragglers, she retreated to the kitchen. Mandy could
serve the final few High Street estate agents.

Frank removed his white hat, still unusually talkative. 'Can
you finish that new ginger and lemon recipe by this afternoon,
Libby? I reckon it'll be a winner.'

'Mmm. Just need to tweak the frosting. A bit over-sweet, I
thought.'

'You're the expert. It'll sell like hot cakes.' Libby grimaced.
Frank made the same joke at least once a week. 'Funny thing,' he
went on. 'Millions of people watch cooking programmes on TV,
and half of 'em don't know how to turn on their ovens. Still,
mustn't grumble. Where would the business be if everyone did
their own baking, eh?'

Frank left to drive the van, loaded with filled rolls, to a nearby conference centre. Libby took a deep breath, drinking in the smell of freshly baked bread. She tied on a clean apron, and set about testing the new recipe, relishing the familiar, satisfying tasks of measuring sugar, beating eggs and sifting flour. She'd persuade Frank to let her put the new confection in her next book.

Mandy joined her. The teenager's earlier good humour seemed to have evaporated. Libby opened her mouth to tell her to stay in the shop, ready for new customers, but the look on the girl's face changed her mind. Mandy's lip trembled. Libby said, 'We'll hear the bell if anyone comes.'

Mandy grunted, tipped a bowl of risen dough onto a bench top and pummelled it as Libby watched. Nothing relieved angry feelings better than making bread. It had been a favourite therapy during her miserable marriage. What had upset the girl?

'Everything all right?' Libby asked.

Mandy said nothing. Libby let it go. She recalled her own children as teenagers, not so long ago, grunting and taking offence at everything she said. At least that phase had passed.

For ten minutes, only Mandy's effortful gasps and the whirr of the food processor disturbed the peace of the kitchen. The corners of Mandy's mouth still drooped. She sniffed. Libby had an idea. 'Why don't you make the frosting?'

As Mandy dumped the bread dough back into a stainless steel bowl for its final proving, she explained.

'I've weighed everything out, but the sugar needs watching.' The teenager scraped dough from sticky fingers, shrugged and picked up a wooden spoon. 'Make sure it all melts before you turn up the heat. That stops the mixture turning into a gritty mess.'

Mandy, eyes on the saucepan, stirred. 'Mrs Forest?' She sounded hesitant.

'Mm-hmm.' Best not to sound too interested, and perhaps the girl would share whatever was worrying her.

'Dad threw a knife at Mum.'

'A knife?' Libby stiffened, sugar spilling from the spoon.

'It was only a knife from the table – not a carving knife or anything.'

Libby gulped. No wonder the girl was upset. 'Is your Mum OK?'

Mandy nodded. 'Think so. She says it's not the first time, nor the last. He missed, anyway.'

Libby lowered the spoon and took Mandy by the shoulders. 'She needs to tell the police.'

The girl shrugged Libby's hands away and swiped a sleeve across her eyes, smudging black mascara across one cheek. 'She won't. I've told her. She says he doesn't mean it. He's sorry, later.'

'Mandy, that's rubbish.' Libby closed her eyes, fighting memories. She took a long, slow breath. 'Of course he's sorry afterwards. They always are, but it happens again.' Fingernails bit into the palm of her hand. 'Has he ever hit you?'

Mandy tossed her head. 'He tells Mum it's her fault for making him angry, but anything sets him off. It was just about watching football on the telly, yesterday.'

Libby pulled out a chair and eased on to it. She'd had just such a stupid row with Trevor. They'd argued – shouted – about nothing, and she'd thrown his dinner in the bin. He'd cracked the TV remote control against her shoulder, all his strength behind the blow. His face, contorted with fury, sometimes appeared in Libby's dreams. She'd been terrified he'd hurt the children.

'Mandy.' She took a moment to control her voice. 'Mandy, if your mother won't do anything about it, then you should leave the house. You're old enough.'

Mandy bent over the saucepan. 'I think the sugar's ready to boil.'

Libby handed over the sugar thermometer. 'Think about it. I've got spare beds at my house if you need them.'

Mandy sniffed and rubbed her nose but said no more. Libby let it go. The girl had to make up her own mind.

The doorbell tinkled. Libby left Mandy at the hob, watching sugar boil in the pan, and stepped into the shop, pulling on a pair of clean white gloves. 'Can I help you?'

Tall, grey haired, a little older than Libby, and dressed in a long blue overcoat, the new arrival smiled. 'Good morning.'

Libby stared. 'It's you. The man with the dangerous dog.'

'So it is. We seem to have got off to a bad start.'

'I should say so.'

He grinned. 'I gave Bear a good talking to before I handed him back to Mrs Thomson.'

Libby's lips twitched. 'Quite right. He needs to learn to behave. Fuzzy's a bit of a menace, of course.'

'Well, to be honest, I liked the look of Fuzzy. I admire a cat that stands up for itself. Bear doesn't agree.'

Libby looked at the blue eyes. Yes, definitely familiar. Where else had she seen them? 'Did you want a sandwich? Or cake?'

'Just a ham salad baguette, please.' He patted his middle. 'Have to watch the weight, these days.'

Mandy arrived from the kitchen. She'd redone her mascara. 'The frosting's ready, Libby.' She stopped. 'Hello, Mr Ramshore.'

Libby looked from one to the other. 'Ramshore. Like the detective sergeant?'

He smiled. 'My son.'

6

COFFEE AND SUSPICION

This new Ramshore's first name turned out to be Max. 'My parents were Norwegian.' That explained the blue eyes.

'I thought I owed you a cup of coffee. I wasn't too gracious, earlier. Bear is much too big and loud, and I should have managed him better, though your cat caused the trouble.'

'He didn't—'

'Anyway,' he broke in, 'let's not argue again. There's a coffee shop further down the road. Can I buy you a coffee?'

'I don't know. Mandy would be alone in the shop.'

'I can manage, Mrs F. We're quiet, now.'

'Well, if you're sure.' There was something very pleasing about Max Ramshore's eyes, and his smile took years off his face. Libby wondered how old he was. Fifty? No younger than she was, anyway. 'Just ten minutes.'

Libby chose a table in a corner of the coffee shop and shrugged off her coat while he bought two lattes.

'What breed is Bear?'

'Carpathian Sheepdog. Very gentle, like many big dogs, but he needs an incredible amount of exercise. He belongs to my neighbour, Mrs Thomson, really. Her husband kept him on the farm, but old Eric had to go into a care home before he died – dementia, I'm afraid. I own the farm now, though I don't work it myself. I look after Bear when he gets too much for Mrs Thomson, which is quite often. She still lives in the old farmhouse, down the lane from me.'

'Well, anyway.' Libby wasn't ready to forgive him, or Bear, completely. Besides, she was suspicious. 'Did you know I worked in the bakery? I'm sure you didn't just happen to walk in today.'

'No, to be honest, my son told me about you.'

'The detective sergeant himself? What did he say?' She glared. 'Aren't the police supposed to keep things confidential?'

'He just suggested I look out for you, on my marathon Bear walk this morning. He thought you might be upset, after that business on the beach. Then, you had your little accident.'

'Caused by Bear.'

'And Fuzzy.' His eyes twinkled. 'I can see we're not going to agree on that. Anyway, I felt bad, so I asked one of your neighbours where you might be going. It's a small town, you know.'

'You can say that again.' Where did looking out for each other stop and nosiness begin? 'Have you always lived here?'

He nodded. 'I went to school with Susie Bennett, you know.'

Libby laughed.

'What's funny?'

'Everyone I've met here went to school with Susie, but she doesn't seem to have many friends.'

'It's a small town. We all grew up together. Susie wasn't in my year, she's a couple of years younger, but I knew her.' Libby waited for the inevitable slur on Susie's character, but he surprised her. 'She was a nice girl. A difficult family, though.'

'Oh?' Libby hesitated. 'You're the first person I've heard say anything good about her.'

'Who have you asked? Wait. Let me guess. The Townswomen's Guild?'

'No.' Libby's face burned. 'The local history society, actually. They all knew her at school.'

'And didn't approve.'

'Maybe they were jealous?' She was thinking aloud.

He stirred coffee with a long spoon. 'Susie was too pretty for her own good, and too ready to believe everything the boys told her. You know how teenage boys can be. They try it on with girls, then if one says yes, they pull her reputation to pieces. That's how it was with Susie. Hardly any friends, just boys who wanted her for one thing. She had a terrific singing voice, though.'

'I hear her album's likely to make a fortune.'

He crumbled a coconut macaroon onto the table. 'I bet the music company are thrilled. They don't care how they make a profit, do they?'

'She went to America, before she became famous, didn't she?'

'It all started here, though. Small local gigs at first. It was Glastonbury where they got their big break.'

Libby shivered. 'Glastonbury. I went once. Cold, wet and smelly, as I remember.'

He laughed. 'Not everyone's cup of tea. Still, it's great place for up-and-coming bands. Mickey Garston, the big American music producer, heard Susie there, signed up the band and married her. It all happened fast. He whisked her away and the next we knew; she was on the cover of million selling albums and on TV.'

'What about her family?'

'All dead or gone away. No Bennetts left in the town.'

'That's sad.'

'Typical story of a small-time girl with a turbulent life, I'm afraid. The marriage with Mickey Garston didn't last long. They split up years ago, but she never married again.'

'No, she wasn't wearing a wedding ring when I found her.' Did Max know about the plastic ring? Had Joe told him she'd moved the body?

Max Ramshore drank the last drops of coffee and set the cup down with care. 'My son mentioned a different ring. He said you seemed bothered by it.'

'Bothered? No, why should I be?' Her face was burning.

'Come on. What are you hiding? I'm not the police, you know.'

'No, but your son is.' She bit her lip. Now it sounded as though she'd committed a huge crime. 'OK. I moved the body. I pulled her hand out of her pocket and the ring fell on the beach. That's all. I know I shouldn't have touched her, but she looked so – well – vulnerable, I suppose. I wanted to help. Does that sound crazy?'

'I told you, I'm not the police.' It was his turn to hesitate. 'Truth is, I know a bit more about Susie than the others around here. It's private information, and maybe I shouldn't tell anyone, but it makes me think there was something more going on than her committing suicide.'

Libby licked dry lips. 'D'you mean, you think she was murdered?'

'Mmm. Sounds a bit melodramatic, doesn't it?'

Libby thought about it. 'That scene at the beach – it wasn't like a suicide.'

'The police have it down as an open and shut case, at least unless the coroner disagrees at the inquest.' He shook his head. 'Frankly, if no one does anything, she'll be a statistic: just another girl who grew too rich and famous and couldn't handle it. I don't want to let that happen.'

'What is it you know?'

The man blinked and looked away. 'Not here. We need to talk somewhere more private. Can I take you to dinner tonight? There's a restaurant near Taunton where they know me. They'll let us have a quiet table.'

Libby bit her lip. 'All right.' She stood up. 'I've got to get back to the shop. Pick me up at seven?'

7

DINNER

Libby changed her dress three times before seven o'clock. It was stupid to feel so nervous. *I'm behaving like a teenager.* She hadn't been out alone with a man since Trevor died. The last thing she wanted was an entanglement. Not now, as she started to build the life she'd always wanted.

The linen shift dress was elegant, and a shade of pale rose that brought colour to her cheeks, but it wouldn't keep her warm, it creased too much, and the neckline was too low. She tossed it on the bed. This wasn't a date, after all. The man had only asked her to dinner to discuss Susie. Maybe she was an old girlfriend.

Libby tried a silk dress with a high waist and flared skirt that made her look girly. 'Mutton dressed as lamb.' she told Fuzzy, who rolled on the linen dress, covering it with ginger and white hairs.

Libby shooed the cat away and pulled out a pair of black evening trousers, matching them with a white shirt. There, that didn't give out any awkward signals. It was neat and business-like, but the trousers were well cut and the subtle embroidery, like damask, made them chic enough for evening. A silver chain round her neck, a heavy silver cuff on her wrist, and a squirt of scent completed her preparation, just in time. The bell rang as she left the room.

He was early. Libby ran downstairs, stomach fluttering, took a breath and opened the door. Mandy, hair wildly back combed into an unruly bird's nest, rested a foot on the doorstep as if poised for retreat. In one hand, she hefted an unwieldy backpack with a black t-shirt spilling out of the top. The other hand was at her mouth, teeth tearing at a black-painted fingernail. She dropped the hand long enough to whisper, 'Did you mean it? Can I really come to stay?'

'Of course you can stay.' Mandy staggered into the hallway and Libby took the bag. 'I don't think it's safe for you to go home, if you're frightened of your father.' She took the bag. 'Good heavens, whatever have you got in there?'

Mandy made a sound halfway between a laugh and a sniff. 'My laptop. And some books.'

Books? Mandy? That was a surprise. 'Well, you're welcome to stay. I could use a lodger, here. There's a spare room. Does your Mum know you're here?'

'I didn't tell her.' Mandy's fingernail was back in her mouth. She looked like a frightened child.

'You should let her know. Won't she worry?'

'I'll ring her later. Dad won't be back tonight. He's going out drinking with his old mates and staying over at the Watson's place.' Maybe Samantha would keep an eye on Mandy's father: help him stay out of trouble. Libby would ask Max Ramshore about Mandy's dad this evening. He'd know what to do. His son was a police officer.

Mandy, gaining confidence once the front door closed, perched on a stool in the kitchen, gazing around the room, eyes wide. 'Wow. What a place, Mrs Forest.'

'Call me Libby. Now, I must go out this evening, but the bed's made up in the spare room. I won't be late. Make yourself at home and help yourself to anything you can find.'

Mandy was scooping walnut brownies from a tin when Max Ramshore arrived. 'Don't worry about me.' She looked from one to the other, the hint of a smile on her face. She'd be on Facebook before they were out of the drive. By tomorrow, everyone in town would know they'd been out for dinner.

Libby's companion drove a comfortable, well-used Range Rover. Bear lay in the back, greeting Libby with a bark. 'Hello to you, too,' she said, tugging his ears.

Max Ramshore raised his eyebrows. 'Hope you don't mind if Bear comes too. He likes the White House.'

The restaurant was by the river, a string of tables lining the bank. There was an autumn chill in the air, but the wind had dropped. Still, it was a good job she'd brought a warm jacket. Libby rejected the polite invitation to eat inside. She liked the dark of the evening, and lights illuminated the scene. Bear made himself at home, disappearing into the reeds on the riverbank, searching for a succession of sticks for Max to throw.

'If you grew up in Exham, Mr Ramshore, you must know just about everybody in town.' Libby had spent all her life, until now, in West London. 'I meet a new person one day, like Mandy at the bakery, and the next day I drop into the newsagent and find her mother works there. It's like a spider's web.'

'I wish you'd call me Max,' he said. 'You're right. We're a small community. If you need a job done, you can always find a friend or relative of someone you know, who can help.'

'I'm asking Ned Watson to renovate my bathroom. What do you think?'

He tapped his fingers on the table. 'He's probably the best option. There's always Bert, Mandy's dad, if you want it done for cash with no questions asked. But I wouldn't advise that. A bit crooked, is Bert. Ned Watson's better. He undertakes building and plumbing. Tell him you know me, and he'll give you a decent price.'

'Tell me more about Mandy's father. Bert, you said?'

Max grimaced. 'The man's a bully. He was like it at school. No one's lunch money was safe.'

Libby peeked at Max's shoulders, broad as a boxer's. Her lips twitched. 'I bet yours was.'

He smiled. 'I can look after myself. Since school, Bert's been on the dole most of the time, though he makes plenty by cleaning windows: cash payments only, of course.'

'Is Mandy's mother safe? Won't he hurt her?'

Max took a sip of Beck's Blue non-alcoholic beer. 'I'm not sure. Bert goes down the pub with a bunch of his loser pals, gets drunk and takes it out on Elaine. The police are called round there from time to time.' He shrugged. 'Usual story. Wife takes him back every time. Refuses to press charges. She's had a black eye or two.'

Max's own eyes glinted, cold as ice. 'I try to keep an eye out for Elaine. Bert listens to me, so long as he's sober. We go back a long way, but I'm not always successful. One day, he'll go too far.'

Libby swallowed. 'Well, she'll be OK tonight. He's staying with the Watsons.'

Max laughed. 'Samantha would never have let Bert stay if she was at home. She ruled Ned with a rod of iron until they split up.'

'Anyway, Mandy's safe with me. Her father won't even know she's there.'

'He'll hear soon enough: you can't keep secrets in Exham on Sea, you know.' Max topped up her glass. 'Don't worry about Mandy. She's eighteen, old enough to make her own decisions.'

He swished beer around his glass. 'What about you? How did you get here?'

'My husband died.'

'I'm sorry.'

She met his eye. 'Don't be. I'm not.' His eyebrows shot up and Libby laughed. 'Sounds dreadful, I know, but he was my big mistake. My parents warned me.' She hadn't listened, and she'd never told them they were right. 'He turned out to be one of those controlling husbands. Another bully, like Mandy's father. That's why I was keen to get her away from their house. I know what it's like.'

'I'm so sorry.' Max's eyes were dark with sympathy, and Libby's stomach gave a little lurch.

'I know it sounds awful, but when Trevor had a heart attack, I cheered inside. At last, I could work, have my own life, make friends and live where I chose. I chose Exham on Sea.'

She raised her glass. 'To my new life.'

'Now,' she put the menu to one side. 'We didn't come here to talk about me. What can you tell me about Susie Bennett?'

Max drummed his fingers on the table. 'The thing is, Susie kept in touch with me after she left. I used to live and work in Bath, in one of the banks, and Susie came in one day, before she left for America, and opened an account.'

'Was she rich?'

'Not rich then, though she was later, but I don't think she ever trusted Mickey. I tried to stop her going away with him.' Max's eyes were focused on his plate. Did he still hold some sort of a candle for Susie? It would explain why he was the only person in Exham on Sea with a good word to say for her.

'She wouldn't listen. Said she could handle herself but wanted to be sure there were funds somewhere safe, that only she knew about, in case she, or anyone else, ever needed them.'

Their steak arrived and Max stopped talking, refilling Libby's glass with wine and taking a deep draught of beer. Libby sliced into her food, watching blood trickle from the rare steak.

'Or anyone else,' she murmured. 'What could she have meant by that?'

Max shrugged. 'She wouldn't say. Just told me it was her

secret and she'd let me know when she wanted the money. That's all there is to it.'

'That's all?'

'I shouldn't even be telling you.' The sharp edge was back in his voice.

Libby ignored it. 'I'm glad you did. What happens to the money now?'

'There's been a pretty big pot waiting for Susie, but she never used it. She never came back, just contacted me from time to time to check on the interest. In the early years, we spoke about every six months. She talked about needing it soon, but after a while, she stopped contacting me.'

'When was that?'

'Oh, six or seven years after she married. It was about the time of her last album. You remember, *Twilight over the Sea?*'

Libby did remember. Susie's dark contralto voice blending with a plaintive guitar in sad songs of love and loss. Her best work, the critics said. 'She never made another album, did she?'

'No, that was it. She lived the rock and roll lifestyle with Mickey: plenty of drugs and booze. They broke up a few years later and she wrote to me again, asking me to keep the account open. She said she'd probably not need it, anyway. That was the last time we were in contact, apart from the statements sent by the bank. I haven't seen her for years.'

Libby took a chance. 'You were pretty close to Susie, then, if she trusted you with her money?'

His eyes narrowed. 'What gossip have you been listening to?'

Libby held his gaze, keeping her voice steady. 'I don't listen to gossip, but you're the only one I've met so far who knew Susie after she left.'

Max picked up a dessert spoon from beside his plate, twirling it in his fingers. His eyes slid away, looking out over the hills. Libby pulled her jacket more tightly round her shoulders.

'Susie and I had a business relationship. It was no more than that.'

'But you'd have liked it to be more?'

Max's eyes narrowed. Libby flinched at the steely undertone to his voice. 'It's none of your business, Mrs Forest.'

She gripped her hands under the table. She took a gamble and murmured, 'Did your wife know how you felt about Susie?' A man as attractive as this must be married. Libby discovered she wanted to know.

Max's eyes were stony. 'We're divorced.'

'Because of Susie?'

He gave a sharp laugh and drained his glass with a flourish. 'Oh, Mrs Forest, how very inquisitive you are. Do you think I murdered Susie Bennett?'

'I don't know, but I'm sure someone killed her. I'm just trying to find out more about the people who knew her. You're one of them. I thought you wanted to help.'

'Of course I do. You'll have to make up your own mind about me, but for what it's worth, I didn't kill Susie, even though I was no model husband. To answer your question, Susie was just one of the reasons my wife and I quarrelled. But there were plenty of others. Now, if you've had enough to eat, we'd better move inside. The wind's getting up and I'm freezing cold.'

Sure enough, a gust of wind blew napkins from the table and raindrops splattered the cloth. Max rose to his feet, calling Bear back from the river. The dog arrived, wet, muddy and smelly. Libby shivered. 'Maybe we'd better just leave?'

9

WALNUT BROWNIES

Max drew up behind the Citroen. 'You'd better get that dent fixed. Try Jenkins' Garage, it's the best around this area.'

'I suppose you were at school with Mr Jenkins.'

'As it happens, I was.'

'Another member of The Band of Brothers?' Libby climbed out.

'I suppose you could call it that. We look out for each other.'

'Well. Thank you for dinner. And, good night.'

The house lay quiet, the kitchen clean and tidy. Mandy was on her best behaviour. How long would it last? Libby, unsettled, fell into bed, her stomach full of good food and wine, and slept heavily until morning.

The phone startled her awake. 'I've been thinking about that money of Susie's.' Max didn't bother to ask how she was. This relationship was strictly business. Libby swallowed a stab of disappointment, yawned and focused on his voice. 'Anything she saved will be part of her estate and go to her heirs. I'm wondering who they might be.'

The smell of burnt toast and the sound of scraping rose from the kitchen, and Libby's mouth watered. She tried to concentrate as Max talked. 'I'm going over to the States. I've got Susie's old address. I think we need to let people know what's happened.'

'Isn't that a police job?'

'No, not if there's no foul play in the case, apparently, and no grieving husband or children. Someone needs to find a solicitor, or attorney, or whatever they're called in the US, and sort out wills and so on.'

'So, you're going to do it?'

'Er – yes. Well, there's no one else, is there? It'll take ages if we wait until after the inquest and anyway...'

He let the words hang in the air but Libby knew what he was thinking. Justice for Susie. 'I'm off to Heathrow now. There's a flight this afternoon.'

'Already? What about Bear? Who's going to walk him?' *Shut up, Libby, what are you saying?*

'I've left him with Mrs Thomson. He'll have to wait for his exercise until I get back.'

Libby let the silence grow. It wasn't her job to look after that huge dog. She groaned. 'I'll go and rescue him. I don't see why he has to suffer.'

'Libby, you're a treasure.'

'I know I am. You'd better let me know anything you find out. And Max, there's one question we have to answer.'

'What's that?'

'If she's been living in the US since the 1990s, with no contact with anyone in England, what the heck was she doing on Tuesday on the beach at Exham on Sea?'

She put the phone down. *And why are you so keen to go to the States? What are you up to?*

She rang Ned Watson, mentioned Max's name and asked him for a final quote for the bathroom. He was business-like. 'I like a week to do a bathroom. You don't want to rush it.' He'd come around tomorrow to get started. Libby, used to long waiting lists for any work in London, was impressed. She couldn't wait to see the back of the orange tiles and avocado green bath.

* * *

Mrs Thomson's old, tumbledown house lay just outside town, surrounded on three sides by green fields, cattle and a green knoll that rose in a rounded hump from the Somerset levels. A flock of sheep and three or four horses speckled the slopes.

Libby peered up the lane. A few stray leaves, hardy enough to withstand the recent gales, still clung to the branches of a row of trees – horse chestnuts, perhaps. The tracery of branches framed a neat, white-painted building. That must be Max's place. Libby whistled. Max Ramshore lived in style. *Mr Lord of the Manor.*

What was it he did, exactly, that he could leave at such short notice to go to the States? He'd left the bank, but he was way off retirement age. Or, was he going to America for some other reason, using Susie as an excuse?

Beyond Mrs Thomson's' house, dunes led down towards the golf club and beach. The nine legged lighthouse must be nearby. Libby dragged on the brake, eased out of the car, tugged the battered boot until it opened with a screech, and rescued a box of walnut brownies. Tucking it under one arm, she scanned the net curtains for signs of occupancy.

She thumbed the doorbell and waited. No answer. She rapped on the wood of the door and leaned harder on the bell. No one in. Maybe she'd do some snooping round Max's house, as he was away.

As she stepped back, Bear bounded around the corner, greeting her with the enthusiasm of a long lost friend. With a super-human effort, she kept her feet, pushing the dog's wet nose away from her face. The door creaked open.

An aged head appeared in the gap between door and frame, hearing aid peeking from behind each ear. Libby recognised the old lady's Victory Roll hairstyle, popular at the end of the Second World War. Her great aunt used to wear one. 'Mrs Thomson?' Libby raised her voice. Deafness must be a blessing to anyone who lived with this sheepdog and his ear-splitting bark, but it was going to make conversation difficult.

The lady of the house screwed up her eyes. 'Are you the dog walker for Bear?'

So far, so good. 'Max Ramshore sent me. He said you'd like me to come and help with Bear while he's away. I've brought some brownies.'

The door closed. A chain rattled and Mrs Thomson pushed the door wide, beckoning with one hand as she untied her apron with the other. 'Come in, come in. I'll make a cup of coffee and see if we've got any biscuits. You must be hungry, coming all this way.' She led Libby through the house, talking all the time.

All this way? From Exham?

'I've brought brownies,' she repeated.

'Yes, we get a lot of townies here. They like to walk on the Knoll.'

10

ANNIE ROSE

Mrs Thomson's long, low sitting room looked out over the dunes. The windows were small and wooden, long overdue an update to double glazing. Libby shivered. The wind from the sea must blow straight through the crumbling wood. She could smell the salt from here.

Mrs Thomson shook her head at Libby's bawled offer of help in the kitchen, pointed to the sofa and went out. Libby tried to remove dog hairs from the tapestry cushions decorating the sofa, changed her mind about sitting down, and stepped over to the window. It took an effort of will to make herself look to the right, along the beach to the lighthouse.

The view encompassed the whole beach, from the pier to the lighthouse and beyond. The tide was out again, leaving the building's stumpy legs exposed in the mud. Libby released her breath in a relieved sigh. There was no body in sight, today.

Mrs Thomson returned, balancing a tray painted with cats. China cups and jugs rattled as she lowered it to one of the side tables. Vases, silver framed photos and dog-shaped ornaments teetered on the piano. Pictures of Bear standing alongside a bent, aging man hung on the walls. Mr Thomson?

His widow poured coffee and brought a cup to Libby at the window. 'We've got three lighthouses in Exham, you know.'

'Three?' Libby sipped the hot coffee.' It seemed the three lighthouses were a source of pride to local people.

'Yes.' Mrs Thomson stretched knobbly, arthritic fingers. 'There's one on the beach, up there,' she nodded to the right. 'That's where they found Suzanne, the other day.' Libby set her cup and saucer down on the table nearest to the hairy sofa and sat. She could brush her jeans later.

Mrs Thomson took a brownie. 'These are nice, dear. Did you make them yourself?'

Libby smiled. 'You've heard about Susie Bennett, then, Mrs Thomson?'

Her companion shook her head, her brow folded into a criss-cross of lines. She looked about to burst into tears. 'Oh, yes. Such a shame, a lovely girl like Suzanne.'

Libby bit her lip. Mrs Thomson was old and widowed. Maybe asking questions, getting her to relive the past, would be cruel.

Before she could decide, Mrs Thomson was talking. 'I knew her before she was famous, when she was a little girl, singing at the Christmas parties the vicar used to put on over there.'

She pointed through the window to a small, squat church that lay almost on the dunes. 'Suzanne, we called her. I don't hold with shortening names that were given at a proper Christian baptism. The young people do it all the time, these days. You never know who's who. My name's Marjorie, and I never let anyone call me anything different, not even my Eric.'

'Did you know Suzanne well?' Libby steered the conversation back to the past.

'My Eric used to play the piano while Suzanne sang. Such a

pretty little thing, she was, all curls and a big smile.' There were tears in the old lady's eyes.

What had she thought when Susie grew up and developed a taste for boys and fast living? 'Did other children go to the parties, too?'

'All the boys and girls were there. There'd be dancing and games, Suzanne would sing, and Maxwell would play the saxophone. You know Maxwell, don't you? Calls himself Max, nowadays. Of course you know him. What am I thinking? It's Maxwell sent you round to walk Bear.' She leaned on the arm of the chair, pushing down for support and staggering to her feet. 'I'm getting forgetful, that's my trouble. Where did I put Bear's lead, now?'

Libby cut in. 'Please tell me more about Suzanne.'

Mrs Thomson narrowed her eyes. 'Why do you want to know about her? From the press, are you?' She pursed thin lips. 'I know the girls from the local paper. You're not one of them. Are you from the Western Daily Press?' Her voice rose. 'Nosey people, those reporters. That Jeremy Abbott from Weston super Mare barges his way in without so much as a by-your-leave. He came yesterday evening, but I didn't open the door to him. Never do, after six o'clock, not at my age. I like to settle down in front of my telly.'

She gave Libby a hard look, as though trying to remember who she was. 'Anyway, I've nothing to say to you, so you'd better be getting off.'

11

PHOTOGRAPHS

Judging by the unhealthy, deep red in Mrs Thomson's face, the elderly lady could be on the verge of a stroke. Libby held out her hands. 'No, no. I'm not a reporter. It's just that – well, I found Susie's body, Mrs Thomson. Suzanne's, I mean. I was walking my friend's dog on the beach.'

'Hm.' Mrs Thomson stopped in mid-gesture. She stared hard at Libby, suspicious. Satisfied, she sank back into the chair, the livid colour slowly ebbing from her face. 'I suppose Maxwell wouldn't have sent you round here if you were with the papers. He has his faults, that one, but at least his heart's in the right place.'

Libby hesitated. She didn't want to risk hurting the old lady, but she needed to know more about Susie. 'You must have been proud of Suzanne?'

'Mr Thomson used to keep all the cuttings from the newspapers when she went to the States. Who'd have thought little Suzanne would make such a big name for herself?'

Libby took a shot in the dark. 'Did she keep in touch after she left Exham?'

'Oh yes, she used to send me all her records. Albums, they call them nowadays, of course.'

'Or downloads.'

'Pardon?'

Libby wished she'd kept her mouth shut. 'Nothing.'

Mrs Thomson was talking again, 'She sent a card at Christmas, as well, every year, regular as clockwork. All except for that one year.'

'Which one was that?'

'The year the little girl died. It must have been, let me see, the little girl was seven, so that was back in the early nineties. She wrote and told me about it, but no cards that year. Not surprising. Poor Suzanne, it broke her heart.'

Coffee scalded Libby's throat. 'Little girl? She had a daughter? That explained the pink ring. Libby had been sure there must be a child.

'Oh yes, she had a daughter in America. With Mickey what's-his-name. Big record executive, he was, or some such. Annie: that was the little girl's name. Annie Rose. Pretty little thing, she was, just like her mother. Here, wait, I've got a photo, somewhere.'

She pattered from the room; old green slippers soundless on the patterned carpet. Drawers opened and closed in a different part of the house. Mrs Thomson returned, clutching a red photo album and Libby shifted along on the sofa, making room. Heads together, they flipped through pages of photos: babies, houses, older children.

'Here we are.' Mrs Thomson pointed at four photos protected by a filmy, plastic sheet.

A neat, handwritten date and caption accompanied every image. 'My Eric put all our photos in an album, labelled and everything. He was like that. Always neat and tidy.' Mrs Thomson peered round the room, maybe half hoping to see the late Mr

Thomson in his usual chair. 'The farm was the best in the county. Our Herefords won prizes.' Her shoulders slumped. She sighed, misty eyed. 'All sold, now.'

Afraid the old lady was slipping into reminiscing about the farm, Libby tapped a finger on the photo at the top left of the page. 'Is this Suzanne?'

'That's her. Still at school, then.' Libby caught her breath, shocked to see a young Susie smiling in the photo, very much alive. Under the lighthouse, she'd been wet, bedraggled and dead. Nevertheless, this was the same person, no question. There was no mistaking the neat nose and arched eyebrows.

Mrs Thomson moved on to the other pictures. 'Here she is, on stage in America.' Two tall youths, one bowing a violin, the other behind a keyboard, each young face taut with concentration, dwarfed the singer. Despite her tiny stature, Susie's personality sprang from the photograph. She glowed, alive with the joy of performance, an enormous guitar slung round her long, white neck.

'This one's her wedding photo.' Mrs Thomson's voice jerked Libby back to the present. 'And this—' one gnarled finger touched the last photograph, light as a caress, 'is little Annie Rose.'

Libby let her eyes slide down to the image of Susie's little girl. The child was a miniature of her mother. Hair so fair it was almost white, she struck a dancer's pose, toes pointed, arms in the air, delicate in a tiny version of her mother's fringed skirt and full-sleeved blouse.

Libby dragged her gaze from the dead child's enchanting dimples and looked at the wedding photo. So, that was Mickey, the husband. He loomed over Susie, heavy arm pulling her off balance, crumpling the puffed satin wedding dress. The bride gazed up at her new husband adoringly, while he smirked at the camera, stealing the moment like a spoilt child.

Still, being self-centred and arrogant didn't mean he was responsible for Susie's lonely death. If Mickey was in Los Angeles on the day she died, he couldn't have killed her. Libby hoped Max would take a good look at the man's alibi. 'Mrs Thomson, do you know how Annie Rose died?'

'Oh, dear. I'm afraid the poor thing drowned.'

Libby's head spun. Perhaps Mrs Thomson was confused. 'No, I mean Annie Rose, not Suzanne.'

'That's right. She fell in the swimming pool.' Mrs Thomson's eyes were very bright. 'They all have swimming pools, out in California. It's so hot, you see. It broke Suzanne's heart.' Her smile trembled. 'We never had children, Eric and me. Suzanne was like the daughter we never had. We'd been so happy for her, with her little girl, doing so well, and then, Annie Rose died. It was quite dreadful. Eric never got over it.'

Libby's stomach lurched. Had she jumped to conclusions? Maybe Susie had drowned herself, after all, still heartbroken, choosing to end her life as Annie Rose had lost hers. Perhaps the police were right.

She struggled for words. 'How did you find out?'

'They rang, from America. Mickey's secretary, I think it was, said Suzanne was too upset to talk but she wanted us to know.' Mrs Thomson took out a tiny white handkerchief and wiped her eyes. 'There, it still upsets me, dear. I'm sorry to make a fuss. You see, it all happened so far away. And now this...'

She blew her nose again, pocketing the scrap of cotton, standing, shrugging her shoulders. 'Well, these things happen. I'll make more coffee.'

Mrs Thomson clattered in the kitchen. Libby flipped backwards through the pages of the album. She found a photo of a Christmas tree, piles of presents and rows of kids. They were about eleven or twelve years old, Libby guessed. The vicar beamed in the centre of the back row. She looked closer. There was Susie – Suzanne – in the front row, a brace running along her teeth.

The tall, gangly boy standing beside Susie looked familiar. Yes. It was Max. Mrs Thomson returned, tray in hand, and leaned over Libby.

'Look, there they all are. Most are still here, or hereabouts. There's Maxwell, of course, and Benedict who's married to Samantha. The one with the broken tooth is Alan – Alan Jenkins. Oh, look, there's Angela...'

She broke off as the doorbell rang. Libby jumped to her feet, glad of an excuse to avoid more coffee. Her insides were awash. 'Don't worry, Mrs Thomson. I'll open the door.'

An elderly woman on the doorstep wrinkled her forehead, perplexed to find an unexpected stranger in her friend's house. 'Oh. Is Marjorie in?' A cake shaped parcel, wrapped in tin foil, peeped from her basket. Libby ushered the newcomer in, made her excuses to Mrs Thomson, grabbed Bear's lead and left them to their memories.

12

BEAR WALK

Libby gripped Bear's collar when they arrived home, hauling him back as she unlocked the door. The last thing she needed was a confrontation with the cat. She shouted for Fuzzy, but as usual there was no response. That animal came only when she chose, and she could be anywhere. Probably out for the day, finding dogs to torment. Libby wasn't about to leave Bear outside, digging up the tiny garden. She wanted the huge animal where she could see him.

She shut the door to the sitting room. He wasn't going in there either, no matter how much he whined or scratched the door. Libby's heart sank. The animal barely fitted into Hope Cottage, and she couldn't let him into the kitchen. Not if she wanted a hygiene certificate so she could sell her own food.

He'd have to stay in the hall. She looped the lead over a door handle to keep him from the stairs.

'Sorry, Bear. It's only for a while.'

He deserved a reward. Food? She scratched her head. She'd never owned a dog. What with Shipley's wild chasing on the beach, and Bear's size and quantity of drool, she was learning, fast.

Did the aging, forgetful Mrs Thomson remember to give him regular meals? That might be why Max had taken the dog under his wing. She should offer him something to cheer him up, and there was steak in the fridge – a treat for the weekend. Libby had planned to share it with Mandy, her new lodger, but the tiny rent she was asking for wouldn't cover it, anyway.

Libby dropped the rump steak in an old bowl and Bear leaped on it with enthusiasm. 'You're either hungry, or greedy.' She set a bowl of water near the food.

The builder, Samantha's husband, arrived on time, built like a wrestler, with enormous thighs and shoulders, his biceps tight inside a sleeveless t-shirt. He squeezed past Bear. Comfortably full, the dog was taking a nap, stretched out along the hall, snoring happily. Ned considered the bathroom, sucking his teeth and accepting Libby's offer of cake. 'These avocado suites were put in during the seventies,' he said. 'Don't see them around very often, these days.' He laughed.

She sighed, 'I can't wait to get rid of the tiles.'

'It'll take me a week,' he announced, once he'd measured the room. 'I'll email the quote for the work, while you choose the units. Here.' He thrust a shiny catalogue in Libby's hands, swallowed her last brownie in one bite, and left.

Head teeming with plans for a spa bathroom that she knew she could not afford, Libby climbed the stairs to the study, opened her laptop and pulled up a list of a hundred and twenty emails. Most were junk. A long page from her daughter tempted her, but she moved on. Ali would ring if there was a problem. This was a news bulletin. She'd enjoy it later.

Ah, there it was. Max had checked in, as promised. She'd exchanged emails with him before he left for the States and been secretly hoping to hear from him. She'd liked the man's eyes, and she was touched that he'd chosen to look after Mrs Thomson and Bear.

She felt like she had as a teenager when a boy she fancied smiled at her. *This is ridiculous. I'm far too old for that nonsense, and a respectable widow of two years. Max and I are collaborating for the sake of Susie.*

She forced herself to concentrate on the email.

Staying in luxury in Hollywood

he gloated.

Contacted Mickey's company and got an appointment to see him this afternoon. Told them I was an old friend of Susie's and it was personal and urgent. Will let you know what happens.

Libby snorted. Luxury in Hollywood would mean five-star glamour. Flowers in the room, champagne on ice. Libby's family holidays had been camping in Scotland or a week in a chilly holiday cottage or, when the kids were teenagers, caravan holidays in France. Trevor never wasted money. Max, it seemed, had plenty.

She knew he had retired early, and she suspected he'd been more senior than a 'bank manager', judging by the sizeable farm he'd bought from the Thomsons. He had contacts in America – maybe he was a kind of consultant, charging thousands for a day's work.

Libby closed the laptop, retrieved Bear from the hall, wiped up the water he'd splashed on the wooden floor and set off, anorak hood firmly in place against the weather. It had turned nasty again. The wind and rain grew stronger every moment. It was going to be a rough afternoon and probably a stormy night. Summer seemed a very long time ago.

She rejected a walk on the beach, heading for the countryside, and choosing a couple of fields with no livestock. She wasn't taking any chances, although Carpathian Sheepdogs, she'd discovered online, were peaceful, placid animals with an affinity for sheep, able to roam long distances in the Romanian hills to keep their charges safe.

She found a stick and threw it. Bear charged away, fur flying, grasped it in his teeth with hardly a pause, raced back and dropped it triumphantly at her feet. Libby laughed aloud, pulled his ears and threw the stick again. Fuzzy would never dream of such undignified behaviour.

'Oi. You.' The voice came from behind. 'What the devil d'you think you're doing?'

A short, squat man wearing a waxed jacket and flat cap appeared at Libby's side. 'We're not doing any harm.' How dare he shout at her? This was a public footpath.

Oh. No. Now Libby thought about it, she realised it wasn't. She'd left the path some way behind. Still, there weren't any crops here to be trampled, and no sheep or cows. She'd brazen it out. The man's face was very red, his nose enormous and lumpy. *Drinks too much.*

'That dog's not on a lead. I could shoot him.' The man's eyes were small. He narrowed them into angry slits.

'You haven't got a gun.'

'Didn't say I was gonna shoot, did I? But I could.'

They summed each other up. Libby stood as tall as her five foot four inches allowed and glared, hiding triumph as the man's gaze dropped. 'What you doin' with Bear?'

'You know him, then?'

"Course I know him.' He called out, 'Hey, Bear.'

The dog raced over to lick his hand, happy to transfer his allegiance from Libby.

'Oh. Well, I'm walking him for Mrs Thomson. Max asked me to.'

'Ah. Max.' He drew the word out. The grin was insulting. 'Friend of yours, is he?'

'Not really. I like walking dogs. I'm just helping out Mrs Thomson while Max is away.'

The man nodded; the smile even broader. 'Gone far, has he?'

About to tell him to mind his own business, Libby stopped. Instead, she tried her best smile, head on one side, eyelashes fluttering. 'I don't know him well. He seems very busy. I've no idea what he does all the time.'

The man laughed. 'Max has his fingers poking into all sorts of pies. You be careful, now, a nice lady like you.' His eyes travelled up and down Libby's body.

Glad of the shapeless anorak, Libby tried another tack. 'Do you live around here?'

'Over yonder, t'other side of the hill. Want to come and see?'

'Why not?' Was she mad? Libby straightened her shoulders. She could look after herself.

They trudged along the lane without speaking. He was definitely the strong, silent type. They turned the corner, but saw was no sign of a house. The edge of the village began a hundred yards down the road, and the nearest building bore a garish sign, 'Jenkins Garage.' Libby's spirits rose, despite the missing apostrophe. That was the garage Max had mentioned. 'Is that yours?'

'Yep. Alan Jenkins at your service, Ma'am.' There was grime under his nails and oil stains on his coat. He was not a farmer, after all. He'd been stringing her along. Libby wouldn't make much of a Sherlock Holmes. She hadn't even recognised him as one of the boys in Mrs Thomson's photo album.

He might be a useful source of information. He knew Max, Susie and the others. In any case, her car needed him. 'Maybe you can help me. There's a dent in the back of my car.'

'Jag, is it?'

'I wish. Citroen.'

'You bring it round; I'll see what I can do.'

Libby took Bear back to the house. She found Fuzzy in the airing cupboard where she'd been hidden in a nest of Libby's towels all the time the builder had been there. She shut the dog in the hall, barricading the stairs with kitchen chairs, and took the car round to Alan Jenkins at the garage.

He pursed his mouth. Ramping up the bad news so he could overcharge her, Libby decided.

'Tell you what,' he said.

'Yes?' She braced herself.

'Seeing as you're a friend of Max's, I'll do it for nothing.'

'What? Don't be ridiculous. Why would you do that?'

He grimaced. 'The thing is, Mrs-er...'

'Mrs Forest.'

'Mrs Forest. The thing is, I owe Max a favour, just at the minute. I reckon, seeing as you and he are good friends, like, this 'ere'll pay it off.'

Libby's blush rose hotly up her neck. 'We're not good friends. I told you, I hardly know him.'

"You were out at the White House t'other night, and that's a fact.'

'Yes, but...' More evidence of the speed of the town grapevine. Libby's words tailed into silence as her brain raced. 'Well, maybe we are friends. Max has plenty of friends.'

'Yes, and I wouldn't want to be on the wrong side of most of 'em.'

Libby swallowed. 'So, what's the favour you owe him?'

'Now, that would be saying.'

The man was putting on a good local yokel act, Libby had to hand it to him. 'Come on, Mr-er-Alan. If you want me to help you get on the right side of Max, you'd better tell me a bit more, or else I'll give you a cheque and tell him you threatened me.'

'I never did.'

'I know that, but Max doesn't.' Libby coughed, fighting a snort of laughter. Alan Jenkins had turned pale.

'All right.' He looked around, to check they were alone. 'There's been some ringing.'

Libby tried to look intelligent. 'Ringing? With – er – um...'

'Broken-down cars fit only for scrap, sold for next to nothing, tarted up, clock turned back, sold on to nice unsuspecting ladies, like you.'

Together, they eyed Libby's car. 'It came from a proper Citroen garage, I'll have you know. A long time ago.'

He wiped his hands on the front of his overall. 'Anyway, the garage got in a bit of trouble with a Bristol gang and Max – well, he sorted it out for me.' Max had enough clout to scare off a gang of criminals, had he? Alan Jenkins picked up an oily rag and polished the wing mirrors of a small Renault. If Libby wanted to know more, it appeared she'd have to ask Max.

'Where are you?'

'What?' The harsh trill of the phone broke into Libby's confused dream of sand, mud and dogs. 'What time is it?'

Marina exhaled loudly. 'It's half past one, and we're all here, waiting for you.'

Libby shook her head to click it into gear. 'I fell asleep.' She never fell asleep after lunch. She wished she'd kept Bear with her, instead of walking him back to Mrs Thomson's house. He would have kept her awake. 'I'm on my way.'

Her heart sank. Today, the local history society was giving a talk about Victorian women at Mangotsfield Hall, the huge mansion nearby, owned by the National Trust, and Marina was planning to demonstrate the clothes a Victorian lady wore. Libby had agreed to be a model chiefly because Trevor's ancestor had worked there as a maid, and Robert, her son, would love to see photos.

Unfortunately, the appointment had slipped her mind. 'You might have reminded me.'

'We talked about it on Tuesday.' Marina dropped the

outraged voice. 'Look, don't panic. Angela's doing the magic lantern show first, so you've got a bit of time. I know how you feel, I've been all of a tizz ever since the Susie thing. Just get here as fast as you can.'

'What about refreshments?' Libby had planned to pick them up from the bakery.

'Mandy brought them over. She said she's staying with you? As a lodger?' The question hung in the air. No problem with Marina's gossip antennae.

Libby ignored it. 'Look, my car's in the garage. Can someone pick me up? I'll be ready in ten minutes.'

She grimaced. She'd agreed to some crazy things since she came to Exham, hoping to fit in with the townspeople, but it would probably take at least twenty years to be accepted as a local. She really ought to spend more time on her career. She was getting behind with the next book, and it was time she booked another cooking course. Baking. That was her future. And chocolate. She ran downstairs. Better not keep Marina waiting.

* * *

Marina's car screeched to a halt at the back of the Hall, at the tradesman's entrance. Libby dashed through another sudden downpour, frantically grasping the edges of an umbrella as the wind threatened to turn it inside out. She pasted a serene expression on her face as they walked in.

'It's OK.' Marina poked her head through a crack in the door. 'Angela's kept them busy.' Laughter blared from the hall, followed by applause as Angela finished.

'Come on, then,' Marina hissed. 'It's us next.' She gave her friend a hearty shove and Libby half fell into the hall.

She was never going to volunteer for anything, ever again.

She really, really hated people staring. What had she been think-ing? Well, too late now. She smiled through clenched teeth, lips stiff, as Marina dressed her up in Victorian costume and make-up, beginning with a cotton shift and working up through layers of corsets and wire crinoline cages. She wouldn't be able to bear the weight for more than five minutes. How did Victorian ladies keep going all day?

Marina attached false ringlets to the sides of Libby's head. 'The Victorians thought it impolite for a lady to show her ears,' she explained, taking a pot of strong-smelling potion and a paint brush, and smoothing oil over Libby's hair. As it dried, Libby shook her head, but the ringlets stayed rigidly in place.

The result was a passable imitation of Queen Victoria. As though that were not sufficient humiliation, the audience gath-ered round, taking photos that threatened to haunt Libby for the rest of her life. They plucked at the costume, lifting heavy layers and letting them fall. 'Look, you can hardly raise your arms, those sleeves are so tight.'

'It's all part of the Victorian way of life,' Marina said. 'In fact, wearing a corset supports your back, don't you think, Libby,'

'I could wear this every day,' Libby lied. 'For one thing, it hides my waist. I could put on pounds and no one would notice.'

Slowly, the audience dispersed, chattering happily. At last, she could get rid of the costume and have a few words with Marina. 'What's in that disgusting stuff you spread all over my hair? You didn't warn me about that. How am I going to get it off?'

The words dried up on her lips as Libby caught sight of Detective Sergeant Joe Ramshore. She shifted, embarrassed. Did Joe know she'd been out to dinner with his father? Oh, well, who cared? She was a grown woman and Max was divorced. It was none of his son's business.

'Mrs Forest, I'm glad to see you.' Joe focused on Libby's hair and smirked. 'So sorry I missed the meeting. That costume looks terrific. And the hair...' He made a noise halfway between a laugh and a cough. 'Actually, I'm one of the trustees of Mangotsfield Hall and it's my day off today, but I'd like to have a word with you.'

Libby swallowed. Was she in trouble? About to be accused of obstructing the police by moving the body and taken into custody?

'Of course.'

'I wanted to tell you we've had the pathologist's report. It's no more than we expected. The cause of death was drowning while intoxicated. He found alcohol in Susie's blood. Probably not a deliberate overdose, just enough to stop Susie taking proper care around the water.'

'No sign of anything else?'

'A bruise on her head, but that would be the tide bashing her against the lighthouse. It was a rough old storm on Monday night.'

Libby tried to think. 'What about the time of death?'

'It's hard to tell. The body was in the water for a few hours, but it was so cold the pathologist can't tell when rigor mortis set in.' Libby winced. It was the stiffness of rigor mortis that had kept Susie's hand in her pocket, until Libby pulled it out to point at the sky.

'Look, Detective—'

'Call me Joe.' The grin told Libby he knew she'd been to dinner with his father.

'Look, aren't you going to investigate further? I mean, you said she was bruised. Don't you think that's suspicious? What if someone else was there?'

Joe sighed, looking suddenly tired. 'Please, Mrs Forest. We're grateful to you for calling us in as soon as you found the body, but now, you must leave it to us. We've seen hundreds of accidental deaths, you know, especially when there's drink or drugs involved.'

The patronising tone infuriated Libby. 'I know that, but common sense—'

'Common sense tells us there was nothing suspicious.' He'd raised his voice. 'Now, let me give you a bit of advice.' Joe's mouth smiled, but the eyes, as blue as his father's but ice cold, told a different story. Libby resisted a shiver.

'You're new here. You didn't know Susie. People feel strongly about her around here. They're proud. Not many from Exham end up famous. Folk don't like anyone suggesting she's more than just unlucky.' The blue gaze bored into Libby. 'We need to keep everyone calm. Talk a bit less about the drink and drugs, if you see what I mean. It was just an unfortunate accident.'

His tone was reasonable. 'Walking on the beach at this time of year is dangerous. The sea comes in fast. Susie's been away a long time and she forgot about the power of the tide.' He leaned towards Libby and spoke with emphasis. 'It was an accident, Mrs Forest. Leave it be. No more gossip.'

Gossip? That was rich. The whole town was abuzz with scandal. Libby shrugged. 'I didn't know her. I just found the body.' She hoped he hadn't heard details of her conversations with Max or her visit to Mrs Thomson.

'Exactly. You didn't know her. I'm just saying, some folks here don't take kindly to a stranger, who wasn't here in the old days, stirring things up.' His words silenced Libby. She tried to think of a sufficiently cutting reply, but before she could gather her wits, Joe walked away, leaving Libby, arms akimbo, mouth open.

Marina took her elbow. 'Are you OK?'

'I don't know. I think I've just been told to keep my nose out of town affairs.'

'By Detective Sergeant Joe?' Libby nodded. Marina waved a hand. 'Don't worry about him. He can't get over his father coming back to town, just when Joe's been promoted to Chief Inspector's bagman. He wants to be top dog around here. You know, a big fish in a small pond. Max tends to cramp his style. It's family stuff.' She laughed. 'He's giving you a hard time because Max doesn't take enough notice of him.'

'Joe knows I've been out with Max,' Libby blurted.

Marina snorted. 'Of course he knows. It's the talk of the town, Libby. That's why the room was packed this afternoon. Everyone wanted to get a look at you.'

Libby's eyes threatened to pop out of her head. 'You mean, they're judging me?' She glanced over her shoulder. The few stragglers remaining in the hall stood in small knots, staring at her, fascinated. Libby choked back her anger, took a breath and stalked, fists clenched, eyes straight ahead, out through the door, as whispers chased close behind.

14

MANDY

The afternoon at Mangotsfield Hall had confirmed every one of Libby's fears about making a new life in a small town: gossip, cliques and the cold shoulder. London neighbours had warned her, but she'd thought she knew best. So much for those great plans for opening a chocolatier here. She was a laughing stock.

Safe at home, she grabbed a bottle of chardonnay from the fridge, filled a tall glass and took a satisfying gulp. As she drained the glass, and tilted the bottle again, ready for a top up, she caught sight of the clock. Mandy would be back soon, unless she'd changed her mind and found somewhere else to live or returned home.

Drinking wouldn't help. Libby had better cook dinner, instead.

She screwed the top back on the wine bottle, replaced it in the fridge and rifled through the shelves, looking for food. She had plenty of vegetables and some chicken. A stir fry, maybe? Something sharp and satisfying, with lovely noodles to warm the stomach.

Libby chopped and tasted, blending soy sauce with chili. She crushed garlic, relishing the sharp scent and the bite on her tongue, her spirits rising.

The door crashed open. Mandy appeared, soaked to the skin, tattooed arms full of flowers.

'These are for you.' The girl blushed crimson to the roots of the unnaturally black hair, plopped the flowers on the kitchen table, dropped a box of chocolates beside them, and walked out. 'For being kind.'

Libby heard the glue of tears in Mandy's voice as she disappeared upstairs.

Libby wiped her own, suddenly damp, eyes, ran cold water into a vase and cut the ends off the flower stems. She went to the foot of the stairs and shouted. 'Thanks. I love Alstroemeria.' She kept her voice matter of fact. 'They last for ages.'

Back in the kitchen, she turned on the radio, humming as she worked. A door closed upstairs and Mandy reappeared in dry clothes, wearing a sheepish grin. Libby longed to take a cloth to the girl's chalky face. Somewhere, under several inches of white make-up and lines of black kohl, hid a pretty face.

Libby reopened the wine, took out a clean glass and filled it, offering it to her new lodger. Mandy barely glanced at it before taking a long swig. Libby winced. Now wasn't the moment to pontificate about wine drinking, but it hurt to see good wine glugged like orange squash.

Mandy said, 'I heard about Joe Ramshore at the Hall.'

'News really does travel fast here, doesn't it?'

Mandy laughed. 'You said it. Anyway, don't take any notice of him. He's a fool. By the way, I told Mum I've officially left home, and you know what? She said, 'Good for you.''

'I'm sure she's glad. She worries about you. I know I—' Libby stopped. Mandy had enough problems without hearing a sob story about Libby's marriage. 'Mothers worry about their children.'

'Hmm. Maybe. Anyway, I told her to come over here if things get worse.'

Libby swallowed. 'Oh. Good idea.'

'Don't worry, she won't come. At least, I don't think so...'

Every scrap of dinner eaten, they lounged around in the sitting room, eating chocolate and watching television. Libby fiddled with kindling and firelighters until a blaze started in the fire. She rested twigs and bigger shards of wood on top in an elaborate cone shape.

'First fire of the year. Bet it goes out.'

The smell of apple wood scented the room. Libby breathed in, tension leaving her shoulders as she curled her feet up on the sofa. Fuzzy lay across Mandy's lap and purred loudly. 'She never sits with me,' Libby said. 'She likes you.'

Mandy dipped her head, cheeks reddening. 'Libby, I've been meaning to ask you something.'

'Ask away.'

'You said you're going to open a chocolate shop.'

Libby groaned. 'That's the idea. Sometimes it seems a very long way away. Don't tell Frank, because I don't want him to think I'm setting up in opposition to the bakery. I haven't decided yet. I've got a course coming up about the business side.' She wrinkled her nose. 'Not my favourite thing. Still, I don't want to be bankrupt in my first week. Then, I need to get more experience, and I've got to finish writing the next book, if I decide to do one. I haven't signed the contract yet.'

It sat on her computer, still waiting for a decision. 'Don't worry, Mrs Forest,' the publisher, a thin, exquisitely dressed young man, with a condescending attitude, had insisted. 'We'll do all the hard work for you. 'Baking at the Beach' was delightful, of course, but just a photo book, you know. Not – er – exactly professional. We're offering real expertise, and the chance for a bestseller.'

Libby had laughed.

'No, no, Mrs Forest – or, may I call you Libby – I mean it. We're one of the foremost publishers of creative crafts in the country. Of course, we can't offer an advance – but we'll bear all the organisation and all the costs.'

'And all I have to do is invent dozens of recipes, and test them?'

'Exactly. Oh, and provide a tiny story for each one – to keep the reader interested. Couldn't be easier.'

Libby told Mandy the story. 'So, we're looking at months, if not years, before I'll be in business for myself.'

'Well, when you do, I wondered—'

The phone rang. Libby, wishing she'd taken it off the hook, made a 'sorry' face at Mandy and answered. 'It's me. In Los Angeles.'

'Max. You're kidding. Really?'

'Really. I thought you'd want a progress report.'

'Report away.' She had things to say to Max when he got back, but they could wait.

He talked fast. 'I saw Susie's husband, Mickey. He's a jerk.'

'As we thought.'

'Quite. Well, he said, and I quote, he was sorry Susie was dead, but he hadn't seen her for years and he's far too busy with a new family to come to the funeral. He doesn't know what Susie was doing in Exham, and by the way, he wants to know if the will's been read yet. I suppose he's hoping to be in it.'

'Is there a will?'

'Your guess is as good as mine. Susie never mentioned it, but if she signed one, she might have left it with a solicitor.'

'What about the rest of her band? Did you track them down?'

'Mickey's assistant gave me addresses.' Libby heard a smile in his voice. 'Nice girl.' He'd have taken her out to dinner and pumped her for information. 'Guy the violinist and James the keyboard player left years ago and went back to England. The addresses may be out of date, but it's a start. I asked her if she knew about Susie's solicitor, but she didn't. Said Susie left all the business to Mickey. I'm heading back.'

'Back to Somerset? Not going to enjoy Los Angeles a while longer?'

He snorted. 'Alone in a hotel? Not my idea of fun. How are things?'

She paused. She wouldn't tell him about Joe. She didn't want to get involved in family jealousies. 'Fine.'

'Good. What about Mrs Thomson?'

'She showed me photos.'

The silence dragged on. 'Photos?'

'Of Annie Rose. Didn't Mickey mention her?'

'Who's Annie Rose?'

He didn't know? 'Mickey and Susie had a little girl who died when she was seven.'

The sharp intake of breath on the other end of the phone told Libby it was news to Max. 'Susie sent cards, and photos of her daughter to Mrs Thomson. Mickey didn't think to mention her?'

'I'm speechless. Look, I'll be home late on Saturday. Let's meet on Sunday: lunch at the Lighthouse Inn.'

'You'll be jet-lagged.'

'I've got through it before. A glass of pinot noir does the trick.'

Used to jet-setting around the world, then. Libby felt suddenly small and naïve. An afternoon in the local National Trust House, playing at dressing up, while Max flew halfway around the world, probably club class. Bet he'd been everywhere. 'Libby?'

'Yes?'

'Thought we'd been cut off.'

'I was thinking. Can't you get back to Mickey and ask him about the little girl?'

'Tell you what. Email a copy of the little girl's photo for me to show him I mean business, and I'll try.'

Libby bit the inside of her cheek. She hadn't thought to ask for the photo, but she wasn't about to admit it. She'd have to nip back to Mrs Thomson's bungalow. She sighed. The car was in Jenkins' garage. 'I'm in the middle of something, I'll send it this evening.'

'OK. No hurry. Mickey won't go to bed at 9 o'clock, I bet. He'll be out on the town with his trophy wife. The secretary will tell me where he goes: I'm meeting her again at one of the bars here later today.'

Of course, you are. She couldn't resist you, could she?

'By the way. None of my business, but what exactly are you in the middle of?'

The cheek of the man. 'Mandy's here. You know, from the bakery? She's lodging with me. She came to-to...'

'To get away from her Dad?'

'Something like that.'

'OK. Good idea. He's a menace. Send the photo as soon as you can, Libby. See you on Sunday.'

Mandy appeared in the hall. Libby grabbed her keys. 'I'm popping out for a minute.'

'Can I come?'

Libby couldn't think of a reason to refuse. 'We'll have to walk.'

15

BREAKING AND ENTERING

'Mrs Thomson?' Libby rapped on the door. The light was on in the house and she could hear the TV. Mrs Thomson must have turned the sound up. Libby banged again, harder, and pressed the bell, keeping her thumb on the buzzer, but no one came.

Mandy spoke from behind Libby's shoulder. 'I'll go around the back.' She disappeared. Libby kept up the banging and ringing, but no one came. Where was Bear? He should be barking his head off by now.

Maybe Mrs Thomson had gone away. She might be visiting a friend, or a sister.

'Libby. Get help.' Mandy was back, panting. 'I looked through the window. I think she's had a fall.'

Libby dialled 999, hand shaking, remembering the last time she'd had to ring the police, on Tuesday. 'Fire, police or ambulance?'

'Ambulance. Police. Both.' Heart pounding, Libby ran with Mandy to the back of the house and peered through the kitchen window. The room gave nothing away: clean, neat and as tidy as before; plates stacked on the draining board; tea towels folded over the sink to dry. Mandy grabbed Libby's arm and pointed. The door to the hall stood ajar, and through the gap, Libby caught a flash of green. She groaned. Mrs Thomson's slippers. She'd been wearing them when Libby visited.

The door was locked. Libby shook it, but it held fast. She stood back, struggling to stay calm and sum up the problem. A pane of glass ran down the middle of the door. Libby gripped her phone in both hands and smashed it hard, into the panel. Broken shards clattered to the kitchen floor. She elbowed jagged fragments inwards, pulled the sleeve of her jacket down round her wrist, and slipped her arm through the door. The tips of her fingers touched the key. Grunting, she forced her shoulder further in, more splinters tinkling to the ground, until she could grasp the key between thumb and finger and turn it in the lock.

Praying Mrs Thomson hadn't shot the bolt across from the inside, Libby leaned on the handle. To her relief, the door swung open. She crunched across glass and pushed open the inner door. The old lady lay at the foot of the stairs, the back of her head angled against the wall. Mandy whispered. 'It looks as though her neck's broken.'

Another body. A wave of nausea struck Libby. She swallowed it down. No time for that, now. She felt Mrs Thomson's neck for a pulse, and fingered her wrist, horribly aware she'd done exactly the same for Susie.

'I think she's dead.'

Mandy's hand clamped to her mouth, muffling her voice. 'She must have fallen down the stairs.' She tugged Libby's elbow. 'Can't we do anything? Shouldn't we put a blanket over her, or something?'

'It's too late for that.' A news programme still blared from the television, echoing through the house. Libby's head pounded. She strode to the sitting room, found the remote control and switched off the set. Silence fell. A cup of tea, half finished, sat in its saucer on the table, next to one of Libby's walnut brownies. No steam rose from the cup. The tea must be cold. Libby knew better than to touch anything. Tears misted her eyes. Mrs Thomson had been alone, with no one nearby to help when she fell. Libby hoped she'd died instantly. The thought of the old lady lying in pain was unbearable.

The house was quiet: too quiet. What was wrong? *Bear.* Where was the dog? Why hadn't he barked when his mistress fell? A cold hand tugged at Libby's chest. She stepped with care around Mrs Thomson and set off up the stairs.

'Where are you going?' Mandy squeaked.

'The dog's missing.' Libby went through the house, opening one door after another. 'Bear, where are you? Come on out, it's me.'

Mandy sat on the stairs, transfixed by Mrs Thomson's body. 'Maybe he's outside?'

Before Libby could search the garden, horns blared, lights flashed, and the emergency services arrived in force. Joe Ramshore was first. 'Mrs Forest. What are you doing here?'

Mandy said. 'We found Mrs Thomson.'

'Did you?' He frowned at Libby, eyes narrowed, suspicious. The ambulance crew whispered in his ear. 'Another body,' he said. 'And once again, you're on the spot.' He took Libby's arm. 'Might I ask what you were doing here?'

* * *

The wooden chair at the police station, designed for utility rather than comfort, made Libby's back ache. She stared ahead at uninviting walls, bare of pictures or notices, painted dull grey. Mandy sat next to her at the plain wooden table, swirling cold, undrinkable tea inside a paper cup. Detective Sergeant Ramshore tilted his chair back, until only two legs touched the floor, waiting blank faced for an explanation.

'We went to the house to look at a photo,' she said. 'Mrs Thomson showed it to me earlier when I visited. To walk the dog.'

His expression didn't change. 'You were looking after Bear?'

'Max – your father – he's away.'

Joe raised one eyebrow in disbelief. 'And he asked you to take over the dog walking?'

Libby held his glance. 'Why not?'

He shrugged. 'So, you came back here in the evening, to visit an old woman? Didn't you realise you'd frighten her at this time of night? It looks like she tried to get to the door, wearing her ragged old slippers, and tripped on the stairs.'

'What?' Furious, Libby leaned forward. 'Are you saying it's my fault?'

'Have you got a better idea?'

'The dog's missing. Maybe she was going out to look for him?'

Joe crossed an ankle over the other leg, tapping his cup with a long finger. 'In the dark? We'd know more about that if you hadn't broken in, making such a mess of the back door, wouldn't we?'

'We had to get in.' Libby was indignant. 'We could see her at the bottom of the stairs. She could still have been alive?'

'OK.' He uncrossed his legs. 'Fair enough, I suppose. Anyway, I'm afraid the poor old soul's gone. She must have been almost ninety, and she lived all on her own. Something like this was bound to happen one day.'

'You think it's another accident, then?'

The detective laughed. 'Mrs Forest, please don't start imagining someone murdered Mrs Thomson. Old ladies fall all the time. It's amazing she lasted so long, alone in this place. No one broke in. The only damage is to the kitchen door, thanks to you.'

'Can we go home, then?'

When Joe smiled, he looked like his father. 'I'll get one of my men to drive you.' Tired, Libby and Mandy trudged along the drab corridor of the police station. 'And Mrs Forest.'

She stopped. 'Yes?'

'Try not to find any more bodies for a few days.'

16

Libby tapped out a brief text for Max before she fell, exhausted, into bed.

Can't send photo after all. Explain later. Please text addresses of band members

She was asleep even before the whooshing noise sounded, announcing that the text had gone.

A series of messages greeted her when she woke.

What's going on?
Hope everything OK.
Here are addresses

She smiled. Max was no more able to use text speak, full of gr8 and thx, than she. She copied the addresses onto a scrap of paper and folded it, sliding it into a pocket in her handbag.

'I'm worried about Bear.' She poured cornflakes into a bowl. Mandy, white faced, a faded grey dressing gown pulled up to her chin, looked like a vampire. She cradled a coffee cup in both hands and grunted. Libby hid a smile. It was good to have a teenager about the place again, failing to communicate. 'I'm going back to see what happened.'

'You know it's not half past six yet, don't you?'

'You can talk.' Concerned, Libby considered Mandy's pale face. 'Couldn't you sleep?'

Mandy shivered. 'I kept thinking about that poor old lady.'

'I know. We'll talk about it later, after you get back from the bakery. In the meantime, I'm going to find out what happened to Bear.'

I can't face Max if something happens to the dog, as well as to Mrs Thomson. She longed to email or ring, to tell him, but she couldn't. It would be unfair while he was too far away to help.

Fiercely, she chopped a banana into tiny pieces and dropped them into her bowl. 'I can't just leave him any longer.' Besides, she wanted to get to the Thomson house early. There was a job she meant to do.

Mandy heaved a sigh and pushed herself up from the table. 'I'll come with you.'

'No.' She wouldn't involve Mandy any further. 'You have to get to the bakery. I landed you in enough trouble yesterday, and I won't do it again. If Detective Sergeant Ramshore finds out we've been back to the crime scene, we'll go straight to the top of the suspect list. That is, when he works out Mrs Thomson didn't fall.'

Mandy's mouth hung open. 'You think she was pushed?'

'Of course she was. How many unexplained sudden deaths does a place like Exham have in the average week? Yet, here are two in a few days.'

Mandy sucked at a corner of toast. 'There are lots of old people here. You know, in Haven House and that new place near the kid's playground. There must be dozens of people dying every week.'

'I hope you're exaggerating. Anyway, Susie wasn't old and it's too much of a coincidence.' Libby stirred the banana into her cereal. 'Think about it. She comes back to Exham for some reason, we don't know why. Next minute, she's dead. Then, one of the few people who really cared about her dies.'

She pointed her spoon at Mandy. 'I was beginning to think the police were right, and Susie's death was an accident, but this is one coincidence too many.'

Mandy got to her feet and stacked her bowl in the dishwasher. 'In that case, I'll definitely come with you. You can't go alone. Someone has to keep you out of trouble.'

Libby choked on her cornflakes. 'Nonsense. I'll be careful. Anyway, Frank can't bake bread and serve at the same time, and we mustn't let him down.'

If she hadn't been so worried about Bear, Libby would have enjoyed the walk to Mrs Thomson's house. The wind had died away overnight, and the rain had stopped. The sun was almost up, peeping from between heavy clouds that threatened more storms before long. She'd offer to take Shipley out soon. She'd been neglecting him, deserting the poor animal for Bear, and she doubted Marina would have exercised him.

They'd have a good run on the beach later, before the weather broke again.

As expected, the police had boarded up Mrs Thomson's back door. Libby walked on, out into the half acre garden. The late Mr Thomson's retirement pride and joy looked neglected, the pond clogged with duckweed and dead leaves. A few remnants of foliage clung to grey overhanging branches. Beds of roses had run to a riot of hips and haws. Something for the birds to enjoy, at least.

Libby called softly. 'Bear?' No answer. She called again and whistled. What was that? She strained her ears. The sound had come from her right, where a sturdy shed nestled against a ragged yew hedge. Libby tugged at the door until it creaked open. Bear sprawled in the corner. He raised his massive head, staggered to his feet, whined, wobbled and lay down again.

Libby's stomach heaved as she caught the acrid scent of sick. A pool of vomit stank nearby. Fresh scratches covered the shed door, where the dog had tried to get out. Bear whined again, and lay, head on paws, exhausted.

'What happened to you, Bear?'

The shed was clean and warm, and a selection of doggy toys suggested Bear sometimes slept there. His basket was lined with old sweaters, positioned close to an empty bowl. Judging by the nearby splashes, it had recently held water. Another bowl held a lump of meat, half eaten. Bear had only taken a bite or two.

Libby rubbed her knuckles against the top of his bony head and the dog nuzzled her hand. 'What did they give you? You seem to be on the mend, old thing. I'll take you home with me and look after you today.' She straightened up. 'But first, I need to get into the house.' There was a toolbox in the shed. This was going to be easier than she'd thought.

The lock on the back door was still broken. The police had nailed hardboard roughly across the opening, half to the door, the rest attached to the frame. She'd better be quick. A locksmith would probably arrive this morning, to secure the house properly.

She opened the toolbox, glanced round to check she was alone, grasped the biggest hammer firmly, hooked the claw behind the first nail and twisted. The nail popped out. So did the second. The third was awkward, bending and sticking, and

Libby's hair was stuck to her head with sweat by the time she wrenched it out.

As she levered out the fourth and final nail, the door swung open and she stepped inside. The broken glass had been swept away. She tiptoed into the front room, stopped and straightened. No need to tread with such care; there was no one in the house to hear her. She let her gaze rove across the crowded tables and shelves. Nothing had changed since she'd been here with Mrs Thomson.

The old lady's presence seemed to fill the air. Libby shivered and whispered, 'I hope they didn't scare you, before they shoved you down the stairs.' How exactly had she died? Libby's head spun with different scenarios. Maybe they took Mrs Thomson by surprise, and she died, mercifully, hardly knowing what happened. Or perhaps the killer was someone Mrs Thomson knew and trusted. Lonely, she might have let them in, just as she'd welcomed Libby.

Libby doubted that. Mrs Thomson had said she never answered the door after six.

'I won't mess up your house, I promise. I just need those photographs.' Libby spoke out loud, as though the old lady could hear her.

The album lay where she'd last seen it, among a pile of note-books and scraps of paper.

'I'll find out who killed Suzanne,' Libby added.

She started to flick through the stack of papers, fingers fumbling. Her head flew up. What was that noise? Someone was outside.

She grabbed the pile of papers and books, along with the album, and thrust them all into her shoulder bag. Just in time. The door flew open.

'What the—' Detective Sergeant Ramshore slid to a halt,

halfway between Libby and the door, arms folded. 'Mrs Forest. I might have known. This is breaking and entering, you know.'

Libby thought fast. 'I'm worried about the dog. I came back to find him.'

Joe hooked his thumbs into his belt. 'Well, one of my men found him in the shed. Looks like he slept there last night, so you can go home again, Mrs Forest, and please, please, just stay away.'

'I was going to take him home with me, if he's well enough.'

Joe's face cleared. 'Good idea. Make yourself useful. And don't come back.' He stood aside and Libby slipped past, making light of the heavy shoulder bag, hoping he wouldn't ask to see inside it. Sometimes, age and gender had its uses. He'd have spent longer talking to a pretty young girl, and he'd have been suspicious of a man, but a woman of a certain age, old enough to be his mother...

Maybe he'd decided Libby was just a foolish, interfering older woman. She bit her lip to keep a tell-tale smile from her face.

'Wait.' Joe held up a hand. Libby stopped, heart racing. She'd celebrated too soon. Was he about to search the bag? She'd have a job explaining the stack of stolen papers. 'I've got some news. I suppose you're entitled to hear it first, as you found her.'

'About Mrs Thomson?' Libby stood sideways, her bag clasped under the arm furthest away from the officer, her body shielding it from view.

'No, about Susie Bennett. The complete postmortem shows more bruising than we thought: more than the pathologist thinks would result from being thrown about in a storm.'

'Bruising? What does that mean?' No harm in continuing to play the innocent woman.

'It means you may be right, crazy as it sounds. Susie Bennett might, just possibly, have been murdered.'

'Do you – do you know who did it?'

He leaned back against the wall, legs set apart, every inch the bold investigator. 'Not yet. I'll be surprised if we ever find out. A body on the beach, in a storm. No evidence, you see. Still, don't leave town, Mrs Forest.'

Libby slipped out of the room, clutching the bag tight to her body.

Joe had already lost interest in her. 'Better get the door fixed right now, Evans, before the rest of the town comes to visit.'

By the time she arrived home, Bear trooping, listless, beside her, Libby's shoulder ached from the weight of books. Her mind raced. As she'd turned to leave Mrs Thomson's sitting room, she'd glanced out of the window. From there, the widow could see right along the beach, to the pier on the left and the lighthouse to the right.

What if Mrs Thomson had stood, looking out into the storm, on Monday night? She might have seen something unusual. More than the storm and high tide. Something that had got her killed.

The faithful old Citroen was due for collection today. Libby checked the time. Yes, if she hurried, she could pick up the car and visit both of Susie's band members today.

Bear recovered fast, growing perkier every moment until he bounded up and down the hall with his usual vigour. How long could Libby keep a dog his size in this tiny cottage?

Oh, well, she'd worry about that later. Meanwhile, she dug out an ancient apple crate from the cupboard under the stairs, dragged it into a warm spot in the hall and lined it with old blankets. 'There you are, my lad.' She took a step into the sitting room and held her breath. Fuzzy lay curled by the door, in one of her favourite spots where hot water pipes lay under the floor.

Bear heaved himself to his feet, looming over the cat, panting.

Was Libby about to witness an epic fight? She grabbed Bear's collar. Fuzzy stood, yawned and stretched her back legs.

Then, to Libby's amazement, the cat began to purr. Libby dropped her hold on Bear. 'When did you two make friends?'

The dog leaned over, touched his nose to Fuzzy, and settled down next to his new buddy.

Libby stashed Mrs Thomson's photo album in a drawer and walked to the garage. She'd spend the evening poring through the book for clues.

Alan Jenkins wiped oily hands on a blue overall. 'Ah. Mrs Forest, there you are. She's just about ready for you.' Why did men always call cars, 'she'?

He still insisted on refusing payment. 'Tell Max it's a present.' He'd even topped the Citroen up with petrol. Was Max some kind of Godfather around here?

Tired of arguing, Libby held out a packet of her homemade shortbread. Alan's eyes lit up.

'You're a good woman.' What was it the old wives used to say about the way to a man's heart being through his stomach?

The road to Bath twisted through tiny villages, along a road too narrow for more than one car. Marina told her it was quicker by train, but Libby needed her own transport. She'd made up her mind to visit both the other members of Susie's old, defunct band, before Max returned. James, the keyboard player, lived just outside Bristol, and Guy, the violinist, lived in Bath.

She'd thrown a ham salad into a Tupperware container before setting off, and she pulled over beside the Chew Valley Lake, to eat. She took a bite and screwed up her nose. The dressing didn't taste quite right. Maybe a little too much lemon juice? Or not enough honey? She'd make up another batch soon.

It was days since she'd had time to potter around in the kitchen, experimenting. Once this business was over, she planned to lock herself in for hours and get on with devising recipes. Before long, she'd have to give Niles Fisher, the publisher, her answer about the book.

Libby felt a twinge inside at the thought. She planned a series of excuses as she ate, opening the door to let a few rays of sunshine warm her. *Dead bodies: that would do it.* At least it had the advantage of being true, and Mr Fisher had no way of knowing the bodies in question were unrelated to Libby.

She threw a crust of bread into the water. Excited ducks scrambled over one another. Libby took out a chunk of sultana cake. The ducks wouldn't get any of this, her favourite comfort food.

Every last crumb eaten, she climbed back into the car, crunching gears in sudden excitement. Maybe Susie's old bandmate, Guy, would have some answers.

His double-fronted Georgian house stood, white-painted, in a block of similar graceful homes. To Libby's surprise, the door flew open almost before she'd had time to drop the brass lion-head knocker, as if he'd been expecting her.

The man's appearance took her aback. She'd been prepared for aging hippy long hair, flares or a tasselled waistcoat. Instead, his short, neat haircut, shirt, and the final touch, a silk tie with a Windsor knot, were conventional enough to have pleased Libby's parents. He was only a short step away from a cardigan.

His lined face wore the slightly anxious look of a middle-aged man whose mirror proves his youth is disappearing fast. He led her inside.

'Max rang to say you'd be coming.'

So, it was Max who gave the game away. Annoying man. Libby had lost the element of surprise.

'Anyway,' Guy shrugged. 'Susie was all over the local news. I thought I'd hear something from Exham. When's the funeral?

Was the man upset? Libby couldn't tell. The pupils of his eyes were big and dark. He pushed wire-rimmed glasses further up a long nose and waved at a selection of wines and spirits on a breakfast bar.

'We don't have a date yet. Not until after the inquest.'

Guy nodded. 'I'd like to be there for Susie. We had some good times together in the old days. Drink?'

The huge, airy kitchen was clean and, unlike Guy himself, at the cutting edge of modern design. Libby flicked her gaze round the room, finding no sign of a wife or children among the uncompromising shine of black granite and glassy smooth white paint.

She shook her head. 'I'm driving, but I'd love a coffee.'

'Ah. Good choice.' Guy clattered around the huge, gleaming chrome of the coffee machine with milk jugs and coffee. Libby hid a smile. Kenco and hot water would have taken half the time.

The coffee, when at last it arrived, was perfect. 'So, you found Susie on the beach. That's sad. Not quite the dramatic end I'd expect of her. She'd have preferred something outrageous, like a mistimed bungee jump.' When Guy smiled, he showed beautiful white teeth. They must be the result of the band's success in America. 'Was it the drink that killed her?'

There was no reason to hide the truth. 'In fact, she had been drinking, but I'm afraid it looks like murder.'

That caught the man's attention. He blinked. 'Seriously?'

Libby pressed on, glad to have dented his calm surface. Now, maybe he'd forget any prepared speeches. 'There are a few suspects. I imagine the police will visit you, soon.'

A flash of consciousness, a widening of the eyes, told Libby she'd hit a nerve. He shot a glance around the kitchen, and she realised what had seemed odd about him. His gaze unfocused, his eyes dark, his behaviour too casual.

The man was stoned. Libby wondered where he kept the drugs.

'Excuse me.' He stepped outside the kitchen, into the hall, and called up the stairs. 'Alvin?'

'Yeah. What is it?' A younger man, in his twenties, hair longer, mussed up, his sleeveless t-shirt showing muscled arms, leaned over the banister.

'Clean things up, will you?'

The younger man frowned, puzzled for a moment, then his brow cleared. 'Right. OK.'

Libby gulped down the coffee. She had to get her questions out before Guy cut the conversation short. He'd want time to clear the house of incriminating drug paraphernalia.

'I just want to find out about Susie. What happened after all those albums, when she came back to Exham, and why? Those sorts of things.'

He shrugged. 'Don't ask me. Didn't know she was here. The band broke up years ago, and we all lost touch. We made a bit of money. I had enough to buy this place.' He looked around the kitchen, beaming. 'Bought a house for my mother, as well. She's in a care home, now, but she had a good few years.'

'What about Susie's marriage?'

The smile faded. He shrugged. 'Usual showbiz thing. Mickey found a newer, younger model. You know – longer legs, blonder hair. Anyway, Susie lost her spark when...'

He stopped, licked his lips and shot a sideways glance at Libby. She let the pause go on as she rinsed her cup and dried it, but Guy offered no more details.

She'd have to prompt. 'OK. I know about the little girl that died. Annie.'

'Annie Rose, yeah. Cute little thing.' The lines on Guy's face softened. Libby glimpsed a warmer, kinder man somewhere under the surface. 'Broke Susie's heart when little Annie died.'

'And Mickey's too?'

'What? Oh, yeah, of course. He was upset. We all were. That's when Susie said she couldn't go on. We tried to talk her out of it, but who could blame her? Something like that cuts you right up.

She left LA, went up north, heading for Canada. She had some sort of connections there; distant family, or something. She was a bit vague.'

'Has she been in touch?'

'Nope. Clean break. I came back to Bath, took an OU course in computing.'

Libby laughed. 'Computing? After life in a band?'

He pushed his glasses up again. 'Well, I'd always done the techie stuff. I played violin a bit, sure, but I preferred to tinker with the sound system.' He shrugged again. 'Not really cut out for travelling. It was good to get off the road and settle down.'

'Apart from the drugs.'

He shuffled his feet. 'Just weed. Nothing heavy.'

'Anything else you can tell me about Susie?'

'She was a nice kid. If I'd known she was in England I'd have got in touch.'

Alvin shambled into the kitchen, scratching at an unshaven chin, and Libby beat a retreat. Guy seemed to know as little about Susie as her old school mates in Exham. It was as though she'd been a ghost, passing through people's lives.

One question above all others hammered in Libby's head. What on earth had Susie been doing in Exham after all those years away?

18

Libby fiddled with the Satnav, planning the route to Weldon on the other side of Bristol, aware that someone, either Guy or Alvin, was watching from a window. They wanted to make sure she'd left the area. She revved the engine and wound down the window, waving with enthusiasm. She'd have time to visit Susie's other band mate if she set off now.

The route to James Sutcliffe's home took Libby down a series of ever more winding, narrow roads. She stopped to check her iPhone. Surely no one lived down this tiny, overgrown lane, hedges high on either side?

No signal. Should she give up, reverse back and go home? A horn blared and Libby twisted in her seat. She flinched. A monster tractor filled the whole of the rear window. The engine ground to a halt at the last moment, inches away.

The driver dragged off a pair of headphones, swung down from the cab, and rolled across to her window. A knitted jumper of indeterminate colour lay, unravelling, over his paunch. His head was stubbly and weathered. He shoved a ruddy, belligerent face close to the glass. 'Where you off to, then?

He'd left Libby no space to open the Citroen's door. Trapped and furious, she lowered the window and used her iciest voice. 'What business is it of yours?'

'If you're on the way to Ross on Wye, you need to go back, turn right onto the main road, and take the motorway. And don't use that Satnav. Can't be trusted.'

'How can I reverse with your tractor practically in my back seat? Anyway,' she remembered why she was here. 'I'm looking for James Sutcliffe. I think he lives nearby.'

'Ah.' The eyes narrowed. 'Huh. Plenty like you come up here on the way to Ross. No more sense than the day they're born. Buy an expensive Satnav, throw away perfectly good maps and get lost here, in my lane. You're going nowhere this way, let me tell you.'

Libby picked out information from an apparently well-practised rant. 'Your lane? You must be Mr Sutcliffe.'

'So, who wants me?' Must they have the conversation here? Libby peered ahead, but she couldn't see around the corner. The cultured voice of the Satnav recovered and broke in, insisting that in one hundred yards she would reach her destination.

Libby pulled out the connection. 'I want to ask about Susie Bennett.'

'Thought so.' James Sutcliffe was triumphant. The colour in his cheeks, previously the sort of dull pink a kind observer would describe as a healthy, open air glow, darkened to purple. Was he about to have a stroke? At least that would stop him blowing Libby's head off with a shotgun. 'Just get off my land, woman. I've had enough of journalists nosing into my business.'

'No, no, I'm not a journalist.' The squeak in Libby's voice was less than convincing.

'Who says so?' The man had a good point. It was one thing to prove you were something: journalists carried ID cards, didn't they, like police officers? Much harder to prove you were nothing special, just a normal person. Not that Libby felt very normal, given the events of the past few days.

She slapped on what she hoped was a non-journalistic smile, aiming for a mix of seriousness and reason. 'Anyway, even if I came from a newspaper, I can't go back until you move your tractor.'

Sutcliffe growled. 'Get yourself up to the yard.' He stomped back to the tractor.

The vast front end was only inches from her car. Libby feared for the newly repaired Citroen. She clashed gears and cursed under her breath, and the car lurched further up the lane, finally rounding the corner to rest on a cobbled farmyard.

Mud, an inch thick, covered uneven cobbles. Libby groaned. She'd chosen her shoes with care: elegant red patent with kitten heels and elaborate holes cut into the sides. Wholly appropriate for the refined ambience of Georgian Bath, they were unlikely to survive an encounter with farmyard muck. The temptation to wheel round and disappear back up the lane was almost over-whelming.

Holding the door for support, feet slithering, she edged out of the car. 'Mr Sutcliffe, I'm honestly not from the media. I've just been talking to Guy. Guy Miles.' The farmer frowned, obviously recognising the name. Libby held out her phone. 'Ring him, if you like.'

Libby had never heard anyone harrumph before, but that was what Sutcliffe did. He brushed past the outstretched phone. 'Better come in, then.'

She ducked under a low doorway that opened into a huge kitchen. Mud from the yard had infiltrated, using the convenient transport of Sutcliffe's boots, through the ill-fitting door. It carpeted the otherwise bare, flagstone floor of a rustic room, apparently undecorated since the 1950s. Rickety orange boxes, stacked underneath and to the side of a huge, pine table, teetered and trembled. Libby caught a glimpse of greaseproof paper and a logo showing a goat's head. Sutcliffe, proving himself to be no more of a talker indoors than in the lane, uttered one word. 'Cheese.'

19

CHEESE

'Dairy's over there.' He pointed through the window. To be sure, behind the run-down farmhouse nestled a contrasting complex of neat brick buildings, doors and windows smart with red paint, enclosing a small yard lined with pristine paving stones. In the distance, a herd of goats tugged up mouthfuls of grass in a paddock, as though on a mission. 'Jack runs the business now.'

The unexpected burst of information brought Libby back to the filthy kitchen. Could that be pride in the farmer's voice?

'Jack?' She guessed. 'Your son?'

'Ah. Lives over yonder with that fancy wife of his.' Sutcliffe's ruddy face had calmed. Social relations had somehow been restored. The farmer gestured towards a battered brown kettle. 'Tea?'

'Yes, please. Let me get the cups.' Many more of these visits and she'd float away on a tide of tea and coffee. She pulled mugs from the wobbling pile on the draining board and seized the opportunity to inspect them for grime. She'd seen worse.

Sutcliffe fiddled with kettle and tea caddy. Libby coughed.

'Susie Bennett. You were in the band, with her and Guy, isn't that right?'

'Ah.' Sutcliffe kept his back turned.

'I found her body.'

He stopped, kettle poised inches above an ancient, cracked teapot. His words were almost inaudible. 'Did you now? All alone on the beach?'

The bluster drained away from the red face, leaving it crumpled, like a crushed eggshell. Libby took the kettle, pouring hot water into the pot, giving the farmer time to blow a loud nasal blast on a grubby handkerchief. 'Little Susie. Who'd have thought it?'

The door opened and a younger, taller, cleaner version of James Sutcliffe strode in. Any hope the son would prove more welcoming than his father evaporated. He threw a cursory glance at Libby. 'What's going on, here, Dad?'

Sutcliffe wiped his eyes. Libby assessed the distance to the door, wishing she could just leave, annoyed to have misread James Sutcliffe. The gruff exterior hid deep feelings.

'I – I'm sorry.' Lost for adequate words, she sniffed a nearby bottle of milk, decided there was life left in it, and poured three cups of tea. 'I came to find out more about Susie Bennett.'

'You've picked a bad time.' The son pulled out a wooden chair and his father sank into it. 'Dad's wife died a month ago. The news about Susie just about finished him off.'

Libby gulped. No wonder the place was such a mess. James Sutcliffe had been running on empty, trying to keep going after the tragedy.

A thought struck. Jack Sutcliffe had said, 'Dad's wife.' She wasn't his own mother then.

He folded his arms. 'What's it all to do with you, anyway?'

'I found Susie's body. On the beach, under the lighthouse. I

just wanted to find out more about her. The police aren't interested, but she'd been away for so long...'

'The lighthouse?' James Sutcliffe interrupted. 'That's where
we used to do our courting, back along when we were lads.
Bonfires on the beach, hanky-panky in the dunes.' Libby studied
the rugged face, searching for a likeness to the youth in the
photograph. Life had been hard for Susie's old friend.

Jack opened a series of tins, peered into one and offered it to
Libby. 'Rich tea?'

She took one, dunking it in her mug. 'I just wanted to find out
why Susie was back in England. I thought her old band mates
might know.'

The older Sutcliffe stuffed his handkerchief in a pocket,
packed a biscuit into his mouth and mumbled. 'Came to see my
Mary.'

His son translated. 'Susie wanted to see my stepmother
before she died. It was cancer. It took a long time for her to go.'

Libby sat back. The answer to Susie's presence in the area was
as simple as that: no mystery, after all. Susie had come back to
visit old friends in trouble. 'I'm very sorry for your loss.'

Sutcliffe's son filled in the details. James married his first wife
in the United States before the band broke up. The marriage
didn't last long: the first Mrs Sutcliffe had a sharper eye for business than for romance and left her husband and young son for a
wrinkled but rich American tycoon. Susie stayed in touch when
the newly divorced James brought his son, Jack, home to the UK
and turned to farming.

'She used to write, now and then.' Jack smiled. 'Even sent me
presents from America. T-shirts and sneakers: things you
couldn't get in England, then. Like an aunt, really.'

'Do you have any letters?'

Sutcliffe shrugged. 'Threw them away. Anyway, they were

private.' Libby held up a hand. 'I'm not being nosy, Mr Sutcliffe. You see, no one knows exactly what happened. How Susie died, I mean. It seemed like she'd been drinking and got caught in the high tide.'

Sutcliffe snorted. 'Susie wouldn't get caught. She grew up in Exham. Knew every inch of the beach. She'd never let the tide catch her like one of those summer visitors. She drank like a fish, mind you, that's true enough.'

Libby smiled. 'You must have known her daughter?' She looked from one man to the other. 'I heard Annie Rose drowned.'

Sutcliffe clenched his fists and hammered them on the table, rattling the mugs. 'If I could get my hands on that man...' He pointed a finger at Libby. 'Neglect. That's what killed Susie's little girl. Mickey Garston let her die because he was too lazy to look after her.'

'Dad.' Jack intervened, one hand on his father's arm. 'No one really knows what happened. Anyway, that was years ago. It's Susie's death we're talking about. You're saying it might have been an accident?'

Libby shrugged. 'No. Murder.' She let that thought sink in.

Sutcliffe clattered the mugs together and threw them in the sink. 'Mickey Garston. That's who's behind it, you mark my words. Susie cursed the day she met that man. Just let me get at him...' Jack laid a hand on his father's shoulder, but the older man shrugged it off. 'Should have dealt with him myself, years ago.'

'Mickey was in America when she died,' Libby said. 'Besides, why would he want her dead after so many years?'

'I'll show you.' Sutcliffe left the room. Libby heard drawers opening, papers being shuffled. 'Here it is.' He held out two pages of writing paper. He hadn't thrown all her letters away then.

Libby glanced at the signature. *Love, Susie, xxx.* She read through the childish script.

Dear Jamie and Mary,

Thank you for the beautiful flowers you sent, and for remembering the anniversary of Annie Rose's death. She would have been ten years old. I still can't believe she's gone.

I miss England very much, but I won't come back. I have friends out here and the sun always shines. Most important, though, is I can visit Annie Rose's grave to talk to her.

You probably heard Mickey and I split up. It's been all over the news programmes. He's going to divorce me. I'd stop it, if I could, but Californian law won't let me. It makes me angry. Why should I set him free to marry someone else, after all he's done? My mistake was marrying him in the first place.

I want him to be miserable...

Libby re-read the letter. 'Divorce?' She let the idea take root in her brain. 'So, Mickey was her ex-husband. And now, Mickey's married to another woman.'

She thought for a moment. 'I wonder if Susie named Mickey in her will, or if she made another after the divorce?'

Sutcliffe rocked his chair back. 'Susie wouldn't let Mickey know how much money she had. I bet she put it somewhere out of his reach.'

Libby was still thinking it through. 'I don't blame her. She wouldn't want to rely on Mickey for alimony.'

Sutcliffe laughed; the sound sharp as a whip crack. 'You have to understand Susie, you see. Most people don't. At school, she was a bit of an outcast, because her parents were travellers. Her mother came from an old gypsy family. As for her dad, he was long gone when she was just a bairn.'

'Susie's parents never bothered to get married. No one knows what happened to her old man: he'll have died, long ago. Travellers live free as air, but they don't live long. Her Ma died while we were in the States.'

'Our Susie was more of a gypsy than anyone I've ever met. She didn't care about money. She did things the traveller's way: with a handshake. I'd be willing to bet my farm she died without leaving a will. Probably didn't even have a solicitor.'

'That means Susie's money...'

Sutcliffe slapped the table with one hand. 'It means Mickey might think he can get his hands on Susie's fortune – but he can't. It'll go to her family, no matter how distantly they're related.'

20

MUSHROOM SAUCE

Libby's bones ached as she turned into the lane leading to Hope Cottage in the dark. She longed to get home, close the curtains to shut out the world, light the sitting room with the gentle glow of table lamps, collapse onto the comfortable sofa and think.

If only Max were here, she could run today's discoveries past him. Had he found out any more about Mickey? Susie's husband had an alibi, but that didn't mean he couldn't mastermind Susie's death from the other side of the Atlantic. It all depended on Susie's will.

She yawned and drove onto the drive. She'd hardly had time to think about Mrs Thomson's fall. Had the old lady been pushed: killed for something she'd seen through the wind and rain of Monday night? Libby shivered. Two women were dead, and the local police weren't bothering to investigate. She felt very alone. If she didn't persist, Susie and Mrs Thomson would be forgotten.

Later, she'd look through the photos in the old lady's album. Who knew what else she might uncover from Susie's past? But first, she needed a large glass of wine. Her mouth watered in anticipation as she parked the car in the drive, fumbled in her bag for keys, and unlocked the door.

As it opened, a wave of noise erupted. Mandy, the Goth. Libby had forgotten all about her. Televisions blared from every downstairs room. Above the racket, Mandy was singing, tuneless but enthusiastic. Libby shouted. 'Mandy.' She waited. 'Mandy.' She clattered up the stairs to hammer on the door of Mandy's room.

The door swung open. 'Oh, hello, Libby.' Mandy, eyes wide, covered her mouth with one hand and pulled an earphone off one ear. 'Sorry, am I too noisy? Mum thumps on the ceiling with a broom handle when she wants me to shut up.'

Libby's exasperation dissolved. Having Mandy around reminded her of the recent, bitter-sweet days, when her own noisy teenagers lived with her, shoes and bags littering the hall-way, damp towels everywhere and the fridge emptied as fast as she filled it. The angry retort died on her lips. 'Is chicken and chips OK for dinner?'

'Wow, wonderful. With some of that special sauce you told me about?'

'Ready in half an hour.'

Bear and Fuzzy were still snoring in the sitting room. The dog had needed to recover and Fuzzy, over ten years old, could snooze for at least three quarters of every day, waking only to eat and wander outside hoping in vain to catch a bird.

Bear woke as she entered the room. 'You can sleep through Mandy's racket, but you hear me come in on stockinged feet?' Dogs, Libby decided, were remarkable creatures.

Leaving the animals, Libby opened a bottle of pinot noir in the kitchen. Mandy was lodging permanently so it was time to wean her off sweet white fizz. Forgetting the tired ache in her back, Libby set about preparations with enthusiasm. She made salad dressing, sliced potatoes into chips, washed vegetables and fried a handful of chestnut mushrooms in olive oil. In a minute or two, she'd add some crushed garlic, a slug of brandy, a whisk of mustard and a dollop of cream, and the sauce would be perfect.

She breathed in garlic and olive oil, the scent of sunshine and happiness. Mandy burst into the kitchen. 'Mm. Smells good.'

Libby handed over a glass, one third full. 'Sit down, Mandy. You're not to take a single mouthful yet.'

'What? Why not?'

'You'll enjoy it more, this way. Trust me.' Mandy rolled her eyes, but waited, glass in hand. 'Now, just circle the glass in your hand, so the air gets at the wine. That's it. Be gentle,' as Mandy's wine threatened to spill over the top of the glass. 'Now, have a look at the colour. Gorgeous, isn't it? OK, now get your nose in the glass and sniff.'

Mandy giggled and put on a fake, affected wine tasting voice. 'I'm getting peaches, brambles and a spot of manure.' Libby threw a tea towel at her. 'Maybe I need another glass to be sure.'

'Wait a minute, here's the food.'

Libby served the chicken breasts. Mandy spooned salad from the oversized wooden bowl onto her plate. 'Mmm. Scrumptious.'

'Had a good day at the shop?'

'Your latest recipe went down well. What about your day? Made any discoveries?'

'Not about Mrs Thomson, I'm afraid, but I found out one or two things about Susie.'

Mandy's phone rang. She bit her lip. 'It's Mum.' She pressed the button and her voice rose. 'Calm down, Mum, I can't hear you.'

Libby could hear Elaine's voice on the other end of the phone. It sounded scared. Mandy's hand shook as she covered the phone to hiss at Libby. 'It's Dad. He's having one of his tempers – stomping around upstairs and shouting.'

'Tell your Mum to come over here. She mustn't stay there. No, wait, I'll go and get her.'

Mandy relayed the message to her hysterical mother. 'No, Mum, stay there, but keep an eye out. Libby's coming.' Her voice rose. 'Mum, I can hear him. Get out of the house, now!'

Libby ran to the car and accelerated away, tyres screaming. The drive took less than three minutes. She screeched to a halt, just as Mandy's mother, coat-less despite the cold, ran out, fumbling at the car door. Libby leaned over to release the catch and Elaine half fell into the car, shivering, cheeks wet with tears, teeth chattering so she could barely speak. 'I s-sneaked out the back door when Bert went to get b-beer from the fridge.'

Bert burst through the front door, bottle raised, and Elaine screamed. Libby stepped on the accelerator.

'Hold tight.' The Citroen roared away from the kerb, heading for home. 'Just in time.'

Home in minutes, Libby slotted the safety chain firmly in place on the front door while Mandy took her mother's arm and settled her in the kitchen, still trembling. 'Did he hit you?' A cut on Elaine's forehead oozed blood.

She flinched. 'No. I – I banged it—'

'Ran into a door, did you? I don't think so.' Libby dipped cotton wool in warm water laced with Dettol and dabbed at the cut. 'It's not deep. I shouldn't think you need stitches, but you do have to ring the police.'

Elaine pushed Libby's hand away. 'No. Bert's had too much to drink, that's all it is. It'll be fine when he sobers up.'

'Mum.' Tears started in Mandy's eyes. 'It won't be fine. It's all happened before. He'll get drunk tomorrow and do it again, you know he will. Please ring the police.'

Elaine shook her head. 'I know what's best, Mandy. Just let him be. He'll cool off.'

A heavy blow shook the front door. Libby leapt to her feet.

'If Bert's cooled off, then who's that?' Another crash echoed round the house, then a third. A male voice bellowed, but Libby couldn't make out the words. The three women were on their feet, searching for something – anything – they could use to defend themselves.

Mandy grabbed Libby's arm. 'He's come after us. What are we going to do?'

'We're going to tell him to go home.' Libby's stomach lurched. Bert was well-built and strong. The bad back that kept him on sick pay was pure fiction. He could stop hammering on her door, though. How dare he? 'Stay here, you two.'

Libby straightened her shoulders, strode to the front door and pulled it open a few inches, the chain keeping it safe. Bert thrust his head into the gap. Libby could make out every mark on the man's red face: black, open pores on a bulbous nose, blobs of sweat above a mean top lip and deep lines on an angry brow.

Spit flew from the thin mouth. 'You little...'

'Don't you dare speak to me like that, Mr Parsons. There are three of us here, and we're phoning the police at this very moment.'

Mandy was close behind, holding a phone to one ear. 'Yeah, Dad. Go home and sober up.'

Bert Parsons swore and kicked the door. The chain rattled. Libby took a pace back, bile in her throat. She was vaguely aware of clattering behind her back, as Bert kicked again. Helpless, Libby watched as the screws holding the chain on the door sprang out, clinking as they hit the floor.

The third kick burst the door open. Bert shoved Libby in the chest. She over balanced, clutching the wall for support. Bert was in the house.

'Get out here, wife,' he roared.

A terrifying growl echoed round the hall.

Libby watched, mesmerised, as mouth open, teeth bared, Bear leapt at the intruder. Bert stumbled back. The dog growled again, and reared up, his enormous paws on Bert's shoulders. Bert tried to turn, slipped, and fell. Bear dropped to all fours, teeth bared, panting and slavering.

Saliva dripped on Bert's face. He struggled to rise, one arm fending off the dog. 'Get that animal away from me.' Bear planted both forepaws firmly on Bert and howled.

'Well done, Bear.' Suddenly, Max was in the hallway, hands on hips. He grinned at Libby and her stomach leaped. 'But it looks as though I've arrived too late for the excitement.'

Heart still pounding, Libby hauled the dog off Bert, and scratched Bear's ears. 'Good dog.' She slipped her fingers through the dog's collar. 'Mandy, take Bear into the sitting room.'

Elaine leaned on the doorway to the sitting room, watching in silence as Bert scrambled up, deflated and blustering. 'That dog's a menace. He needs putting down.' He shot a venomous look at Elaine. 'And you just wait 'til I get you home.'

'I won't be coming home, Albert Parsons. Not tonight, and not ever again.'

Max gripped Bert's jacket and turned the man to face him. He grabbed both lapels and tugged, forcing Bert on to his toes. Their noses almost touched. 'You'd better leave, Parsons, or you'll be the one that gets hurt.'

Bert looked from Max to Libby. 'So that's what you're up to, Max Ramshore.' His words were slurred. 'Got a new woman in town. Well, you're welcome to the ugly cow.' He shook off Max's grip and lurched down the path, stumbling and muttering.

Libby held out her hand, struggling to stop it trembling. 'Your timing is excellent, Max. Come on in and join the party.'

She stretched the meal to four, adding extra salad leaves, cutting chicken breasts in half, slicing chunks from a loaf of Frank's finest rustic bread, and opening another bottle of wine.

They ate in the kitchen. Bear settled down on the sofa in Libby's sitting room, a gentle giant once more. She hadn't the heart to move him. 'Just this once,' she said, 'Since you're a hero.'

The cat had disappeared, keeping away from the disturbance. Elaine, shaking with relief, refused to go to Accident and Emergency or call the police, but swallowed aspirin and let Mandy lead her upstairs to make up a bed.

'I'll go to my sister's in Bristol, on Monday. Bert won't come back tomorrow, not while the dog's here. And not if it means losing drinking time.'

Libby stacked plates in the dishwasher, while Mandy and her mother talked upstairs.

'Now, Max, why are you back so soon, and what did you find out?'

He insisted on making coffee, talking loudly over the grinder and frothing milk with enthusiasm. 'Well, I heard about poor old Mrs Thomson. It looks like all the action's over here after all. What is it?'

Libby was laughing. 'Mrs Thomson told me your name's really Maxwell.'

'Anyway,' he glared, 'I was worried about you. I wasn't sure how you and Bear would get on, after that business with your car. I can see I needn't have worried.'

They moved to the sitting room, where he stretched out in an armchair. 'That was a wonderful meal, by the way: better than a restaurant. I'm bushed. Jetlag, mostly. Wake me if I fall asleep.'

Fuzzy appeared from under the settee, stretched and sauntered over to sit on Max's knee.

Libby said, 'The car's been fixed and Bear's looked after me. He's even made friends with Fuzzy. I'll tell you about Guy Miles and James Sutcliffe in a minute, but first, what did you find out in America?'

'I didn't take to our friend Mickey, that's for sure. Too rich for his own good, that one, with a trophy wife, a mansion in Beverley Hills and a great opinion of himself.'

'Did you see his house?'

Max laughed. 'No, he graciously offered me half an hour of his time in a hotel. But I'd hired a car, so I did a little snooping around the area. You know, see how the other half live?'

'And?'

'I never would have thought I'd say it, but the heat was too much for me. It's good to get back to some Somerset weather.'

Libby shivered. 'Gales and rain, you mean. I suppose, at least we don't need air conditioning. Anyway, was Mickey what we expected?'

'Exactly so. I met his latest wife, by the way. Maybe you've seen her? She's starring in that sci-fi blockbuster that came out last month, and she was giving interviews at the same hotel. Mickey whisked me in and out of the room. I think he was trying to impress me.'

'Hm. He was rattled?'

'Hard to tell. Trouble is, he's got a great alibi. He spent most of Monday night at a televised award ceremony. Even with the time difference, he couldn't have attacked Susie and got back to the States in time. In any case, he hasn't really got any reason to want her dead, what with the sparkly new wife and all.'

Libby sat in silence, thinking. 'Doesn't her money go to her ex-husband if she doesn't have a will?'

Max shook his head. 'Afraid not. I checked with an online solicitor, and even if she'd left money to her husband in a will, and hadn't cancelled it, he wouldn't get it when she died. The law treats the estate as though her husband was already dead. That cancels out any financial motive for our friend, Mickey.'

'Hm. So, who would be entitled to her money?'

'It depends on whether she had children, or parents, or brothers and sisters, or maybe aunts and uncles.'

'Wow. That's complicated, and it gives any of those people a motive for murder. Oh!'

'What is it?'

'I didn't tell you the police think we're right – she could have been murdered.'

Max yawned. 'That's good. We can let them chase down Susie's relatives.'

'So, that's it? We leave it to them?'

'Not quite. What about Mrs Thomson?'

Libby gasped. 'You're right. How could I have forgotten? They insist she fell down the stairs, for no good reason.'

'But you think her death's connected to Susie's?

'Of course it is. Mrs Thomson loved Susie. She showed me photos – you were in them, by the way.'

'I was? Hope that doesn't make me a suspect.'

'It seems we need to think again. I'm sure Mrs Thomson was killed because she knew something.'

Max removed Fuzzy from his knee, stretched, and crossed the room to poke at the logs on the fire, prodding until flames shot up the chimney. 'There are plenty of reasons people kill each other. Money, of course, but then there's jealousy, and revenge, and a sudden burst of uncontrollable anger – and that's even before we get to sheer craziness.' He looked up at Libby, and his voice was gentle. 'I don't want to worry you, but Mrs Thomson died after talking to you. That might mean—'

'That I'm in danger too?' Shocked, Libby sat upright, rigid. Suddenly, the investigation had taken a terrifying turn.

Max was yawning again. Libby said, 'You need to sleep. Go home. We'll be fine here.'

Max frowned. 'I can't leave you like this, but you're right, I'm bushed. Maybe I could sleep on the sofa...'

'No, you need a proper night's sleep.' She had an idea. 'Why don't I keep Bear?'

A smile transformed Max's worried face. 'That is a brilliant idea. He's already proved his worth as a guard dog. You'll be safe with him – safe from angry husbands and,' another enormous yawn overtook him, 'and whoever killed Susie. Let's have a drink tomorrow and talk further.'

As if on cue, Bear awoke, shook his head, and walked over to Libby, settling down at her feet.

She stroked his head with one hand, grabbing her phone

from the coffee table with the other. 'I'm calling a taxi. You can't possibly drive..'

As she locked the front door, Libby suddenly felt lonely, despite the presence of Mandy and Elaine upstairs. She whispered to Bear. 'Don't tell anyone, but I'm sorry he's gone.'

22

THE OTHER LIGHTHOUSE

Mandy and Elaine slept in on Sunday morning. Libby enjoyed a quiet breakfast with Bear and Fuzzy. Last night's fears had disappeared and her usual good humour prevailed. She'd see Max again today and Bear would look after her. Her stomach performed an odd little flip. Exham had suddenly become a much more interesting place.

He'd phoned to suggest they meet in the Lighthouse Inn for Sunday lunchtime drinks, and something to eat. The venue seemed appropriate. Determined not to make too much effort, Libby wore a minimum of make-up: just mascara and lipstick, with the slightest blush of pink on her cheeks. Well, she excused herself, no need to go around looking tired. She pulled on jeans and a raspberry coloured sweater, brushed her hair until it shone, shrugged on a light grey jacket, loaded Bear into the Citroen – a considerable squash – and drove to the Lighthouse Inn.

Pre-dinner drinkers crowded the bar. Libby recognised some of them. Samantha Watson was in one corner, head bent close to

Chief Inspector Arnold. She waved a limp hand in the air without meeting Libby's eyes.

'We must have lunch some time, Libby.'

Bear turned his back on the solicitor. Libby murmured, 'Good dog,'

Max leaned on the bar, an air force blue sweater picking up the colour of his eyes. Libby slid onto a stool. 'You look as though you slept well.'

'I'm still a touch jet-lagged, to be honest. I need a beer.'

She waited until they'd ordered. With an orange juice and lemonade in her hands, she asked, 'Why did you want to meet here?'

'I thought we should talk to a few of Susie's old friends. See who you might recognise from Mrs Thomson's photos.'

He hadn't asked her out to enjoy her sparkling wit, then. Libby asked the barman for a bowl of water for Bear, and the animal was soon surrounded by a circle of admirers.

Libby slipped the Christmas photo onto the bar. 'Mrs Thomson told me some of the names. The full names, of course. No nicknames. I wonder if Bert still answers to Albert?' She pointed to one of the boys in the picture, 'Who's that, with black hair?'

'That's Chief Inspector Arnold.'

Libby snorted. 'He's changed a bit. I suppose the beard makes a difference, and the thinning hair. I suppose everyone's changed since this was taken all those years ago, but I can recognise you. You're just the same.'

'Apart from the wrinkles.'

'I guess Bert won't be coming in today?'

'Don't bet on it. He'll be looking for sympathy. He thinks he's untouchable. There he is, with Alan and Ned.' The garage owner waved. Ned winked. Bert kept his eyes on his shoes.

Samantha, elegant in tight white jeans and a navy cashmere sweater, looking years younger than her age, with not a trace of grey showing through expensive highlights, left the inspector and shimmied over to kiss Max on both cheeks.

'Libby and I know each other.' Her eyes picked out every detail of Libby's appearance, before she turned her attention back to Max, eyelashes aflutter. 'We're in the history society together.'

Max grinned. 'History society. Really?'

'One has to find something to do here.' Samantha heaved a heavy sigh. 'It's not Bath, you know.' Her voice held a bleak note and a little of Libby's antagonism drained away. Samantha had no children. Libby's two had left home, but they phoned regularly. Lately, she even seemed to have found a surrogate child in Mandy, but Samantha, with her lovely face and figure and lucrative career, was sad, bored and lonely. Ned joined them at the bar, but his wife's lip curled in contempt.

One of the drinkers Libby had never seen before slid his pint mug along the bar. 'Is there a date for Susie's funeral, yet?' Another of Max's old friends, Libby supposed.

Max shrugged. 'Not until the police release her body.'

'Your lad, Joe, was round at our place,' the man went on. 'Asking whether we'd seen her lately.'

Samantha tossed her head. 'She pretty well walked away from us all when she was famous.'

'She was back recently.' Libby spoke without thinking. Max glared, sending her a silent message. Maybe she'd stolen his thunder. Samantha blinked, but her forehead stayed smooth. With a flash of inspiration, Libby realised why she looked so young. *Botox.* She stifled a laugh.

Max said, 'Libby, this is Ollie. We were—'

'Don't tell me. You were at school together.'

Ollie chuckled. 'You say Susie was back here? When? Did anyone see her?'

'She went to visit a member of the band. James Sutcliffe's a farmer now, making cheese, out in the sticks beyond Bristol. Susie came back to visit his wife before she died.'

Ollie whistled. 'Phew, wish we'd known. Could have had a reunion.'

Samantha laid a manicured hand on his arm. 'I don't think Susie would want to be seen with us these days, Ollie.'

Libby felt an absurd need to defend Susie. 'She kept in touch with Mrs Thomson over the years, you know, sending photos.'

Samantha's tinkling laugh jarred on Libby's ears. 'I don't know why Susie would bother with that nosy old woman. Such a busybody.'

Max's eyes flashed steel. 'Haven't you heard?'

'Heard what? I've been away the past few days. I only got back from London yesterday.' Samantha edged closer to Max, her elbow almost touching his.

He took a step away. 'Mrs Thomson's dead. She fell down the stairs.'

'Oh.' Samantha recoiled. 'Well, how would I know that? Anyway, it's true, she was a busybody, standing at that window of hers, spying on us all. She used to tell tales to my parents.' She looked round the circle of faces registering their distaste, and her voice changed to show sympathy. 'It's very sad, all the same.'

Libby said. 'Anyway, she seems to be the only one in Exham that Susie told about her—' She broke off as Max repeated the glaring routine. She coughed. 'About her visit.'

Max took her arm. 'If we're going to do that walk, Libby, we'd better get going. Joe will let us know as soon as there's a date for the funeral; either of the funerals.'

Ollie raised a refilled pint glass. 'We should all chip in, give Susie a proper send-off.'

23

Libby's back tingled as they walked away. She could swear Samantha's eyes never left her. She hissed, 'What was that all about, Max?'

He grinned. 'I wanted to see some reactions.'

'Not about Susie's daughter, though. That was what you stopped me saying, wasn't it?'

'I thought we should keep that under wraps for a while.'

She waited, but he seemed in no hurry to explain. 'OK, Max. What aren't you telling me?'

'Let's get out of here first.'

Ten minutes later, they arrived at the foot of the Knoll. Max let Bear out of the car. He jumped up, panting at the prospect of a walk. Libby wasn't so sure. The hill was steep.

'You said we were having lunch.'

'We'll do a round trip and finish up back at the pub, when everyone's left. We don't want half the town eavesdropping.'

She shrugged and set off. 'Then why did we come to a pub where you knew we'd find all your school friends?'

'Told you: for reactions. Like Samantha's. What did she have against Mrs Thomson?'

'Or against Susie?' Libby shot a glance his way. 'Max, why didn't you let me tell them about Annie Rose?' The hill grew steeper. Max's legs were long and Libby found it hard to match his stride.

'Can't we slow down a bit?' she puffed.

'What? Oh, all right.' He slowed the pace a tiny fraction.

'You're blushing, Max. Come on, spill the beans. I thought we were supposed to be working together.' She was tired of wondering about Max's history. A hint here, a tiny piece of information there: he was so secretive. 'What happened with you and Susie when you were growing up together?'

'Susie and I were good friends, back in the day. Before she left school. I suppose you'd call us childhood sweethearts.'

'And Samantha was jealous.'

He stopped, looking out over lush green fields, the motorway purring faintly in the distance, and chuckled. 'A bit, maybe. Susie and I were together for over a year. She was a dear, sweet girl. At first, anyway. She was always musical, unlike me, and loved to sing. Guy asked her to join the band. That was fine, at first, but then the band took off and things changed. Susie started to drink too much – even for a teenager. She started smoking pot. Everyone was doing it in those days. Well, not everyone. I wasn't one of the cool kids.'

Libby laughed. 'Me, neither.'

Their eyes met. 'I wish I'd known you then,' Max said.

Libby swallowed.

Max set off again, slowly. 'Sorry, where was I?' He coughed. 'When Susie drank, she was wild. She didn't seem to know when to stop.'

'I suppose it's easy to get carried away if you're in a successful band.' Libby's breathlessness had nothing to do with the incline.

Max walked faster. 'Guy didn't go to our school. He was at a public school in Bristol: his father was a wealthy man. Guy kept Susie supplied with pot, I'm afraid. She started to spend more time with him than with me. I suppose I could see the writing on the wall.'

Max's face took on a faraway look, as though he was reliving the past: a past when he was in love with Susie. He breathed hard. 'Susie had a Saturday job in the newsagents. One afternoon, I went in to get cigarettes.'

He glanced sideways, caught Libby's eye, and grimaced. 'Everyone smoked, back then. The owner went into the back room. When Susie put my money in the till, she lifted a handful of cash. It wasn't much, but it gave me a jolt. We had a row, and I accused her of being a drunk and a thief. She laughed at me.'

Max bent over, picked up a handful of stones and tossed them into a hollow. 'She said: "You go around with your eyes shut, Max. If you only knew..." I had no idea what she was talking about. I suppose I was a bit dim in those days. I wouldn't let it go. I got mad, accused her of preferring Guy to me, of sleeping with him. She just roared with laughter and I stormed off. Neither of us apologised and we broke up. That's it, really. An everyday story of teenagers.'

Libby stopped walking. 'But you must have known she wasn't sleeping with Guy.'

'What? Of course, she was. She didn't deny it.'

'Max, he's gay. He's living with a man called Alvin. They're a couple.'

'You're kidding.' He scratched his head. 'Guy? Who'd have thought it? Are you sure?'

She nodded. He gave a crack of laughter. 'More fool me. Well,

Susie and I didn't get back together.' He stopped, frowning, as though thinking hard. He murmured, 'Not Guy? Then who?' He shrugged. 'Well, the band played at Glastonbury, Mickey came along, whisked her off to the States and married her.'

Libby's head was spinning. 'Can we sit down for a bit?'

They were almost at the top of the knoll, and the wind whipped at their clothes. Bear galloped up and down, full of energy, while they perched on stones. Libby's heart rate slowed to something more normal as she gazed out across the patchwork of fields. Rooks swooped, cawing, high above. The wind blew Max's hair over his eyes and he shoved it back with an impatient hand.

Of course, Max still had a soft spot for Susie, his first love. It was touching, really. Those teenage years, when life was so intense. That must have been around the time Libby met Trevor. She shook the thought away and spoke lightly. 'Well, that's quite a story. I guess we all have stuff in our past. Anyway, did you see Susie again after she left the country?'

'No. I was too proud. I wasn't going to chase after her. I wish I had. Not to get back together again, we'd grown too far apart, but to keep an eye on her. She could have used some real friends, I think.'

'My mother used to say, "If wishes were horses then beggars would ride". Come on, I'll race you to the top.'

Max overtook Libby easily. She stood and watched as he climbed on, towards the summit. What were those motives he'd mentioned? Money, jealousy, revenge. Max could have nursed his anger at Susie all these years and seized the opportunity for revenge when she came back.

She clenched her fists. Surely not Max? It couldn't be...

He turned to wait for her, and she remembered he'd been abroad when Mrs Thomson was killed. Relief left her legs shaky. She closed her eyes for a moment. She'd been in danger of letting imagination run away with her. She put on a spurt of speed to catch up.

Bear reached the summit first. He rolled in a patch of hazy sunshine. Max reached back to pull Libby, panting, up the last few yards. She groaned. 'I need to get into shape.'

'You look good enough to me.' She blinked, surprised, and a little warm glow ignited inside.

To cover her confusion, she told Max about her visits to Guy and James yesterday. 'They both cared for her and James kept in contact. He showed me a letter she wrote, just before the divorce. He said losing Annie Rose broke her heart.'

'Losing a child. Nothing could be worse,' Max murmured.

They sat quietly. Libby thought she'd rarely been happier than today, with Bear and Max.

'What do you do for a living, Max? You said you had business in America.'

'Finance stuff. I consult, which sounds much grander than it is. I work for organisations that need my rather dull ability to trace financial transactions.'

'Oh.'

'Exactly. Not exciting at all, but I get to travel from time to time, although most of the work can be done online.' He plucked a handful of grass and threw it into the wind. 'Which is a good thing, at my age. Jetlag's a killer.'

Libby watched as the grass blew away.

Max said. 'I've been thinking about Mickey again.'

The autumn sun warmed Libby's face as she leaned her back against the jutting rock. 'Sorry, what did you say?'

'Mickey. I'd crossed him off our list of suspects, but I'm still not sure. He was shifty when I met him. We may not know of a motive for him, but that doesn't mean one doesn't exist, and a man with his wealth can have a long reach. He may not need money, but what about jealousy, or revenge?'

He sat up, leaning on his elbows, his eyes on Libby. 'You should take care. I'll leave Bear with you for a while. Keep your eyes open and don't go out alone, especially at night. Meanwhile,' he jumped up, brushed mud from his trousers and pulled Libby to her feet. 'Let's have that lunch.'

A weak autumn sun shone above Exham the next morning. A niggle of dread had haunted Libby after the conversation with Max, but it evaporated with the night. Of course, she was in no danger. They'd been over-dramatising.

She hummed as she showered and dressed, before driving Mandy and Elaine to Exham on Sea station for the first leg of their journey to Bristol. They waved as they crossed the railway bridge to the east-bound platform. Mandy planned to stay, settling her mother in with her aunt before returning in a day or so. 'I'll try to get Mum to talk to the police.' She had a determined glint in her eye.

Libby planned to take Bear back to Max. She'd kept him here for one last night, but there was no space in her tiny house for such an enormous animal. She could look after herself, and Bear needed to run free in Max's grounds.

'Make the most of it,' she told Fuzzy as she gathered up the day's post from the mat. 'We're both going to miss that dog.'

She flipped through the handful of letters: a catalogue, two flyers and something official from Trevor's solicitor, acting as his executor. More on the slow progress of probate, presumably. It seemed to take forever, even though he'd left everything to Libby.

She ripped the letter open.

Dear Mrs Forest...

She sank on to the bottom stair, deaf to the racket Fuzzy and Bear made as they chased one another round the house. The letter shook in her hand.

Nausea gripped her stomach as she read the words again, hoping she'd misunderstood.

We regret to inform you...

The solicitor used careful, legal language, but the meaning was clear. There was no money. Trevor had spent every penny, and more. He'd had accounts in places Libby had never dreamed about, all with overdrafts and loans. The solicitor had tracked them down, paid back as many as possible and set out the account for Libby to see.

Trevor's debts far exceeded the total of the estate. Libby was broke. What's more, she owed several thousand pounds to Trevor's creditors. Shakily, she heaved her body up. A headache gripped her temples. She threw the letter on the kitchen counter, mechanically spooned instant coffee into a mug, searched for aspirin and wondered what in the world she was going to do.

It was already late. She had to go to work. She couldn't afford to lose the job: in fact, she'd have to ask Frank for more hours.

She brushed her hair and found a coat. Recovering from its temporary paralysis, her mind buzzed. The business course would have to wait. Thank heaven she'd sold the London house. It had been in both names. Trevor had slipped up there. This house had been much cheaper, so Libby had some funds in her bank account, but not many. Would they be enough? Not for a new bathroom.

Profits from 'Baking on the Beach' were tiny. They wouldn't last long. She'd have to sign Mr Fisher's contract.

Susie's death had taken over Libby's life this past week. She'd become obsessed with Susie, Mrs Thomson and Max. She needed to sort out her life, fast.

The morning at the bakery passed in a fog. Business had returned to normal; the excitement over Susie's death little more than a nine day wonder. Libby could hardly talk for the knot in her stomach. She had no clear idea, afterwards, who she'd spoken to or what she'd said. She'd ask Frank about extra work tomorrow. She'd burst into tears if she tried to broach the subject today.

She left as soon as her shift ended and drove home, where Bear and Fuzzy snored, curled together in a bundle of fur, in Bear's apple crate. Libby pulled out the contract, signed it, stuffed it in an envelope, sealing the flap in place so she couldn't change her mind.

Committed to the new book, she started the computer, dragged a file full of her original recipes from a shelf and stared at a blank page, watching the cursor flicker, telling her brain to concentrate on recipes.

After two hours, depression set in. How could she concentrate on rosewater and lemon sponge cake with the horror of her financial position hanging over her head. She couldn't bear to sell Hope Cottage, the home she'd loved since the moment she saw it, despite its horrendous bathroom. The house's rickety charms had wrapped themselves around her heart.

Her shoulders ached and a lump of cement seemed to have settled in her stomach. She should eat, for she'd had no lunch, but she needed to work. Her stomach rumbled. Maybe sucking a mint might help stave off the hunger pangs. She pulled out the drawer where she kept a supply of blindingly strong mints in a tiny green tin.

Mrs Thomson's papers lay where she'd dropped them, on top of the tin. Not now. Libby slammed the drawer shut. She had no time to think about Mrs Thomson. She had a living to earn. She'd spent far too long trekking through the countryside and discovered precious little for her pains. She was no nearer finding the killer of Susie than the day she found the body.

The police, or Max, or someone else – anyone – could find out what happened to Susie without her help.

She leaned both elbows on the desk. The cursor still winked, relentlessly, but she ignored it. Guilt had brought on a cold sweat. She'd visited Mrs Thomson, talked about Susie, and the old lady had died. Was that a coincidence, or was the death connected to Libby's visit?

Libby groaned. She had to know. She ran her hands over Mrs Thomson's possessions. They looked trivial; the usual random collection of documents found in any house. The police, busy with Susie's death, believing the old lady fell down the stairs by accident, would be likely to stuff them in a file and forget them.

That wouldn't do. Someone pushed Mrs Thomson downstairs and thought they'd got away with it. Libby meant to prove they were wrong. She would hand the documents over to the police, like a responsible citizen – but first, she'd read every word. She owed that to Mrs Thomson.

She cleared a space on the desk, lifted the heap of papers and books from the drawer, and laid everything in neat piles; the photograph album on the right, with a couple of notebooks on top. Holiday brochures for self-catering apartments in Cornwall, advertisements for pain relief gels to relieve rheumatism, and an invitation for Mrs Thomson to attend the hearing clinic at the local War Memorial hospital on the left.

She flipped through that pile first, found nothing remotely sinister, and dumped the pile back in the drawer.

Now, she could concentrate on the album and the two notebooks.

She lifted the first, a small blue book, each page dated like a diary. Lines of small, crabbed handwriting covered most pages.

Libby chose a page at random.

Monday 15 March
2.30 p.m. Judy Roach took her three boys down to the beach. They walked all the way to the lighthouse. Philip had a new red bucket and made sandcastles, but his older brothers kicked them down.
7 p.m. Five girls ran wild on the beach this evening, trying to light a bonfire but the driftwood was too wet. Too young to be out alone – never mind playing with matches. Do their parents know what they're up to? Note: mention it in the office at St Mary's school.

So far, so dull. An everyday story of a sleepy seaside town before the summer visitors arrive, written by a lonely old lady, a busybody, watching the children she cared about and trying to keep them safe.

A flash of inspiration set Libby's pulse racing. She turned to the back of the book, fingers fumbling. What if Mrs Thomson saw what happened on the day Susie died? Her house was ideally situated, with that view across the expanse of sand. Libby herself had seen the lighthouse while Mrs Thomson had been in the kitchen. Perhaps Mrs Thomson had noticed something important and recorded it here, in the diary.

Libby checked the dates on the final pages. The notes stopped the day before Susie's death. Disappointment kicked in. She read the last few pages, but as far as she could see, there was not a single clue to be found in the book.

She tossed the diary on the desk in disgust and trailed down to make a sandwich. Fuzzy appeared in front of her from nowhere, running around her legs as she negotiated the uneven stairs. 'Be careful, Fuzzy. I don't want to be the next to fall downstairs.

She picked up the cat and buried her fingers in soft fur. 'You're friendly, today. Bear's having a good effect on you. By the way, if you've been wondering what's going on, you're not the only one.' Bear snored in the apple crate downstairs, twitching, dreaming of bones or chasing rabbits. With a sudden wail, Fuzzy leaped from Libby's arms. She ran back up the stairs to the study, Libby close behind, wondering what had got into the cat.

Fuzzy leapt on the desk. 'Watch out.' Libby grabbed the cat's tail as papers slithered across the surface on to the floor. Fuzzy settled on the shambles, rolled on her back and purred. 'Oh, they smell of Bear, do they? Is that what you're telling me? Well, I'll be finished with them soon. There aren't any clues there, after all.'

Libby retrieved single sheets of paper from the floor and tapped them into a neat pile. Two smaller pages had slid away. She gathered them up, noticing the ragged edges where they had been ripped from a spiral notepad, similar to one a journalist might use – like the second notebook she'd found with the diary.

The pages in that notepad were blank, but the two loose pages bore Mrs Thomson's unmistakable scribbled writing, complete with dates.

She set the notebook to one side and examined the loose

pages. Dated 6th and 7th June, each page bore random letters and numbers.

Libby thought for a moment, then picked up the blue diary and shuffled through until she found the entries for June, comparing them with the single letters.

10 p g

Mrs Thomson had scribbled in her notebook. From the diary, Libby discovered the playgroup had been on the beach at ten in the morning.

If only she had entries for the day Susie died.

She laid the books and papers back on the desk, the notebook open at the blank page. The light from the computer monitor reflected back from the paper. Libby squinted. She could see indentations on the notebook page – the kind left by pressure from a pen. That meant there must be another sheet of paper somewhere – the page where Mrs Thomson had scrawled her note.

She searched through the pile of papers, hope flickering only to die a moment later. There was no sign of the missing top sheet. Frustrated, Libby grabbed the indented page and held it up to the light. An S and a couple of numbers. 14? She peered more closely. Yes, and those marks were W and E. Try as she might, though, Libby failed to make out any full words.

The doorbell rang. Annoyed at the interruption, convinced she'd made an important discovery, she weighed down the loose pages with the tin of mints and scooped up the cat.

Max, a worried frown on his face, stood on the doorstep.

'I came to say you should hang on to Bear a little longer, until this business is over. He'll keep you safe.'

Libby, not listening, grabbed Max's arm and tugged him inside the house.

'Never mind that, now. Follow me.' She led him upstairs, ignoring his protests. 'Look. Can you see?'

She thrust the blue notebook under Max's nose. He squinted. 'Looks like a diary. Is it yours? Are you sure you want me to see it?'

This was no time for jokes. 'These are Mrs Thomson's notes. She watched the beach from the window, writing about everything she saw in the spiral notebook, in a sort of shorthand. Then she transcribed it in full into her diary and made notes to herself. She worried about the children in the area.'

She opened the spiral notebook, laid it on her desk, then rustled through the blue diary to find the right page. 'You see the dates. They cover most of September...' She pointed to each book.

Understanding lit Max's eyes as he read the short entries in the notebook. 'These are from the week before Susie died.' He flipped to the end. 'The last day's missing. What a shame she didn't make any notes on the day Susie died.'

'I thought that, but I was wrong. She did make notes, but they've gone.'

Libby took a breath, desperate to make Max understand. 'At first, I thought she hadn't been watching the beach that day, but then I saw these marks on the next page of the notebook. You see, the page for 14th September has gone – it's been torn out.'

'How do you know?'

'You can make out some of the letters on the blank page, where she pressed down hard.' She stabbed at the blank page. 'I think maybe the – the killer took the page for that day when he killed her?'

Max's eyes narrowed. 'We have to know what she wrote. The police have specialist equipment so they can read it. We'll take all this to Joe.' He waved a hand at the papers.

It was an anti-climax. Libby murmured, disappointed. 'Can't we try to understand it ourselves?'

Max laughed. 'You're not a fan of the police, I take it. Well, since they're convinced her death was an accident, I don't suppose they'll be in any hurry to look at her notes. How did you get these, by the way?'

Libby's face burned. 'I suppose I stole them from Mrs Thomson's house.'

'Did you, indeed?' Max shook his head. 'Joe will have something to say about that.' He grinned at Libby, looking ten years younger, as excited as she. 'Well, before we confess to my son, who'll make a song and dance about it, let's see what we can read.'

Taking a lead pencil from the pot on Libby's desk, he rubbed it lightly over the surface of the paper, leaving the indentations visible.

'You can't see all the letters, but there should be enough to tell us if it's useful.'

Libby, reaching over his shoulder, grabbed a sheet of copy paper and wrote:

4 J boys castles.
5 rain.
5.15 T walking L
6 Windy, wet. B rubbish.
7 Tide.

They stood side by side, considering the letters.

Libby said, 'I think that's right. I can guess at some of the words, but it still doesn't make much sense.'

Max grinned. 'It's Mrs Thomson's own shorthand. All we have to do is crack the code. How are you with crosswords?' He reached over the table. 'Maybe the diary will help.'

He opened the blue notebook and, heads together, they pored over the pages from March, comparing them with the shorthand.

Max said, 'I see. She notes the time of day, who came to the beach, and what happened. It's not too complicated.'

They turned to the page of indentations from 14th September.

Libby stabbed at the first entry. 'The J is Judy Roach, like in the earlier entry. She walks on the beach with her three boys and they build sandcastles.'

'At five o'clock, it rained,' Max murmured.

Libby said, 'At a quarter past five, T was walking L – a dog, I suppose. Do we know who that might be?'

'We should be able to find out easily enough. It's probably a regular.'

Libby remembered. 'There's a lady with a dachshund called Lily – the dog, not the lady. I don't know her name, but I've met her on the beach when I've been walking Shipley.'

Max frowned. 'Shipley?'

'He's the dog I walk sometimes for Marina. It's not important.'

'Right. Ever thought of getting your own dog?' Max turned back to the code. 'At 6 o'clock it was windy and wet. Wasn't it getting dark? How could she see?'

He pulled out his phone. 'I've got an app for sunrise and sunset.' Libby laughed. 'Robert – my son – has dozens of apps.'

'Sounds like my kind of chap. Does he look like you?'

'Not in the slightest. He's my husband's child. Ali, my daughter, takes after me.'

'Lucky girl.'

'Anyway,' Libby returned to business, secretly delighted. 'What does your app tell us?'

'Sunset was at 7.35 that evening. So, at six, it would still be light enough to see anything interesting on the beach.'

'And the lighthouse flashes regularly. That would help.'

'Good point.' Max nodded. 'This B must be another name, someone around in the dusk. It could be a teenager, or an adult. I can't imagine mothers were bringing their children out at that time in the wind and rain. So, what was B doing, and what does *rubbish* mean?' Libby shook her head.

Max waved the problem away. 'Never mind. We can come back to that. There's just one entry left. At 7 o'clock, she wrote *tide*. I guess she means high tide. It came right in, that night, to the dunes.' He straightened up, rubbing his back. 'We have a couple of mysteries left. On the night of Susie's death, Mrs

Thomson saw B just as the tide was coming in. B must be a person. I wonder what B was doing. Mrs Thomson just wrote *rubbish.'*

Libby looked through the notebook, but there was no other entry like that. B must be an initial, like J and T. But why *rubbish?* After an hour, they'd pored over every word in the blue book. There were lots of names beginning with B, but there was no way to know who'd been on the beach on the day Susie died, or why.

Max sucked a mint. 'It could be someone who's never appeared in the book before. That would mean they don't often come to the beach. It rules out dog walkers.'

Libby said, 'I think this is important. Someone tore the page from Mrs Thomson's notebook. She wouldn't have taken it out until she'd transcribed it into her diary. She was fanatical. All the other pages match, except this one. It makes me think...'

Max said, 'Me too. I'm going to take an educated guess – I think she saw someone dumping what she thought was rubbish, and she recognised him – or her.'

He perched on the edge of Libby's desk. 'Maybe I'm jumping to conclusions, but why would anyone dump rubbish under the lighthouse.'

Libby shivered. 'What if it wasn't rubbish, but something else in a bag.'

'You mean...'

'Could it have been – been a body in the bag?'

'Rubbish, or a body. I wonder which?'

'No one would go to the trouble of dumping a bag of rubbish on the beach – it would be far too much effort.'

Max nodded along. 'Let's assume for a moment it was Susie's body. It would be heavy. Susie was small, but she'd be a dead weight. I think it must have been a man. Someone Mrs Thomson knew as B.'

Libby shivered. 'B could have looked up and seen her at the window. He knew she'd seen him, and, from that moment, Mrs Thomson was in danger.'

Max agreed. 'She knew the murderer. She thought he was dumping rubbish – bad behaviour, illegal, and enough for her to make a note of it. She didn't realise he was dangerous, so she didn't tell the police or worry about it...'

'Until B called on her, a couple of days later, to check that she hadn't put two and two together.'

Libby said, 'Susie wasn't in a bag when I found her.'

'No, but the tide was high that night, and the wind blew a gale. Between them, they could easily have ripped the bag away.'

Libby remembered the missing boot. If the storm tide had enough strength to wrench a leather boot from Susie's foot, it could easily shred a thin black plastic bin liner. She bit her lip. 'So, B was getting rid of the body, knew he'd been seen, and visited Mrs Thomson to make sure.'

'She knew him, let him in, and probably gave him a good telling off for dumping litter.'

'He could ask her to fetch something from upstairs – a jacket, perhaps, saying he was cold. He'd follow her upstairs and shove her down. She was a frail old lady, left alone to die.' Libby blinked away sudden tears. 'I wonder how long she lay there.'

Max's face was grim. 'Let's hope she died instantly.'

Libby said, 'I think we should call the police.'

Detective Sergeant Joe Ramshore called at Libby's house within the hour. Libby confessed to taking Mrs Thomson's papers, and Max chimed in to relate their theory.

Joe scolded Libby for interfering with a police investigation as if she were a naughty schoolgirl, scowled at his father. Max's involvement seemed to infuriate him even more.

'You're not above the law, either of you.'

'I'm very sorry,' Libby mumbled, humbly.

Max said, 'But you wouldn't have looked through Mrs Thomson's belongings. You were so sure she died from an accidental fall.'

'Hm. Well, we won't charge you for removing evidence. At least, not yet.'

'Can you find out who B is?' Libby asked.

'We'll check on the electoral register. You see,' he lectured, 'it's the day-to-day police work that will solve this, Mrs Forest, not amateur dabbling.'

Libby kept her temper in check, fighting the urge to point out the days he'd wasted.

Once Joe and Max had left, Libby undertook a whirl of activity. She phoned Ned, the builder, to explain she couldn't afford to go ahead with the alterations to the bathroom.

'Don't you worry about it, Mrs F. I'll keep the plans we made, and you let me know as soon as you want to start.' Libby felt dreadful. That was the trouble with a small town: you knew and liked the people who worked for you.

She wrote to the solicitor, asking for suggestions as to how to sort out the mess of Trevor's debts, and sent emails to Robert ad Ali. There, they won't think I'm just an aging mother, she thought, jabbing 'send' with a triumphant finger. Then, needing a break, she went to the local history society meeting, bearing the latest version of the lemon and rosewater cake.

The group, between mouthfuls, reviewed the recent event at Mangotsfield Hall.

'It was a huge success.' Angela was the treasurer. 'We split the profits with the Hall, and we've made enough to pay for a year's worth of speakers. Not that we don't have some excellent ones of our own.'

She nodded at Beryl, an elderly lady dressed in grey, who sat in the corner fingering a stack of notes.

'Everyone loved Marina's talk.'

'I thought I'd die when Libby was down to her shift,' There was a ripple of laughter. Libby had almost forgotten those awful Victorian clothes. There were so many layers. She frowned. A thought tugged at the back of her mind but she couldn't get hold of it. It was about the costume. Or, was it? She concentrated, but she couldn't recall. Oh well, maybe it would come back to her.

She kept silent about the discoveries she'd made. She'd annoyed the police enough, for now.

Bear stayed with her, 'For protection,' Max insisted. He

popped in, every evening, and took Bear for a run. 'Is he behaving,' he asked.

'Good as gold,' Libby said. 'Fuzzy gives him a smack on the nose if he gets too excited. But he can't stay for ever – he needs room to run.'

'Only until the police make an arrest,' Max insisted. Libby didn't argue. She enjoyed the giant dog's company, and secretly liked Max to visit.

With a spurt of hard work lasting well into the small hours of every morning, Libby settled down to write the cookery book, praying for an early publication date and the chance to pay off some of Trevor's debts. Frank, thrilled with sales for her recipes, had taken her on full-time, given her a rise and a new job title: Development Consultant.

She still felt sick when she thought of the money Trevor had owed. The bathroom made her want to cry, with its bright orange tiles, a shower that dripped slow, barely warm water, and a cracked window. She'd have to live with it for at least another year. She could almost believe Trevor had planned it all out of spite. It was like a final insult from beyond the grave. Libby would work her socks off to get free of him.

At last, the coroner released Susie's body, and the funeral was arranged for the next day – Thursday afternoon. Mandy, having arrived back from a stay with her mother and aunt, insisted on making dinner, using Libby's sausage casserole recipe.

'Oh, it's so good to be back.' Mandy groaned. 'They drive me mad, those two. Always on at me for my tats, and the piercings.'

Libby kept silent about the tattoos that climbed Mandy's arms and encircled her neck. 'Mandy, you're old enough to look after yourself. Get a flat.'

Mandy blushed and cleared her throat. 'I don't suppose you'd like me to stay – be a permanent lodger, would you?'

'I'd love it, but that's not exactly standing on your own two feet, is it?' *But I could use the cash.*

'I can't afford a proper flat of my own.'

'Well, in that case. Just for a while.'

* * *

The evening before the funeral was dark and still. The storms had passed over, and another flurry from the Atlantic was not expected for a while. Libby stood at the window of her study and stretched, muscles tense from an hour at the computer. There was so little light pollution that stars filled the whole expanse of sky. Maybe she'd get a telescope, one day in the distant future when she'd cleared the debts, and learn more about them.

The street lay deserted. Only one car passed, turning into a nearby driveway, its engine dying. Libby heard the clunk of a garage door. She opened the window to smell the sea and took a deep breath. This beat London's bright lights.

A movement on the left caught her attention. Instinctively, she drew back inside the window as a figure crept, soundless, close to the wall of the house, around the corner and past the sycamore tree, finally disappearing into shadow. That was odd. Libby didn't expect a visitor. Ears straining, she listened for a knock on the door, but all was quiet. She slipped downstairs and hovered just inside the front door, watching through the tiny pane of glass, but there was no sign of a caller.

Uneasy, heart pounding, she crept past the sitting room where Mandy was watching a game show, into the kitchen. The curtains and blinds were drawn tight against the autumn night. With a clatter, Bear brushed past, almost knocking Libby off her feet as he leaped at the back door, barking, the noise battering

Libby's ears. He'd heard a noise, too. Libby scrambled to the door, fumbling with the lock, and flung it open.

There was no one there. One hand on the dog, the other clenched tight, Libby stepped outside into cool, still air. She sniffed. Was that a whiff of beer? She hadn't imagined it, then. Someone had been here.

She tiptoed round the side of the house and back again. The stalker was long gone. In the distance, a car engine revved and faded. Mandy was at the back door. 'What was all that about? I heard Bear going crazy.'

Libby hesitated. Mandy needed to be on her guard. She shrugged. 'I thought someone was outside.'

'Who'd be creeping about in the dark?'

'I don't know.' She locked the door, shaking it to check it was secure, sat Mandy down and told her what they'd found in Mrs Thomson's diary. 'Maybe whoever was sneaking around knew I took it from her house.'

'It's a good thing Bear's staying.' Mandy shrugged, unfazed. 'He won't let anyone near you.'

Libby lay awake for a long time that night, chills running up and down her spine. If the stalker was the same person who'd pushed Mrs Thomson down the stairs, the mysterious B, both she and Mandy were in danger.

Her brain whirled, images chasing each other in a confused kaleidoscope of the past few days. There was Susie, slumped under the lighthouse like a sack of rubbish; Mrs Thomson, gazing out of her window at a world that passed her by; the local history group, gossiping; the 'Band of Brothers' of local men, looking to Max for guidance; James Sutcliffe and Guy each living a new life as though the wild days of the band had never happened.

In her mind's eye, Libby recalled the pictures of Susie, with

Mickey on her wedding day, and of her daughter, Annie Rose. Sleep wouldn't come, now. Libby pushed back the duvet, thrust cold feet into slippers and softly, so as not to wake Mandy, slipped along to the study. She grabbed a clean, fresh sheet of copy paper and began to write.

27

FUNERAL

The weather forecast for Susie's funeral promised a day of cold, watery sunshine. Libby, torn between an old grey trench coat and the long, formal, black wool coat she'd bought for Trevor's funeral, peered anxiously at the sky.

'I'll wear the wool coat, otherwise I might never use it again.' She winced as Mandy, appropriate for once in her customary head-to-toe black, fiddled with her latest piercing at the top of one ear. 'Doesn't that hurt?'

At the church, Max squeezed Libby's arm. 'Every shop in Exham must be shut.' The town streamed in past a phalanx of photographers. 'Even the national newspapers are here. Pity Susie isn't around to enjoy it.'

'There's Guy.' Guy brushed past the photographers, eyes straight ahead. Alvin stopped to flick a speck of dust off his jacket. James Sutcliffe was there, too, his son steering him past the press who were, in any case, far too busy interviewing Samantha Watson to notice, let alone recognise, the once famous members of Susie's band. Tossing her fringe, one elegant foot in front of the other, Samantha nailed, with ease, the self-appointed role of Susie's best friend.

After the service, a smaller band of mourners met at the crematorium to say a final goodbye to their old friend. As the coffin slid behind the curtain, Susie's voice followed them from the room, swelling through speakers, filling the building with her most famous song, 'What's In a Name'. James Sutcliffe blew his nose and a lump lodged in Libby's throat.

The local hotel, efficiently run by Marina's sister, put on a spread, the garden bathed in Indian summer sunshine. Libby juggled a plate and glass, leaning on a wall at the front, watching the other mourners.

Max took a place by her side, 'It's good to see the hotel packed with Susie's old friends.'

As he spoke, a black stretch limousine screeched to a halt outside the hotel. The uniformed chauffeur leaped out to fling open a rear door and a middle-aged, overweight man eased from the car, long grey hair caught in a ponytail. Gold earrings flashed and a medallion sparkled at the neck of his open-neck black silk shirt.

Max murmured, 'There he is: Mickey Garston himself.'

Two thick-set men, startling with shaved heads and earpieces, leapt from a second car and took up positions close behind Mickey, eyes hidden by reflective sunglasses. Mandy let out a low whistle. Mickey's transatlantic accent, loud enough to rattle glasses on the wooden tables dotted around the hotel garden, boomed over the crowd.

'Hey, I guess I missed the funeral. That's too bad. Caught up in your English traffic. You need some system around here.'

Max's mouth was close to Libby's ear. 'What do you think he wants?' as the man approached.

The newcomer stretched out an arm. 'Max, my old buddy,

good to see you again.' He grabbed Max's hand, the other arm snaking round his shoulders. 'Won't you introduce me to Susie's friends?'

Max extricated himself, unsmiling. 'I see you came after all.'

'Max, introduce me. Who's this gorgeous creature?' Samantha, white teeth flashing, poised on four inch stiletto heels. She extended one graceful arm, tinkling with bracelets, to take the flabby hand.

Light bulbs popped. Bored journalists set down half-eaten sausage rolls, flipped their note pads to clean pages and pulled out cheap pens.

A hoarse bellow splintered the air. 'What the hell are you doing here?' James Sutcliffe, fists raised, elbowed past Libby. 'Get back to the pond you crawled out of.'

Mickey's bodyguards rearranged themselves on either side of the boss. Max's single step dissected the space between James and the Americans. Jack Sutcliffe grasped his father's arm. 'Come away, Dad, it's too late for that. Leave it.'

James shook the arm away, his face purple. 'You've got a nerve, Garston, showing your face here after what you did.'

Mickey flinched. 'Come on now, no need for this. I'm just paying my respects—'

James shook his fist. 'You should be in prison for what you did.'

Max and Libby exchanged a look. What was James talking about? Did he think the fat American killed Susie?

'What I did? What...'

James bellowed, 'You killed your little girl.'

In the sudden silence,, someone dropped their drink, the glass shattering on the stone path.

Mickey swallowed. He raised his hands, palms out, bluster gone. 'No need for that, now.' He leaned forward, peering at

James. 'Is that you? James Sutcliffe? After all these years?' He let his hands fall. 'Now, come on, man. It wasn't my fault the little girl died. It was an accident. Why, I was as upset as anyone.'

James's voice shook. 'Susie trusted Annie Rose with you, just for one day. All you had to do was play with the child and keep her safe. So, what did you do?' He clenched his fists. Tears soaked the weather-beaten cheeks.

'You sat in front of the TV, drinking beer and eating fast food like a pig.' A sob sounded in his throat. 'How long was Annie Rose in the pool, dead, before you even noticed she'd gone?'

Mickey shifted, edging backwards towards the car, shooting a look at his bodyguards. 'Come on, now, James. The kid could swim. She was fine, playing with the dog I gave her as a present. I guess he jumped in the pool and she followed. It wasn't my fault,' he blustered. 'Susie had no right to leave the kid with me, anyway. She wasn't even mine.'

'Not yours? What do you mean, not yours?'

Mickey laughed through twisted lips. 'You still don't know, do you? Susie fooled us all. She sure made a monkey out of me. Yes, your precious Susie Bennett was already pregnant when we met. She tried to pass the baby off as mine. Made out the birth was premature. I was a sucker.'

Someone gasped. Guy's face creased in a frown. He broke the stunned silence. 'We never knew. She didn't say. It was that summer at Glastonbury. Susie was sick every day. Do you remember, James?'

'We thought it was the mud.' James Sutcliffe shrugged. 'It rained so hard, that year, there was mud everywhere. Couldn't get away from it. Slept in it, sat in it. It got into the food, the beer. In the end, we gave up trying to keep clean. People were ill, plenty of 'em, not just Susie. Caught things from the bacteria in the mud.'

'And we thought Susie had a bug.' Guy pushed his glasses up his nose. 'But maybe we were wrong. Maybe she was sick because she was pregnant.'

Max joined in. 'Susie left town suddenly after Glastonbury. No one expected it.'

Guy said, 'She was excited about our big break. She couldn't wait to get over to the States. She left with him,' he gestured at Mickey, 'and we followed a few weeks later.'

Libby studied the puzzled faces of Susie's old school friends. Most registered shock and surprise – but not quite all. A bubble of excitement grew inside Libby's chest.

'You all knew Susie, you'd grown up with her, but she didn't trust anyone with her secret.' One pair of eyes slid away. Libby's pulse raced. Could she be right?

Mickey folded his arms. 'Yeah. She was expecting someone else's baby, and she kept it a secret until after she'd got me up the aisle.'

His lips twisted. 'She thought she was so clever, putting one over on me. But I'm no fool. I wouldn't have got where I am, if I couldn't work a few things out. That was no premature baby, I can tell you.' He pointed a finger at Guy. 'Soon as the kid was born, I put two and two together, and they made five. Anyway, Annie Rose looked nothing like me. She had blue eyes. Nobody in my family ever had blue eyes.'

He swaggered past the security guards. 'I did right by Susie. I was straight with her and she made a fool out of me, but even then, I didn't kick her out.'

'Course you didn't,' Guy jeered. 'You were making a fortune out of her – out of us all. She was your meal ticket. Because of Susie, you were rich enough, and powerful enough, to keep the scandal out of the press.'

Mickey called to the bodyguards. 'Come on, boys, let's get out of here. I came over to pay my respects, and all I get is abuse—'

'Who are you trying to fool, Mickey?' Max said. 'You don't care about Susie. You came over here to find out if she left you any money. Well, she didn't, but you'll go on getting what you always wanted from her — money. Her songs are already climbing the charts. For you, she's the gift that goes on giving, so clear on out of here, and don't come back. Count your dollars on the other side of the pond.'

Mickey paused, one foot in the limousine. His lip curled in a snarl. 'She owed me.'

Clouds scudded across the sun and heavy drops of rain spattered the tables. As guests ran for cover, the gossip began, eager questions fizzing in the air. Guy's voice rose above the others.

'If Mickey wasn't Annie Rose's father, then who was?'

Max's spoon clinked against a glass. Slowly, the hubbub died away. 'Guy, that's a very good question, and it's at the heart of the mystery of Susie's death.' He encompassed everyone with a sweep of his arm.

'Nearly everyone from the old days is here today. Susie's death was a shock for most of us. But not for one. Not for the father of Susie's baby.'

A murmur rose, almost drowning Max's words. He raised his voice.

'Susie never told anyone the child wasn't Mickey's, but she had a plan, just in case he found out. She put money away for her little girl. It was insurance, in case Mickey found out he'd been tricked into marrying Susie and left her to provide for the child. She never needed it, because Annie Rose died.'

He beckoned to Libby. 'Why don't you tell them the rest? You've worked it all out.'

Libby cleared her throat. 'The person who killed Susie and dumped her body under the lighthouse came from this town.' On Libby's left, Mandy clutched her mother's arm, white knuckles bright against Elaine's black jacket. To her right, Susie's old schoolmates clustered together, faces registering surprise, excitement and, for some, horror.

Libby studied each face in turn. Alan Jenkins from the garage, scrubbed and clean in his best suit, had removed every trace of oil. Samantha Watson leaned her head close to Chief Inspector Arnold, taking no notice of her husband, Ned, who stood on her other side. Angela, Marina, George, Beryl and the others from the local history society gazed at Libby, eyes wide. Bert, Elaine's husband, rested against the wall on the far side of the room, as far from his wife and daughter as possible.

Guy and the two Sutcliffes, father and son, stood a little apart from the townspeople, while Joe Ramshore took up a stance near the door, puzzled eyes fixed on Libby. She took a breath.

'Susie drowned, just like her daughter. It looked like an accident, or suicide. A woman still grieving for the loss of her daughter: who'd be surprised if she chose the same way to die? She was bruised. Again, you'd expect that, what with the way the sea lashed the shore on the night she died. It didn't prove she was murdered. But one thing made it certain.'

Feet shuffled. A forest of faces goggled at Libby. 'You all knew old Mrs Thomson. Lonely, missing her husband, she spent her days watching the world go by. She saw everything that happened on the beach, from her window. Some of you called her a nosy parker.'

More than one pair of eyes slid away. Libby said, 'You were right. Mrs Thomson watched what went on down at the beach, and she kept a diary. She saw the murderer dump the body under the lighthouse, that Monday evening, and she made a note of it, though she thought they were dumping a bag of litter. I found some of the notes in her house, but someone had been there before me. That person shoved the old lady down the stairs and took the notes, because they told us the name of the killer.'

In the sudden hubbub, Joe Ramshore pushed himself away from the door and cleared his throat. Libby shook her head. 'Luckily, the police didn't lock me up for removing the evidence. The notes were missing, but the murderer left behind the second sheet of paper from the pad, and we could make out the words.' Someone moved nearby. 'Unfortunately,' Libby went on, 'they were in Mrs Thomson's own brand of shorthand and she didn't write the full name of the murderer.'

'Well,' Samantha said. 'In that case, we're no further forward.' Her voice rang with disdain. 'Perhaps you should leave the investigation to the police, Libby. After all, they know the town. You've only lived here five minutes.'

'But she's been a good friend to us,' Mandy's voice shook with rage. 'Better than you, with your posh clothes and—'

Libby waved a hand. 'It's all right, Mandy. Samantha does have a point. I haven't lived here long, but as an outsider, perhaps I could see what was going on more clearly than the rest of you.'

She waited for the murmurs to die down. She couldn't care less if people thought she was interfering. Susie deserved justice. 'At first, we suspected Susie's husband. We thought he might have a financial motive, but we were wrong. They were divorced, legally, although against Susie's will. He wasn't entitled to her money.'

Faces that had brightened briefly, fell again. The townspeople wanted Mickey to be the murderer, so everyone else would be off the hook. Libby continued to talk.

'In any case, why would Mickey attack Susie in England? Wouldn't it have been far easier to have his wife killed in his own country?'

She had their full attention. 'I found Susie. I owed her something, and I wanted to know more about her. What she was like when she lived here, in Exham, where she died? Why was she killed here? Why now, when she'd come home?'

Libby's throat was dry. She took a sip of water, listening to the awkward shuffle of feet, the sharp intakes of breath. 'Everyone I spoke to filled in another part of the jigsaw. I discovered the men here seemed to like Susie, but the women didn't.' Someone giggled and was hushed.

'I heard how Susie left Exham in a hurry, and I began to wonder why. Max tracked down her daughter's birth certificate, and sadly, found another – for her death. I looked at Annie Rose's date of birth, and the date of Glastonbury that year, and realised Susie must have been pregnant before she left Exham. That led to another question. Did the father know about the child? What would he do, if he ever found out?'

She had everyone's full attention, now. 'At last, I understood. Susie's murder had nothing to do with money. It was about Annie Rose: about children, parents and jealousy. Susie loved Annie Rose – that's why she carried a child's plastic ring in her pocket until the day she died. I found Annie Rose's ring, with Susie, on the beach.'

'The murderer reckoned without Mrs Thomson. She knew everyone in town, and she recognised the murderer. In the twilight, as the sun went down, she saw someone she knew, carrying what looked like a sack of rubbish and leaving it under the lighthouse. That's what got her killed. She had no idea of the importance of what she'd seen, but the murderer caught sight of her, in the window of her house.

'Mrs Thomson left a clue, but it was tricky to decipher. When she made her rough notes, you see, she used an initial, as she always did, to remind her what she'd seen when she came to write up her diary.'

Libby raised her voice, to make sure everyone in the room heard. 'The killer's name begins with B.'

She waited as first one head, then another, turned, every horrified face pointing in the same direction. It was Alan Jenkins who blurted out the name. 'Bert Parsons.'

Mandy's mother screamed; the sound muffled by a clenched fist stuffed into her mouth. Bert raised red-rimmed eyes. 'It wasn't me, Elaine.'

Alan said, 'We all know you're not afraid of a spot of violence.'

Bert's head flicked from one side to the other, searching in vain for a friendly face. 'No-no. I didn't k-kill Susie,' he stammered. 'I never even went out with her. I was about the only one that didn't. I was already with you, Elaine. You know that. We got married just after we left school.'

Elaine ran at her husband, outstretched fingers curled like a cat's. 'That doesn't mean you weren't going with Susie at the same time.'

'Wait.' Max's voice rang out, and Elaine stopped in her tracks.

Libby said, 'Bert seemed a very likely suspect, but I saw a photo of Susie's daughter in Mrs Thomson's album. Annie Rose was very fair, with blonde hair and blue eyes.'

'That proves it.' Bert pointed at his own head. He was turning bald, the remaining hair thin, but still dark brown, almost black. His eyes were brown, like Mandy's. 'She can't be my daughter.'

Marina said, 'It doesn't prove anything. Susie had blonde hair, so of course Annie Rose did.'

'No.' Angela stepped forward. 'Not necessarily. Susie had blonde hair when she was small, but hair often darkens as you get older. Don't you remember at senior school? Susie's hair began to turn brown when she was about fifteen. She was devastated, and she started dyeing it. All that blonde hair came out of a bottle.'

Libby raised a hand to interrupt the arguments. 'Angela's right. Anyone can dye their hair any colour they choose, but Annie Rose's hair was unusually light in colour, sandy really. What combination of genes would give her such pale hair? And she had very blue eyes. Not green, or hazel, but bright blue. Her colouring doesn't rule Bert out, but maybe he wasn't the only man having an affair with Susie just before she left town.'

She looked straight at Samantha. 'Tell me, Samantha. What's Ned's real name?'

Samantha's head jerked up, face contorted. 'Wh-what do you mean? Ned, his name's Ned.'

'No, Samantha.' Angela said. 'Ned's family thought themselves a cut above the rest of us, descended from ancient Scots and the former owners of Mangotsfield Hall. They wouldn't give their son an ordinary name, worker's name, like Ned.'

Every eye was on Angela. 'I remember the day we started primary school, when the teacher took the register for the first time. She read out his name and we all laughed. Ned cried; he was so embarrassed.' She put an arm around Samantha's shoulder. 'Samantha, my dear, I'm afraid you already know this. Ned's real name is Benedict.'

Wild eyed, face purple, Ned stared from one face to another.

With a roar, like an animal in pain, he dashed for the door. Guy stuck out a foot and Ned fell, heavily, on the plush carpet. Samantha said. 'Your hair's that pale, sandy colour, or it used to be, before you lost most of it. It's your Scottish family.'

Libby said, 'Most people had forgotten you were called Benedict, but Mrs Thomson always used full names. In her mind, Susie was always Suzanne, and Max was Maxwell. To her, you remained Benedict, even when everyone else called you Ned.'

Joe Ramshore tightened his grip on one of Ned's arms. Max had grabbed the other, but after that first dash for freedom, Ned gave up the struggle. He was crying, his words muffled by sobs.

'I never knew Annie Rose was my baby. Susie should have told me.' He cried louder, 'I never knew I was a father.'

He took a long, shuddering breath. 'Susie came back to England, to see Mary Sutcliffe, James's wife. Mary was dying. Susie was her friend, and she wanted to see Mary one last time. I bumped into her in Bristol.' He wiped his nose on his sleeve. 'She still looked the same: still the Susie I'd loved. She never really cared much for me – anyway, not once she'd met that American and been swept off her feet. We met up, just for a drink, one night. Not around here – we went over to Wells. Susie didn't want people to see her in the Lighthouse Inn.' He glared at Samantha. 'You were out with your fancy man, that policeman, pretending to be at work. You must have thought I was stupid.'

Chief Inspector Arnold stepped closer to Samantha and slipped an arm round her shoulders.

Ned's lip curled. 'I drove Susie back to Bristol. She'd had a lot to drink, and it loosened her tongue. She told me everything. All about my little girl: how cute she was, that Mickey never really took much notice of her, and how she died all alone in that swimming pool. I think I went a bit crazy. I couldn't think straight.'

Libby strained to hear Ned's words through his tears. 'Susie had taken my little girl away and left her with a man who let her die. I was so angry; it was like they say in stories – a red mist in front of my eyes.'

He raised his head. 'I wanted to avenge the daughter they stole from me.' He stood tall, his head straight on the broad shoulders Mrs Thomson had recognised. 'I grabbed the Satnav and hit Susie with it. It smashed into the side of her head. I hadn't even stopped the car – it skidded all over the road before I got my foot on the brake. I could have been killed, as well.' He rubbed clenched fists into his eyes. 'All I could think of was my little girl, drowning. Susie deserved to pay for Annie Rose's death.'

He took a breath, shuddering. 'I drove to Exham, pulled out a bin liner from the boot of the car, put her in so no one would see her, and carried her out to the beach. It was already blowing a gale and she was heavier than I thought. I left her under the lighthouse; tucked her in between the supports. I didn't kill her. I gave her a chance – left it to fate to decide. She might have woken up in time, before the tide came in.' He looked at the ring of horrified faces and pleaded, 'I didn't kill her. You can't call me a murderer.'

A burst of anger overcame Libby. 'How dare you. You didn't just kill Susie – you pushed a helpless old woman down the stairs and tried to poison poor Bear.'

The look on Ned's face chilled Libby's bones. 'That stupid old woman, watching everything, telling tales. She deserved all she got.'

He sneered at Libby. 'I saw her looking out of the window. I hoped she hadn't realised what was going on. She was a decrepit old bag – I thought she couldn't know who I was, even if she knew it was Susie in the bag.

'But it nagged at me – did my head in. What if she did know – what if she went to the police.'

He shrugged, cold eyes glittering. 'There was only one thing to do – get rid of her. It was easy enough – one little shove and she somersaulted down the stairs.'

He chuckled, the sound sending a shudder through Libby. 'You were lucky, Mrs Forest. You and your fancy ways – my aunt told me you were at the old woman's place.'

'Your aunt?' Libby screwed up her eyes, trying to think. 'Oh, the woman who visited Mrs Thomson while I was there. She's your aunt?'

Max said, 'I told you, half the town is related to the other half.'

Ned hadn't stopped talking, saliva flying from his mouth as he spat the words out. 'I came to your house to finish you off, but that stupid dog made such a racket, I didn't get the chance.' He swore. 'What do you mean by coming here, lording it around town, making out you're better than the rest of us?'

'That's enough.' Joe pulled Ned away. 'We've heard more than enough to get you put away for years.'

'How could you do such things, Ned?' Samantha called, as Ned was led away. 'How could you kill two people?'

Ned glowered at his wife, hate in his eyes. 'They deserved it. I wish I'd made it three.'

Libby curled up on the sofa while Max stretched out in an armchair. Both nursed large glasses of wine. Bear and Fuzzy jostled for position on the floor, in front of the fire. Mandy had taken her mother back to Bristol on the train. 'I'll be back the moment she starts nagging,' she whispered to Libby. 'Her sister can look after her. See you tomorrow, probably.'

'The town will pay for Susie's headstone,' Max said. 'It's going to say, *Loving Mother of Annie Rose*. We won't take the money from her estate. Everyone wants to chip in.'

'I'm glad about that. I'm sure Annie Rose was all Susie really cared about in the end. If only she'd known how many people still cared about her.'

Max asked, 'How did you guess Susie was pregnant when she left Exham? You weren't here then.'

'I remembered dressing up in a Victorian costume at Mangotsfield Hall. It was the costume, you see. There were layers of clothes; petticoats and skirts and corsets. I think I said, 'I could put on pounds and no one would notice.' The point was, you could hide anything under there. It rang a bell, because my son had told me about one of my husband's ancestors, a maid, who "got into trouble". But I didn't put it all together at first. I didn't think about Susie hiding her bump to trap Mickey into marrying her and then believing he was Annie Rose's father.'

She took a large mouthful of wine. 'About you.' Max raised his eyebrows and he looked wary. 'You loved Susie.'

He nodded. 'You're right again,' he said. 'Bert, Mickey, Samantha, Ned. You've understood them all. You're right about me, too. I never quite got over Susie. I met my wife in Bath, but our marriage was a mistake. Joe grew up living with my wife. I don't think he ever forgave me, even though she was the one who left. Divorce is tough on a child.' He shrugged. 'I concentrated on my career, made some money on the stock exchange – quite a lot, as a matter of fact – enough to buy my house, and the Thomson's farm, and retire. But there was always something missing. I grew bored.'

He smiled. 'I looked around for something else to do – something that could give me the buzz banking lacked. I found some consultancy work. I'm something of a whizz with figures. I specialise in following financial trails, tracking how money moves from one hand to another, and how criminals hide it inside legitimate businesses. I love travel, and I have clients all over the world.'

Libby smiled. 'Including America. You were going over on business as well as seeing Mickey.'

He laughed. 'I took the opportunity to visit one of my clients, as well as our friend Mickey.'

Bear raised his head, lurched to his feet and collapsed with a sigh at Libby's feet. She leaned over to stroke him. 'Tell me about Alan Jenkins. I know he's one of your old mates, but you wouldn't have been able to get him out of trouble with the police if you didn't have contacts.'

'You're quite a sleuth, Libby. The ringing gang was part of a vehicle fraud, where the proceeds were laundered and sent to Latin America to finance the drug trade. Joe discovered it, and he was on the point of arresting poor Alan, who had no idea what he was getting into. An innocent, is Alan Jenkins – he's happiest with his cars. I did some research into the gang and persuaded Joe to drop the case against Alan, in return for information. It was a pretty flimsy case, anyway. Joe's bosses were far more interested in the men behind the fraud and didn't want to expose them too soon. They'll be arrested, soon enough.'

'That gave Joe another reason to be mad at you. No one likes their parents interfering at work.'

Max drained his glass. 'True. I'm not easy to know, Libby. You'll find that, if you let me stick around.' He stood up. 'Do you want me to go now, and let you get on with your new life? What's it going to be: writing books, or a chocolatier, or both?'

Libby's body ached with tiredness. Her brain had all but stopped working, but at least she knew she didn't want Max to disappear from her life.

'I don't know at the moment, but I'll think about it all tomorrow. For now, let's just finish the wine.'

MURDER ON THE LEVELS

AN EXHAM-ON-SEA MYSTERY

1

FOREST CHOCOLATES

The warm tang of yeast percolated through Brown's, the Exham on Sea bakery.

'This must be the quietest place on the planet.' Libby Forest didn't mean to complain, but there hadn't been much excitement here lately. Not since she'd found local celebrity, Susie Bennett, the rock singer, dead under the lighthouse on the beach. At least she'd finally tracked down Susie's killer.

Frank Brown, owner of the business and master baker, dumped a pair of disposable gloves in the kitchen bin, hoisted a crate of fresh loaves onto his shoulder, grunted and shuffled backwards through the door to the car park. 'Time to revamp the bakery. Make space for those *Forest Chocolates* of yours.' Libby's knife clattered to the table. Had she heard right?

'Seriously? You're not kidding?'

Mandy, Libby's lodger and Exham on Sea's resident teenage Goth, hooted. 'When does Frank ever kid anyone?' She pumped a tattooed arm in the air. 'Our very first proper chocolate shop. Great stuff, Mrs F. The place will be famous in no time.'

A big fat grin forced its way across Libby's face. It was weeks since she'd presented her business plan. Frank had sucked his teeth, scratched an ear and mumbled, 'We'll see,' in the way people spoke to children when they asked for unlikely birthday presents. Libby had given up hope and spent several waking nights wondering how she could find another outlet for her home-made creations. She'd even pondered setting up her own website.

Maybe it was the constant supply of free samples that had worn Frank down.

His head bobbed back around the door. 'Fancy a drive, Libby? Those cyclists left their sandwiches in the shop.'

He thrust packages into Libby's arms. She'd made them to order not half an hour ago while the cycling club members boasted to each other about the miles they'd ridden. She'd packed them carefully into separate bags; cheese and pickle, egg and cress, and ham salad.

Mandy giggled. 'Too busy stuffing themselves with free chocolates to care about lunch. Kevin Batty gobbled up at least three lemon meringue truffles, and some of his mates put them in their pockets. They'll be growing out of their Lycra before they know it. Mind you,' she added, 'my clothes are getting a bit tight, too.'

Still in a happy daze, thrilled by Frank's offer of space to sell her chocolates, Libby loaded the packets of sandwiches into her ancient purple Citroen, crunched the gears and drove out onto the Somerset Levels. She followed the cyclists' route through corkscrew lanes beneath a broad blue spring sky filled with blackbird song, head whirling with plans for packaging, marketing, future outlets and exotic new chocolate flavours. Her second cookery book, unimaginatively called *More Baking at the Beach* was half written, and she spent at least one morning a week fending off phone calls from the elegant Christian Fortescue, her publisher, begging for updates.

'Not that I'm pressuring you, but your readers are clamouring – clamouring, I tell you – for more of your perfectly scrumptious recipes.'

Mr Fortescue would have to wait.

Libby turned up the CD player and bellowed 'We Are The Champions' at the top of her voice. Why not? No one could hear it, in this peaceful corner of Somerset.

The car squealed round the final corner, narrowly avoiding a row of bicycles propped against a wooden fence. It lurched to a halt and Libby jumped out. Beyond an open gate, clumps of sedge and willow lined the placid waters of a stream. Moorhens ducked in and out of overhanging branches and a pair of geese honked in the distance.

Libby slithered on the grass. Patches of mud, still damp from a brief overnight rainstorm, squelched under her feet. Not quite a country girl yet, then. Just a year since she'd left London, and she still had plenty to learn. She'd keep a pair of wellies in the car in future.

A hand grasped her elbow. 'Careful.' A few years older than Libby, Simon Logan had pleasing salt and pepper hair and a warm smile, and almost managed to make Lycra look elegant.

Mandy, Libby's lodger and self-appointed dating advisor, had pointed out, 'He's divorced, no children, retired university lecturer, conductor of the local orchestra and much richer than Max Ramshore. He'll do for you, Mrs F.'

Enjoying her sudden, welcome independence, since her husband's heart attack ended their unsatisfactory marriage, Libby had scoffed at the idea. Intent on building a business and a new life, she didn't need male complications, thank you. Max Ramshore was hardly more than an acquaintance. She'd worked with the secretive ex-banker on Exham's recent celebrity murder investigation but he'd left town without so much as a word soon after Susie's funeral.

Still, she admitted to herself, Simon Logan was very attractive.

'Lovely morning.' His deep brown voice resonated pleasantly in Libby's ears, but she had no time to reply, for Kevin Batty intervened, wiping streaks of sweat from sallow cheeks. *Ratty*, Libby thought. His pointy chinned, pink eyed face lacked only a set of stiff whiskers to complete the resemblance to an over-friendly rodent.

He stood so close Libby could count the pores on his nose. She took a sideways step.

Kevin followed. 'Mrs Forest. I see you've brought our sandwiches. Why don't you join us?' He snickered. 'We could do with some female company.' What's more, he'd been eating garlic.

Libby glanced at Simon. He rolled his eyes and she had to stifle a laugh.

He joined the appeal. 'The least we can do is offer you some of our lunch, now you've come all this way. Come and sit over here.' He pointed over her head. 'I saw a heron in that elm tree, the other day. Look.'

He offered her a pair of binoculars and, as she searched for birds, spread a rug on the grass.

The heady smell of still warm pastries made Libby's stomach growl. 'Well, I suppose Frank can manage without me for a few minutes longer. Maybe I'll have an Eccles cake.'

* * *

A smile still hovered over her face as she drove back to Exham. Mandy was taking the afternoon shift at the bakery, so Libby had the rest of the day free. She collected Shipley, a friendly, noisy springer spaniel with far more energy than training, from her indolent friend Marina, and let him loose on the beach.

'Hi, there.'

Libby's sunny mood evaporated in a flash. 'Max.'

'Still mad at me? How many times do I have to say I'm sorry? I had to leave town at short notice.' Max threw a stick for his dog, Bear, the owner of four vast paws and the shaggiest coat Libby had ever seen. He'd looked after Bear since his owner, Mrs Thomson, died. No one had claimed the huge Carpathian Sheepdog. Mrs Thomson's only relative, a distant, aging cousin, lived in London and maintained she was far too old for such an enormous creature.

'He'd pull me over, so he would.'

Bear loped steadily along the sand to fetch the stick, while Shipley raced back and forth, barking ineffectively, and wild with excitement.

Max didn't look sorry. In fact, he'd gained a light tan that made his Scandinavian eyes gleam brighter and his thick silver hair shimmer. He was grinning, expecting to be forgiven.

Libby exaggerated her shrug. 'It's quite all right. You don't have to answer to me when you go away. Anyway, it wasn't you I missed. It was Bear.'

Max threw the stick again. 'I couldn't leave him with you. He's too big for Hope Cottage so I sent him off to have a little holiday with a farmer friend of mine.'

'Well, I'm glad he's back.' Of course, Max was right. Bear had stayed at her cottage before, and the carpets had never been the same since, but Libby cared more for the giant animal than she did for home furnishings, and her cat, Fuzzy, had struck up a surprising friendship with Bear.

Max pulled a box from the pocket of his waxed jacket. 'I

brought you a present. It's a peace offering.'

Libby narrowed her eyes, suspicious. 'What is it?'

'OK, if you don't want it...'

'Of course I want it. I make it a rule never to refuse presents.' Libby unfolded layers of tissue paper inside the little blue box. 'A fridge magnet. How nice.' Not jewellery, then.

'Look what it says. *World's Greatest Cook.* That's you. I've tried your cakes.'

She tried not to laugh. 'You think flattery will get you anywhere. My son gave me one just like it, years ago, when he was about twelve.'

'I may be childish, but am I forgiven?'

Why be grumpy while the sun's shining? 'Maybe. My book's doing well, by the way. My publisher re-issued it. *Baking at the Beach* is now available world-wide and it's coming out in hardback. I'm just waiting for my own copies to arrive and I'm thinking about a follow-up.'

'No. Really? Why didn't you tell me? Wait, because I wasn't here. Now I really do feel bad.'

'Good. Then I forgive you.'

'To make up, I'll buy the first hardback copy.'

Libby snorted. 'Can't imagine you baking cakes, somehow.' She found a length of driftwood and called to the spaniel. 'Shipley, here's a stick, just for you. Bear, leave it alone.' She held the sheepdog back, fondling the giant ears.

They'd already wandered past the nine legged lighthouse where Libby had discovered Susie's body last year. Exham on Sea disappeared, hidden by sand dunes, as they rounded the bend.

Max cleared his throat. 'Libby, there's something I need to—' He broke off and sighed as his phone trilled. 'Sorry.' He stiffened. 'What? How many?' A sharp intake of breath. 'I'll be there.'

'What's the matter?'

'There's been an accident. The cycling club, out on the Levels.'

That couldn't be right. Everyone was fine when Libby left. 'What sort of accident? A road crash?'

'Apparently not.'

'Then what? Wait!' Max was already pounding back along the beach, dogs galloping behind. Libby followed, scrambling awkwardly across the sand. Panting, she struggled up the steps from the beach to the road.

Max threw open the door of his Land Rover to let the dogs pile in. 'That was Claire, Joe's wife, on the phone. She's meeting us at the scene.'

'Is it serious?'

'Claire doesn't know. They're all out at the wildlife reserve.'

'I know. I took their sandwiches. I saw Joe there.'

Libby had exchanged a distant nod with Joe, Max's son. Their relationship was tricky. A detective sergeant in the local police force, he had little time for her and even less for his father.

* * *

An ambulance drove away as Max and Libby arrived at the river. 'There he is.' Joe lay on the grass, face chalk-white, eyes closed. A paramedic nearby saw Max and came over, squatting beside Joe.

'Looks like a touch of food poisoning, sir. Half the club have keeled over.'

'Food poisoning? Could it cause all this?' Max waved a hand at a scene of disaster. A few hardy cyclists hadn't passed out, but lay awkwardly, their backs propped against tree trunks, clutching silvery blankets and shivering.

Over by the stream, Simon Logan wiped his mouth. Had

everyone been poisoned? Libby's own stomach lurched, and she swallowed saliva. The sandwiches? No, surely not...

The young paramedic struggled to her feet. 'Poison is poison. No idea what caused it, but the police will want to take the remains of those sandwiches. My job is to get people to hospital, then we'll know more.'

The officer in charge, Chief Inspector Arnold, nodded to Max. 'Sorry to see that lad of yours is involved, Max, but we need to treat this as a crime scene until we know otherwise.' He peered at Libby. 'Ah, Mrs Forest. I gather most of the cyclists bought their sandwiches at Frank's bakery?'

The knot in Libby's stomach tightened. 'Well... yes, they did.' She licked dry lips. 'I brought the food out here—'

Max broke in. 'Don't say any more.'

Libby gulped. 'You mean...'

'Don't say anything that might incriminate you. Or the bakery.'

Libby's breath caught in her throat. 'Do I need a lawyer?'

The Chief Inspector's face was inscrutable. 'We'll talk to you properly, later. There's no need to worry, Mrs Forest, until we find out exactly what happened here.'

Libby shivered. 'The people in the first ambulance. Are they OK?'

'I'm afraid not. Kevin Batty and Vince Lane are dead.'

2

ECCLES CAKE

A small Ford Fiesta screeched to a halt and a woman leapt out, brown hair flying wildly in the spring breeze. 'Claire. Glad you're here.' Max hugged his daughter-in-law awkwardly, as though they rarely touched. He proffered a set of car keys to Libby. 'Would you do me a favour and take the dogs back to Exham in the Land Rover? Claire and I need to get to the hospital, see about Joe.'

Libby scrambled into the car and set off with a succession of kangaroo hops. She wriggled, uncomfortable. Her trousers felt tight. She undid a button and laid one hand on her bloated stomach.

Her head was swimming, but she had to get back to the bakery, to warn Frank about the food poisoning. Or, maybe she should go to the police station? It was so hard to think. Her cheeks burned. Beads of sweat broke out on her forehead and the stomach pain stabbed, sharp as a knife.

Libby slammed on the brakes, heaved open the door and fell out, just in time to empty her stomach with long, painful gasps against the wheels of the car.

She groaned, leaned against the car to counteract rubbery legs, fumbled for a handkerchief and scrubbed at her streaming eyes. Another wave of nausea engulfed her body. Finally, exhausted, every scrap of her stomach contents now decorating Max's previously shiny wheels, Libby sank down on the verge beside the road. She was only halfway home, but she couldn't drive like this. Maybe someone would come along in a minute and offer her a lift?

The peace and quiet of rural Somerset, she discovered, had its disadvantages. No cars passed. Not even a bicycle appeared. Another wave of sickness came and went, leaving Libby even weaker. Too tired to sit, she lay on one side, tears of self-pity sliding down her face. Was she going to die like the cyclists? This would be even worse, all on her own out here.

The dogs barked, furious at being left in the car, and Libby had an idea. If she could get to the door and let them out, maybe they'd run away and find help. She could reach the car if she moved slowly enough. She ground her teeth and shakily staggered upright, trying to keep her head steady.

The walk to the car might as well have been a mile, over grass that waved and rippled. She'd never make it. Her head span, and she almost fell. 'Looks like you're another victim.' Someone had an arm round her, and relief flooded Libby's body. Maybe she wasn't going to die, just yet.

She tried to focus through a yellow haze. 'Max?'

With Max supporting one side, Claire the other, Libby stumbled to the Land Rover. She collapsed back into the passenger seat; dimly aware Max was talking.

He didn't sound sympathetic at all, just furious. 'Why didn't you tell me you were ill? You shouldn't have been driving. What were you thinking?' Libby gulped air. Talking was too difficult.

'Here.' Max offered a bottle of water. 'Just a sip, mind.'

Libby scrubbed a hand across her face. 'What about Joe?'

'He's comfortable. Sick as a dog in hospital, but not in any danger. His heart rate's up, but the doctors say it's not serious. They just want to keep him in until it slows. We left him there to get some sleep.'

Claire, apparently deciding Libby would survive, returned to her car, hooted, and drove off, waving one hand out of the window. Libby fought back another surge of nausea as Max studied her face, his eyes narrow. She could almost see him thinking.

'Did you eat or drink anything with the cyclists?'

Libby let her eyes close, and the sickness receded. Max shook her arm. 'Come on, try to concentrate.'

'No.' A memory surfaced, and her eyes opened wide. 'At least, just one bite from an Eccles cake. But there was nothing wrong with it. I should know. I made it myself.' She shuddered.

The very idea of pastry tightened the knot in her stomach. 'I feel better now.' That was a lie. She longed, more than anything, to crawl quietly into her own bed.

'We need to get you to the hospital. I want you checked out.'

'You think I've been poisoned, too?'

He leaned over to fasten her seatbelt. 'Pretty obvious, I'd say, but we'll find out for sure.'

Libby lay back, the chaos in her stomach subsiding. 'I only had one small bite.'

'Just as well. Luckily, Joe only ate half a sandwich. Cheese and pickle.'

'Poor Joe.'

'I thought you didn't care for him.'

Libby grunted. 'Well, of course I care. He's your son, after all, and...' Exhausted, still nauseous, she couldn't think of the right words. She let the sentence tail off, too weak to follow through. 'You know what I mean.'

'He's prickly, that's the trouble with Joe. And a policeman, which makes it worse.'

They drove in silence. Libby felt better, so long as she kept both eyes fixed on the road ahead. 'I don't want to go to hospital.'

'Too bad.'

She tried again. 'I was on my way to the police station. I want to find out what happened.'

Max snorted. 'Do you think the police will tell you anything?'

'Probably not. They think I'm a busybody.'

'I'd call you interested and inquisitive, but I know what you mean. Can't blame them, really, after the Susie Bennett affair.'

'It wasn't my fault the police didn't take her death seriously. Come on, Max. You were in it with me. You found out all sorts of things from your strange foreign contacts.'

Several seconds ticked by before he answered. 'Libby, you're talking about my other – er – responsibilities. You know I try to keep my distance from police work in Exham.'

'Yes, I know. You have very important work forecasting financial trends for your clients. I found out about it, remember?' It hadn't been too difficult. All the signs had been there. Early retirement from high level banking, regular trips abroad to conferences, and easy access to foreign authorities. Everything pointed to a second career. Max was either a criminal or some kind of civil servant.

'Keep it to yourself, there's a good girl. Super-forecasting gets a bad press. People think it's some sort of witchcraft. Actually, it's just logical thinking and ability with numbers.'

A good girl? There it was again – Max's unthinking arrogance.

Was it just being a man that caused it? Whatever the cause, it never failed to rub Libby up the wrong way. 'I'm not a child, Max. By the way, you never did say why you had to leave Exham in such a hurry.'

'I didn't, because,' he drawled, 'if I told you...'

'I know, you'd have to shoot me.'

'Seriously, it was a new client. When people buy my services, they don't want their competitors to know. It's a cut-throat business, finance.'

'Just tell me if your other responsibilities have anything to do with the dead cyclists, will you?'

He threw a lingering glance in her direction before he answered. 'Good Lord, no. You're imagining things. Still, I want you to be careful, Libby. Please don't go poking your nose in where you shouldn't.' He waited a beat. 'I know you can't resist a mystery, but at least let me know what you're up to.'

Max said no more, and Libby fell into a kind of hypnotic daze. Half-formed thoughts chased through her head. She'd love to know more about Max. He was handsome, wealthy, and long divorced, but showed very little interest in local women. Or men, for that matter. Maybe there was a secret mistress somewhere else. Libby could imagine Max with someone exotic, all long legs and tanned skin, from South America – Brazil, perhaps. Brazilian women were gorgeous.

Displeased with the idea, she turned her attention to their short relationship. For a while, she'd thought they were getting close, but long walks and longer evenings, with a meal and a bottle of wine or two, had ended in no more than a chaste peck on the cheek. Was that part of the reason Libby found Max so unsettling? Because he didn't want to take things further?

Although she didn't either.

Maybe she should start something with Simon Logan. He seemed flatteringly keen and he was a fine looking man. Would Max be jealous? Libby couldn't decide. His eyes were fixed on the road, his jaw clenched. Libby's eyelids grew heavy. She didn't want any complications. She drifted into sleep.

3

FOXGLOVES

At the hospital, a serious young doctor with floppy hair and horn-rimmed spectacles, tie tucked between two shirt buttons, examined Libby, declared her out of any danger and decreed she could go home.

'The hospital's full to bursting today, after the poisoning. No beds free at all.' He yawned. 'We think we've pinpointed the poison, though. Digitoxin. It's a compound made from digitalis.'

'I'm sorry? What's digitalis? Or the other thing?'

The doctor nodded, brow furrowed in a scholarly expression, transparently gratified to have the chance to explain his newly acquired, expert knowledge. 'Digitalis is found in the common foxglove, *Digitalis Purpurea*. That's the Latin name. You can find them easily in woodland.'

'Or in people's gardens?'

'Exactly. You'd be surprised how many everyday plants have serious toxic effects. Foxgloves can be both poisonous and beneficial, especially the leaves. Digitalis affects the heart rate.'

He thrust his hands into the pockets of crumpled trousers as he lectured her. If the situation hadn't been so serious, Libby would have laughed. The doctor looked hardly older than Robert, her son. What a pity medical staff no longer wore white coats. It gave them so much more gravitas.

The doctor went on, 'Digitoxin must have turned up in the sandwiches or cakes. I believe you only had a small bite, Mrs Forest?'

'From an Eccles cake.' Libby shivered. She'd never eat one again.

A bleep interrupted. The doctor pulled a small device from his pocket. 'Sorry, have to go. Just take it easy for a few days, and you'll be fine. Your heart's steady enough.'

Max took Libby's arm and walked her to the car. 'I suppose you realise what this means for the bakery?'

She closed her eyes. 'I've been trying not to think about it, but it's going to be the first place the police look. Frank will be beside himself with worry. How could foxglove leaves get into the cyclists' food? Was it deliberate, d'you suppose, or a terrible mistake? Oh dear, I can't seem to think straight.'

'Leave it for now. Get a good night's sleep. Things might seem clearer in the morning.' Max drove her home.

Mandy was in the kitchen, eyes on stalks, bursting to gossip, but Max cut her short and steered Libby upstairs. 'Do you need help getting to bed?'

'I can manage.'

'Oh.' He leaned forward and kissed her on the cheek. 'Sleep well.'

* * *

It was the hammering that woke her. Surfacing from a dreamless sleep, Libby groaned and rolled over. Early light filtered through the curtains. The noise started up again, thudding in her head. Someone was banging on the bedroom door. 'What is it?'

Mandy's head appeared. 'Sorry to wake you, but your daughter's here.'

'Ali?' Libby sat up. That was a mistake. Her head thudded harder. She grabbed the water glass by the bedside table and sipped. Empty. She must have drunk it in the night. With care, she slid one foot out of bed, feeling for the floor. Her stomach lurched.

'Here's the bucket.' Mandy was by her side. 'Max said this might happen. He said you're to stay in bed. I wasn't going to wake you, but Ali...' Ali was away at University in Bristol, wasn't she? It couldn't be the holidays already.

'Hi, Mum.' Her daughter's head popped round the door. 'Your friend, Max, rang. Mandy gave him your number. He said you'd been poisoned.'

Libby lay back against a pile of pillows. 'It's not serious. He shouldn't have worried you.'

Ali, eyes wide, hair tousled, grinned. 'Of course he should. I've come to look after you. By the way, who was that girl? Why is she dressed like that, with all those studs?'

Guilt crept over Libby. She'd meant to tell Ali about the lodger sleeping in the bedroom she'd used at Christmas. 'Mandy works at the bakery with me. She's staying here for a while.'

'And when were you thinking of telling me?' Ali raised an eyebrow and leaned over to plump her mother's pillows.

Libby pushed her hand away. 'We haven't spoken recently.'

Ali's eyes avoided her mother. That last phone call had been heated. She heaved a familiar, exaggerated sigh. 'OK, I know I should have rung at the weekend. I was busy.'

'With John?' Libby tried to sound non-committal, but the

words arrived laced with disapproval. She winced, as Ali's eyes narrowed. It was so easy to say the wrong thing.

'Busy with work, actually. John's been away in Dubai, if you want to know.'

'Oh.' Libby said no more. Was she being unreasonable? John was a wealthy, sophisticated man, more than twenty years older than her daughter. Ali had met him when he lectured at the University. He was an expert in philanthropy, apparently, which seemed to be an excuse for the rich to get even richer without feeling guilty.

'Look, Mum. I can see you're feeling lousy. We won't argue just now.' Ali bustled about the room, straightening curtains, smoothing the duvet, dusting a mirror with a tissue.

Libby closed her eyes. 'I think I'd like to go back to sleep.'

'Dry toast. That's what you need.'

'Lovely.' Anything for a moment's peace. Drowsy, Libby twitched awake as the bedroom door clinked shut. She sighed, closed her eyes and drifted away.

* * *

Hunger kicked in and she woke. A tray on the bedside table held a slice of cold toast. Libby took a bite. Delicious. Just what she needed, after all. Ali was right.

Libby looked at the clock and threw back the covers. What was happening at the bakery? She reached for her dressing gown and stopped; eyes fixed on the hugely expensive silk pyjamas she was wearing. She'd bought them a few Christmases ago, as revenge when Trevor gave her a wok. Had Mandy undressed her? *Oh, no. Not Max, surely?*

She winced, struggling to remember. She tugged open a drawer, shuddered at the jumble of clothes inside, and slammed it shut. Max had seen this muddle? And undressed her while she was asleep? She'd never look him in the face again.

Tying the dressing gown tightly, Libby set off downstairs. 'Watch out.' Fuzzy, her marmalade cat, offered daily evidence of despising Libby by disappearing every time she approached, except at feeding time. Now, she shot out of the living room and up the stairs, disappearing into the airing cupboard. 'That was deliberate, Fuzzy. You nearly threw me down the stairs.'

A vacuum cleaner hummed as she approached the living room. Ali had wasted no time getting to grips with the cleaning. Resisting the temptation to tiptoe past into the kitchen, Libby opened the door and planted a kiss on the back of her daughter's head.

'Thank you for coming home.' She took a breath. 'Does your brother know about the – er – the accident?'

'I rang him. He's going to phone you later.' Ali switched off the machine and wound the cable neatly. 'I hear you poisoned everyone in Exham with your baking, yesterday.'

'Not me. At least, I hope not.'

'Of course, I know it wasn't your fault. I was joking.'

'Not very funny, actually. Two people died.'

'How awful.' Ali's eyes were huge. 'Did you know them?'

'Not really. Don't be a ghoul. I don't want to talk about it.'

Her daughter pouted. 'Very well. Did you know your vacuum cleaner needs bags? I'll pick some up this afternoon. Now, what do you want for lunch? I can stay for a day or so to look after you.'

'That's kind of you, but I'm going to work.' Libby sniffed the air, scenting coffee.

Mandy arrived, holding the door open with one foot, balancing three mugs on a tray. 'You'd better have this before we go to the bakery. I have a bad feeling about this morning.'

4

COCOA BEANS

The small yard behind the bakery heaved with police. Libby recognised a middle-aged, overweight constable, all pudding face and small eyes, as one of Joe's team. He held up a hand the size of a dinner plate. 'You can't come in, ma'am, I'm afraid.'

Frank handed the bakery keys to a tall woman in white overalls. He looked terrible, his eyes red-rimmed, his brow furrowed. Mournful, he shook his head at Libby. 'They're going to search the bakery.' He'd aged overnight and become an old man. His voice quivered when he spoke. 'This will put us out of business.' His lip was trembling. 'I'm sorry, Libby. Just when you were about to get started.'

It was true, then. The police were blaming the bakery for Kevin's and Vince's death. Frank's business, built up over dozens of years, had hit the dust, and both Libby and Mandy were out of a job. The shock punched Libby in the chest. A closed bakery meant the end of the chocolate project, as well. Her wonderful new career had died before it even came to life. Mandy's eyes, lined with black kohl, were enormous in her white face. 'What will we do?'

The constable – Ian Smith was his name, Libby remembered – looked vaguely sympathetic. Frank was well known and popular in the town. 'We need to ask you some questions at the police station, sir.'

Frank's body slumped. Libby forced a cheerful smile as she patted his arm. 'Don't worry, we'll find out what happened.'

Constable Smith's concern failed to extend to Libby. 'Don't go interfering, Ma'am. We'll be talking to all of you, and you'll be better off waiting quietly at home until then.'

'Last time—' Libby bit off her words. Reminding the police officer how badly they'd failed before would just antagonise him. 'Are you suggesting we're all suspects?'

'We can't discuss it yet. We'll talk to you later today. Now, let me have your phone number and go on home.'

Mandy's mouth hung open as the police hustled the baker away. 'They can't think it was Frank?'

'It looks like it. Come on, let's go. We need to find out what really happened.'

* * *

Libby's year in Exham had taught her who was likely to know most about the area. In a moment of genius, she lured Ali out of the house, sending her to Bath in search of new curtains for the living room, picked up the phone and issued an invitation to Marina.

While she waited, Libby started on her new, hastily formed plan. The moment of despair at the bakery had soon passed – at least, so far as her own career was concerned. She had no idea how she was going to sell her wares, but she wasn't about to give in and abandon the chocolate dream at the first obstacle. She was going to make up a new batch and find an outlet somehow, even if she had to hawk her wares all over England.

She worried more about Frank. How would he manage if the bakery went out of business? Would the people of Exham rally round him, or buy their bread and cakes elsewhere?

Mandy wandered aimlessly round the house, switching on televisions and turning them off again. Libby tracked her down in the bathroom and grabbed an arm, just in time to stop her painting each nail a different shade of mauve.

'Mandy, come and help me in the kitchen. I'll need an assistant if I'm going to make this project work.'

'Not giving up, then, Mrs F?'

'You bet I'm not. Did you see how those free samples disappeared? There's a real market for original chocolates. We're going to make them, even if we can't sell them at Brown's. Maybe some of the shops in Bath will stock them, instead.' Libby set up the chocolate grinder and tipped warm beans inside.

As they worked, the hours raced past, meals forgotten, until Marina arrived. She wafted in on a cloud of Youth Dew, resplendent in a purple kimono, amber beads jangling on her spectacular chest.

'Darling Libby, you look ghastly,' she gushed. 'We were all so worried.'

'Actually, I'm perfectly all right now, thank you.'

'Well, if there's anything you need, you only have to ask. Though I've only got a few minutes. I'm getting my hair done soon.' Marina settled herself more comfortably on the sofa and got down to business. 'Now, do tell me everything. I heard it wasn't food poisoning, but real poison. How extraordinary. Just imagine.'

Marina wore the permanent air of unconscious, effortless superiority of someone who'd spent her life nurtured and cherished and never denied any pleasure she desired. As a result, good humoured, extravert, and a pillar of Exham society, she provided a never ending source of the very best gossip. Libby forgave Marina's sloth, although one day she'd pluck up the courage to tell her friend to take her own dog for walks. Poor Shipley would never get beyond the garden gate if Libby didn't take him.

Marina sipped at a glass of sherry. 'Who would have thought it of Frank?'

'Don't be ridiculous. Frank wouldn't kill anyone.' Kind, fatherly Frank could hardly bring himself to squash a wasp.

Marina helped herself to a cupcake. 'Who else could it be? One minute, everyone's buzzing along the road like a swarm of starving bees in Lycra, and the next, they eat Frank's food and half the cycling club ends up in hospital. Everyone knows Frank quarrelled with Kevin Batty, years ago. He must have decided to get his own back.'

A chill crept up Libby's neck. If Frank had a motive, he was in big trouble.

'What did they fall out about?'

'Well.' Marina sat forward, settling the heavy orange beads more comfortably, her face animated. 'Kevin was a very rich man. One of the big farmers in the area. Plenty of land, darling, all in the family. Of course, he didn't farm it himself. He rented most of it out.'

Libby blinked. 'You're kidding.' She'd only met the rat faced Kevin a few times, but anyone looking less like a wealthy landowner would be hard to find. Everything the man wore seemed to be made for someone ten pounds heavier, as though he bought every item of clothes second-hand.

Marina's laugh tinkled. 'You'd know if you'd grown up around here. The Battys own half the county, and my husband handles their affairs. Kevin's finger was in plenty of pies; sheep farms, dairy, and just a few acres of wheat.'

Libby topped up Marina's glass. 'Come to think of it, I've seen Batty lorries on the motorway.'

'That's right.' Marina wrinkled her nose. 'Not the cleanest on the road, I'm afraid. Now,' she swept on, 'where was I? Oh, yes, Kevin used to supply flour to the bakery, years ago. Then, he had the falling out with Frank. It started with darts, in the pub. Kevin accused Frank of using weighted darts. Or was it Frank accusing Kevin? Can't quite remember. Anyway,' Marina shrugged, dismissive of such details. 'They had a fight. They were both drunk, and Frank gave Kevin a bloody nose. The next thing Frank knew, Kevin hiked the price of his flour sky-high and nearly bankrupted the bakery.'

Mandy called from the kitchen. 'The grinder's finished.'

Chocolate scented the air as Libby opened the huge metal grinder and scooped out the paste. Marina rustled, close behind. 'Oh, I didn't know you made your chocolates from actual cocoa beans. Can I taste?'

'Not yet, I'm afraid. It's too bitter at this stage. Inedible.' Libby let heavy blobs fall onto a vast marble board.

Marina glanced at her expensive watch. 'Look at the time. I'm going to be late.' She gathered up scarves and bags. 'Now, don't worry, I'll let myself out.' She was gone, slightly unsteady, leaving a heavy trail of perfume.

Libby swooped on the heap of chocolate paste, scraping and turning it with vigour, watching for the shine that would tell her it was ready for use. 'I'm afraid everyone in town knows it's poisoning, now,' she told Mandy. 'The bakery's getting the blame.'

Mandy's eyes were huge. 'I don't know what I'll do for money, without that job.'

'Well, I'm sure it won't be for long. Everyone knows Frank's fanatical about hygiene.'

Mandy was biting her thumbnail. 'It's not just Frank. We're all under suspicion. And no one's going to want our chocolates, either.'

5

PIZZA AND SALAD

Ali arrived back from Bath early. 'I found just what you need in the first shop.' In minutes, she was bent over the ancient, barely used sewing machine, shortening curtains.

Too restless to stay indoors, Libby made an excuse. 'I need Marmite to settle my stomach,' she announced, and drove to the supermarket. The place was overheated and crowded. Libby leaned on the trolley, wishing she'd stayed at home.

'What are you doing here? You should be taking it easy.'

Libby jumped. 'Max? How do you manage to keep creeping up on me like that?'

'You were miles away. Did you mean to put five boxes of corn-flakes in your trolley?'

How did that happen? 'I'm hiding from my daughter's minis-trations.' That was unkind. 'Oh dear, I didn't mean that the way it sounded. It's just that Ali's very organised. Unlike me. She arrived yesterday and she hasn't stopped cleaning yet. She's hanging curtains as we speak.'

Max replaced cornflake packets on the shelf. 'Heaven help anyone who tries to organise you, Libby Forest.'

'What's that supposed to mean?'

'No need to get on your high horse. I mean you're a very capable woman who knows what she wants. By the way, how's the stomach?'

'Better. I suppose I should thank you for putting me to bed.' Now she sounded ungracious. 'Sorry. I really am grateful.' Libby couldn't forget the silk pyjamas, but if she didn't mention them, maybe Max wouldn't either.

'If you want to get away from your daughter for a bit, come over to my place for an hour or so. There's pizza in the freezer.'

'Pizza? Really?'

'Forget your culinary standards for once and come down to my level.'

'I should stay with Ali. Could she come too? I could cook.'

He raised an eyebrow. 'If you like. You choose.'

Why was she making work? The habit of a lifetime. Crazy. Time to stop trying to please everyone. 'Pizza sounds wonderful.'

He grinned. 'That wasn't so hard, was it? You don't have to be perfect all the time, you know.'

* * *

Libby concentrated on the pizza on her plate. She'd made a salad, squeezing lemon juice into olive oil, adding a touch of honey and mustard and a pinch of salt, grateful Max hadn't refused to eat the food she made. At least he didn't think she was a poisoner. 'You're looking better,' Max said. 'Nothing like junk food to settle the digestion.'

Ali chuckled. 'After all those times you grumbled at Robert and me for eating pizza.'

Libby swallowed her last bite. 'How's Joe?'

'They're letting him out in a couple of days, and I said I'd go and visit. We're almost on speaking terms now, so long as we don't mention anything about his work or mine, especially the local thugs he's been watching.'

Libby shivered. 'I've got an interview with one of Joe's colleagues, soon. Ian Smith. About the Eccles cake.'

'Are you interviewing the police, or they, you?'

'Very funny. Apparently, I'm a suspect.'

'Gosh, really, Mum?' Ali was wide eyed.

Max shook his head. 'Everyone knows it wasn't you. Do you want to talk about it?'

'With the police, or with you?'

'Either. Both.'

'There's not much I can say. It's all a complete mystery to me. I mean, poisoning a whole cycle club! Who'd do that? It's ridiculous to suggest it's Frank. It'll ruin his business.'

Ali looked from her mother to Max, calculation in her eyes. 'Do you mind if I go home? I'm expecting a phone call. I'll get a taxi.'

'Of course, you can go if you want. Anyone I know?' Libby was dying to know about the phone call. Ali obviously didn't want her to hear it.

'Just a friend from Uni.' Ali beamed and disappeared, phone in hand.

Max took the plates out, returning to ask, 'You're sure the poisoning's deliberate, then?'

Libby followed, a wine glass in each hand. 'Well, I can't believe the food was contaminated by mistake. We're always so careful. I'm sure it's not the sandwiches, but that doesn't stop people blaming the bakery. We could be shut down for good.'

'How do you know it's not the sandwiches?'

Enraged, Libby glared. 'Of course, it wasn't. I made them.'

'You don't want it to be them, but someone else could have

added the poison apart from you, Mandy or Frank. Come on, Libby, put that mind of yours to work. Digitalis, or digitoxin, or whatever that doctor called it. How would you get hold of it?'

Libby thought hard. 'He said it was used as medicine, so presumably, you could get it from your GP. There's always the chemist, but you'd need a prescription.'

Max chimed in. 'Or the internet.'

Max stacked plates in the dishwasher. 'It sounds as though we're investigating again. Ramshore and Forest, private investigations a speciality. No stone unturned. We should join forces and start a business. You'll need a second string if the bakery has to close. Apart from your second best-selling cookery book, that is.'

Libby put her head on one side. 'Forest and Ramshore sounds better. Anyway, we can't just leave it to the police. Manpower's always short, and unless they're convinced it's nothing to do with the shop, I don't think they'll look too hard elsewhere.'

'Forest and Ramshore it is, then. Where shall we start? With the poison?'

'It's as good a place as any, though there are a couple of other things we ought to think about.'

'Like, what do Kevin and Vince have in common that made them targets? Why were they both killed?'

'Exactly. And what about Joe and the rest of the club? It could have been a random attack, maybe trying to frighten them, that went too far.' It was a mess. 'How could the poisoner even be sure anyone would die? This is going to take a while.'

She rang Ali's mobile. 'I'm going to be later than I thought. Max and I are going over ideas for the chocolate business.'

'Yeah, Mum.' That was a snigger. 'Are you coming home tonight?'

'Of course.' Libby's face burned.

'Mandy and I are fine. She's been filling me in on a few things.' That sounded ominous. 'Oh, and Fuzzy's sitting on my lap.'

'That cat never sits with me. She hates me. She tried to trip me on the stairs again this morning.'

'See you later, Mum.' Ali was laughing as she broke the connection.

Max didn't bother to pretend he hadn't heard. 'I take it you have permission to stay out late?'

Libby dropped her phone in a pocket. 'Fire up that laptop. We've got poisons to trace.'

Poison hunting on the internet revealed few new facts. Digitoxin could be easily extracted from the crushed leaves of foxgloves and was found in some prescribed medication for heart disease.

Several cups of coffee later, with little more to show for their efforts than a list of medications containing digitalis extract under a confusing number of names, Libby sighed and stretched. 'We're not really very much farther forward. We need a better plan.'

Max flipped the lid on the laptop. 'Suggestions?'

'Well, the poison's just the method. What about a reason for killing Kevin and Vince? I suppose you weren't at school with half the cycling club?'

'Afraid not. Most of them moved here in the last twenty years or so. Your friend Marina's husband's a member, though.'

Marina hadn't mentioned that. Presumably, Henry had been at work, not cycling through the lanes that day.

Max cleared his throat. 'There's something I was going to tell you before, on the beach, when my phone rang.'

'Yes?'

He wouldn't meet her eyes. 'I've got to go away again, tomorrow. Just for a day or two.'

'Oh?' What did he expect her to say?

'Well, there's Bear.'

'Not leaving him with your farmer friend, this time?'

'Can't keep abusing the hospitality. For one thing, the animal eats like a rugby player.'

Libby wasn't going to make it easy for him. 'So, what are you suggesting?'

'Bear's used to you. I wondered if you'd come over to keep an eye on him. He lives outside in the shed unless it's freezing cold. That double layer of fur keeps him warm, but he needs company and plenty of exercise, and he likes you.'

Libby laughed. Bear was fast asleep, his massive head trapping her feet, as if he'd already claimed her. 'Let him stay with me for a while. We managed before, and I'll take him for a long run every day.'

'What about your carpets?'

'I'll get them replaced and send you a bill.'

'It's a deal.'

Max thumped the dog gently on the shoulder. 'See, Bear, I told you she'd take you in. Be a good guest. No chewing the furniture.'

'How long will you be gone?'

'Can't be sure, I'm afraid. As a sweetener, would you like to borrow the Land Rover? Better than letting Bear drool all over your car. And, I'll bring you back another fridge magnet.'

'I can hardly wait. You won't need the car?'

'It's quicker by train.' Heading out of the country, then. Libby knew better than to ask where he was going. She was pleased they were back on some sort of steady footing. Good friends, nothing more. Wasn't that just what she wanted?

'Thanks. My car's desperate for a service. I'll get Alan at the garage to pick it up tomorrow.'

6

BREAKFAST

Mandy and Ali gossiped in the kitchen the next morning, brewing coffee, eating breakfast cereal and giggling.

'Morning, Mum. Did you have a good evening?' Cue more giggling.

'Hangover, Mrs F?'

Libby heaved a heavy sigh, feeling like a visitor in her own house. She'd rise above it. She kissed Ali on the cheek, smiled at Mandy, grabbed a mug of coffee, scooped up Fuzzy and retired to the sitting room. Bear padded behind, tail wagging.

The house had seemed quiet when Libby first arrived a year ago but then Mandy moved in as a lodger and brought it back to life. Now, with Ali home and Bear visiting, the tiny cottage seemed full to overflowing.

Ali joined her mother on the sofa. Fuzzy jumped down from Libby's arms to rub herself against Ali, purring, orange tail flicking in the air. Bear, making himself at home, stretched out across the floor, filling the room from door to window. Libby watched her daughter stroke the side of Fuzzy's face and wondered how she'd ever managed to produce a child so unlike herself. Where did that ash blonde hair come from? It was cut short and spiky, emphasising Ali's round cheeks and full lips. Her daughter had turned into a beauty.

'What's wrong, Ali?'

Instead of answering, Ali wrinkled her nose and pouted. Libby recognised that expression. She'd seen it first when Ali, aged three, struggled with an early drawing of a house. It came back whenever she was anxious or faced with a difficult challenge.

'Was there another reason you came home? Apart from the need to look after your sick mother?'

Ali looked guilty. Libby had hit the nail on the head. 'I was worried about you, Mum, truly. Dad always said you can't look after yourself.'

'Well, that's what he thought.' Libby shrugged. No need to dump her feelings about Trevor on their daughter.

She kept talking, giving Ali a chance to collect her thoughts. 'Anyway, I'm glad you get on well with Mandy, though she'll be moving out soon, I expect. She's only staying here until she can afford a flat of her own.'

Ali's eyes were suspiciously shiny. Libby stepped over Bear and dropped on to the sofa, one arm round her daughter. For once, Ali didn't shrug it off or move away.

'Tell me what's going on. Is it boyfriend problems?' That older man. She'd known he'd break Ali's heart. 'Is it John?'

Ali raised a watery laugh. 'No, Mum. We broke up ages ago. I told you.' She hadn't, but Libby let it go.

Ali grabbed Fuzzy and buried her face in the cat's fur. 'John wasn't really that interested in philanthropy. At least, not for himself. He just liked to give lectures about it. Well paid lectures.'

'Good job you saw through him, then. But, if he's not the problem, what's wrong?'

'I don't think I'm doing the right thing.'

'You mean, at Uni? Is it the course?'

Ali blushed. 'History's all very well, and it's interesting, up to a point, but I want to make some sort of a difference. How's history going to help when children are starving on the other side of the world?' She looked up, straight into Libby's face, her own cheeks glowing. 'I want to do something really useful.'

Libby chose her words with care. 'I think that would be very worthwhile. You could get a job in the voluntary sector when you finish your degree.'

Ali rolled her eyes. 'I knew you'd say that. Just because you always did what people told you to, doesn't mean we all have to.'

Her words struck home. Libby had been brought up to expect good behaviour to lead to happiness. She'd been obedient with her parents, and at school she'd followed the rules diligently.

Looking back, she wished she'd had Ali's determination to follow her own path.

Ali spoke slowly, as though Libby was very old or deaf. 'I'm nothing like you. I want to do things that matter while I'm still young enough. Not live a boring life like you and Dad, and then get old and die. I don't want to waste any more time doing something I don't care about, like history.'

Was that truly how Libby's life seemed to Ali? Boring and useless? Libby counted to ten and kept her voice level. 'Why don't you carry on at Uni to the end of the year, then see what you want to do?'

Before the words left her mouth, she knew it was the wrong thing to say. Ali's face flamed.

She pushed her mother's arm away. 'I knew you wouldn't understand. Anyway, it's too late. I've already left Uni.'

Libby stared. 'Left? You mean, officially?'

'That's right.' Ali was defiant, eyes blazing. 'I can't go back, even if I wanted to. And I've got a job.'

'A what?'

'That's right, a job. I'm going to help build schools in the rain forest. I've come home to pack and then Andy's coming to pick me up. Today.'

'You mean, you're leaving the country? And who's Andy? You can't just go. I mean, what about planning...' Libby was struggling to take it in.

'Andy's a friend. He finished at Bristol last year and he's been organising this for months. Why shouldn't I go? I'm not a child any more.'

Before Libby could gather her arguments, Ali dumped the cat on the floor, flounced out of the room and stamped upstairs.

* * *

Libby needed time to think. 'What am I supposed to say, Bear?' The dog whined and nuzzled her legs. 'She's just throwing away her life. She hasn't even discussed it before.'

Libby would never have defied her own parents. Things were different in those days. She'd gone to University, taken a degree in social science, met Trevor and slipped into a quiet domestic life, managing the house and bringing up the children. She'd never even used that degree. Maybe Ali had a point.

Bear was pacing round the room. Fuzzy had disappeared, probably sulking in the airing cupboard. Libby longed to talk to someone. She needed advice, but there was no one around to help. She shooed Bear out into the garden, following behind, hoping fresh air would bring inspiration. She snatched weeds from the border, tossing them on the compost heap.

The breeze blew hair into her eyes, and she pushed it away,

irritated. Of course, she didn't want Ali to turn into a doormat. Libby kicked a stone. She'd wasted a lot of her own life. The only things she didn't regret were her children. Bringing up Robert and Ali to healthy adulthood, with strong minds of their own, were the only achievements she would always think of with real pride.

She needed to make peace with her daughter. Ali had left Uni, and she'd be leaving, today, for South America, whatever Libby said.

She wiped her hands on her jeans and went back indoors, to tap on Ali's bedroom door. Ali, red eyed, blocked her way, preventing her from entering the room.

'Maybe I'd better help you pack, if you're really going.'

Ali stared, frowning. 'Seriously?'

Libby nodded.

'You're not going to try and stop me?'

'Ali, I don't want you to spend your life trying to please other people. If you're determined to do this, and you're doing it for you and not for this Andy, I won't try to stop you.' *But I'll worry about you every moment you're away.*

'I just wish you'd told me before, so I can look into the company you're working for. I suppose plenty of people take gap years, don't they?'

Ali wiped her nose on her sleeve. 'Good.' She muttered. 'I thought you were going to cause a fuss. I'll leave you information about everything. And, I'm sorry I didn't tell you before. I thought you'd stop me going.'

'You're nineteen years old. You're an adult. But, please keep in touch properly, while you're away.'

An hour later, Ali sat on her rucksack while Libby eased the zip round the lumps and bumps of t-shirts, earphones, boots and the other essentials of life in the wild. Ali had all the kit. It was obviously true she'd been planning this for weeks, if not months, ever since she met Andy.

'You'll like him, Mum. He's very quiet. Thoughtful, you know. He's from Canada and he got me the job.' She showed Libby the paperwork. Tickets, letters of introduction, a signed contract, schedules and maps.

Libby couldn't find anything wrong. 'I just wish you'd told me sooner.'

'You'd have tried to stop me.'

'Will I see him?'

'Soon. He's coming here, then we're catching the train.'

The doorbell rang. Ali opened the door and a tall, thin young man with a beard and an enormous backpack came in.

'Hey, Mrs Forest. Good to meet you.' He stuck out a long arm. Speechless, Libby shook hands.

'I guess it's time we were off. Ready, Ali.'

Libby, close to tears, stammered, 'This – this is such a rush...'

Andy frowned. 'You knew we were going, didn't you?'

She shook her head.

He groaned. 'Ali, you said you'd fixed things with your Ma.'

Ali had the grace to blush. 'I thought a *fait accompli* would be easier on everyone.'

There was nothing else for it but for Libby to kiss her daughter and watch her hoist her rucksack on her back, wave to a stunned Mandy, and disappear.

Libby climbed the stairs, head reeling. It had happened so fast, she couldn't take it in. Slowly, painfully, she tidied away the few remaining bits and pieces Ali had failed to stuff in the rucksack and left in the tiny box room she'd slept in last night. A lump of iron seemed to have stuck in Libby's chest, making it hard to breathe. When was she going to see her daughter again?

She blew her nose, determined not to cry. She could see, now, that the cleaning, the fussing over curtains, had been Ali's way of saying goodbye. If only Libby had understood. She stretched, relieving the ache in her back.

Cleaning had worked for Ali. Perhaps it would have the same effect on Libby – take her mind off the shock of her daughter leaving the country.

A few of Ali's belongings remained in the box room – things she'd had to leave out of the rucksack; books and cards, mostly.

Libby gathered them into a pile and looked around. She couldn't bear to throw them away.

In the corner was the old red chest of drawers Libby had long wanted to paint. It was a dreadful colour, but Ali had insisted on it when she was a child, and Libby had kept it when she moved.

So far as she remembered, it was empty.

She pulled out one of the drawers, shoved Ali's bits and pieces inside, and pushed the drawer back in place.

It stuck.

She tried again, pulling it back and forth, but something prevented it from shutting properly.

She pulled the drawer right out and there, caught between the drawer and the back of the chest, was an old brown envelope. It must have been there for years.

Libby pulled it out, laid it on top of the chest and slid out a bundle of papers tied with red tape.

The envelope contained the deeds to a house, made out in Trevor's name.

Libby sat for a long time in silence, shocked to the core.

The house was nothing special; just the kind of lofty Victorian building often divided into flats for students. But in Leeds? The family had no connections there.

The house belonged to Trevor, there was no doubt about it.

If he'd bought the place as an investment, why hadn't he told her. Her heart leapt. Maybe he hadn't left her broke, after all.

But why Leeds? They'd lived in London all their married life.

Libby shook her head, perplexed by yet another shock from the grave. Who would have thought it of rigid, respectable Trevor? Six months ago, she'd discovered he'd emptied his bank accounts and left nothing but debts. It had meant Libby couldn't redecorate the ghastly bathroom, but she'd survived. Now, this?

What else had he hidden from his wife?

There was only one reason she could think of for a man to keep his wife in the dark about a house he owned.

Trevor had been having an affair.

She read the deeds again and started to laugh. She lay on the bed, roaring until tears ran down her cheeks. Who would ever have imagined Trevor had it in him? Dull, bespectacled Trevor. The hysterical laughter soon faded, and a bubble of anger grew inside Libby's chest. She threw the deeds across the room.

She sat on the bed, legs crossed, thinking. Trevor was a control freak. He'd kept her under his thumb, refusing to discuss work or anything else with her. As a result, she had little idea what his job entailed, except that he was an insurance agent.

Somehow, he'd bought a house and set up home in Leeds, and Libby had known nothing about it?

She retrieved the deeds, replaced them in the envelope and took the package to her room, sliding it into her handbag. She straightened. Were there any more surprises from Trevor? She still had a few of his things. Maybe she should check.

She returned to the box room. She'd kept some of his old clothes here. Full of shocked horror at her husband's sudden death, she'd left them in the wardrobe in the London house to deal with later. When she came to Exham, the removal firm had bundled them up and hung them straight in the wardrobe. She hadn't touched them since. Maybe there were more clues to the Trevor she'd never known among his old clothes.

She caught her breath, smelling the faintest trace of Old Spice that clung to an ancient corduroy jacket. Trevor had worn that old brown favourite every weekend, refusing to let Libby throw it out even when it grew old and shabby. She'd bought him a new one, identical, once, as a birthday surprise. Trevor had told her to take it back to the shop.

Pictures flashed behind Libby's eyes. She remembered Trevor one Sunday, complaining that the roast potatoes were cold, retiring to his study, shoving papers swiftly into his briefcase as she brought his coffee. The image lingered. He'd looked annoyed, his cheeks unusually flushed. Did the papers belong to his insurance clients, as she'd always supposed, or were they something less innocent?

Libby tossed the jacket on a chair. It was going out, along with anything else that reminded her of her husband. She grabbed one item after another, shaking them, feeling in the pockets for any stray clues to a secret life.

When Trevor's solicitor had told Libby she was broke, she hadn't thought to investigate. She'd just accepted that her husband had indulged himself, while at the same time complaining about every penny Libby spent on anything he called a selfish luxury – clothes, for example. Now, she had to know more.

Slowly, a pile of old receipts and train tickets grew on the desk, but nothing unexpected. She smoothed out a crumpled slip of paper, a receipt from a hire car company in Leeds. More evidence of a secret life?

Trevor had a mistress, living up in the north of the country.

The thought made Libby burn with fury. He hadn't cared much about his wife's security, leaving her broke, while his mistress lived in his house.

She bundled the pile of clothes into a plastic charity bag and dumped them beside the front door. A plan was forming in her head. She had clues, now. All she had to do was follow them to find out what Trevor had been up to. She'd give it a few days, until she had her car back, all serviced and ready for a trip to Leeds. Then, she'd make the trip and surprise whoever lived in the house.

8

MUSHROOM OMELETTES

Looking after Bear gave Libby the perfect excuse to wander along the seafront the next day, doing nothing in particular. She planned to pick up the car later, ready for the drive to Leeds.

The Exham promenade bustled with early seaside visitors. It was too early in the year for families with children, who were still in school, but the pavement filled with older people more interested in the coffee shops in the High Street than the stalls of plastic spades and Union flags.

Libby strolled in the sunshine, Bear at her side, head so full of mixed speculation about Trevor, Ali and the cycling club, that at first she didn't hear the voice calling her name.

'Libby. Over here.' Angela Miles, grey hair piled on top of her head, wire-rimmed glasses dangling on a string round her neck, poked her head out of the door of the seafront cafe.

Libby liked Angela, who never asked for favours, or bullied people, or expected her to supply free cake. 'Sorry. Thinking about something.'

'I see Max Ramshore's gone away again and left you with his dog.'

'I'm just looking after Bear for a few days. I like his company.'

'Mandy's still staying with you too. I don't know where you get your energy.' Angela ducked as a seagull swooped past on the look-out for easy food. She sounded odd, off balance.

Libby examined her friend's face. Her eyes looked brighter than usual. 'Is there something wrong?'

'Not at all.' Angela beamed. 'In fact, I'm doing something I should have done years ago. The trouble is, it's making me nervous.'

'Sounds exciting.' Libby steered her friend towards the tables set out at the entrance to the pier. 'We need coffee while you tell me all about it.'

'I've just had some.'

'There's always room for another cup. Or,' scanning the list on the blackboard, 'even better, hot chocolate.'

Settled at a corner table, a steaming cup stacked with calories in front of her, Libby could wait no longer. 'Now then, out with it. What's up?'

'It's all your fault, you know.'

Libby blinked. 'Me? Why? Have I offended you?'

'No, of course not. Quite the opposite. I've been watching you since you came to Exham. You dash about, doing what you want, whether other people approve or not. Your book's been published and you're a proper author now, working on your second. You solve mysteries, and you're starting up in business.'

Angela stirred her chocolate. 'Watching you made me realise I don't have to slow down, just because I'm not thirty any more. I'm going to do something with my life.'

She finished her drink and set the mug down on its saucer. 'Did you know my late husband, Geoff, was a composer?'

Libby racked her brains. Geoffrey Miles. The name rang a

bell. 'Not the Geoffrey Miles who wrote music for that film that picked up all the Oscars? What was it called?'

'An Honourable Gentleman.' Angela trailed one finger in a splash of milk on the table. 'I need to explain. When I married Geoff, I was very young. He swept me off my feet with his genius. He was a lecturer at Exeter University and I could see he would make his name in the music world. I was just a student.'

She drew a shape in the spilt milk. Libby thought it was a treble clef. 'My music always came second, of course, because he was a rising star and I was just competent. His friends, fellow lecturers, were all brilliant, but he stood out.'

Angela used a paper napkin to mop up the drops of milk. 'You see, unlike me, you've been brave enough to start again on your own.' She turned bright green eyes on Libby. 'You've shaken up Exham, that's for sure.'

Libby drained the last drop of cream from her mug and wiped froth off her lips. 'And upset a few people.'

Angela piled their cups on a tray. 'I've decided not to waste any more time. I'm starting a series of concerts.'

Libby shooed away a couple of hopeful pigeons. 'Sounds exciting. If you've got time, let me cook you lunch, and you can tell me more. Mandy's out and my daughter's flying visit is over.'

Angela beamed. 'That would be wonderful.'

* * *

Libby tossed a salad, flipped mushroom omelettes and poured chilled white wine into two large glasses. Angela rooted in her giant tote handbag and pulled out a thick file. 'I wanted to show you this. Geoff died ten years ago, but I only found this the other day, when I was up in the loft. I've been carrying it around, wondering what to do. Now, I know.'

She laid the papers on the table. Libby leaned forward. 'Man-uscript paper?'

'Some of Geoff's music. I had a call from his old agent the other day. First time I'd heard from him for years. He wants to do a memorial concert, ten years after Geoff died, using Geoff's old friends. I said no, of course. I'd have to persuade people to join in, organise rehearsals, help with the arrangements for the concert. It all seemed too much bother.'

She grinned. 'I've changed my mind. I used to manage Geoff, when we were younger. I dealt with his travel, the venues, sched-ules, everything. Why shouldn't I do it now? I've decided to put on concerts in Somerset and use them to raise money for charity.'

Angela looked ten years younger. She rustled the manuscript paper. 'I thought I'd start with this quintet. It hasn't been played in public often. It was one of the last things Geoff wrote. We were about to perform it, the day he ran his car off the road.'

'Wow. That's some undertaking.'

'I've already got the performers to agree. Geoff's sister's coming, she's a violinist, I still play the violin a bit, and Geoff's nephew will play clarinet. Geoff would have liked that. It's all on track.'

'When's the concert?'

'In a few weeks. Do you think I'm doing the right thing?' Angela frowned, suddenly anxious.

'Of course you are. It's a wonderful idea.' Libby flicked through the papers on the table, one finger following the lines of notes, wishing she could read music and hear the melody in her head.

She tried to figure out the directions scribbled above the lines. *Allegretto. Diminuendo.* 'I wish I knew what all these Italian words mean.' Her finger stopped moving. 'That's funny.'

'What do you mean?'

'Look. On the last few pages, the handwriting's different. I can't make things out at all.'

Angela balanced her reading glasses on her nose and squinted at the manuscript. 'I see what you mean. I hadn't noticed before. How very odd. Geoff was meticulous. His notation was always neat and tidy.'

She flicked from one page to another. 'Wait.' Her brow cleared. 'I remember now. Geoff must have been working on this when he sprained his wrist skiing. Look, see how shaky that crotchet is?'

Libby hardly knew a crotchet from a croquet mallet, but even she could see the composer had struggled to write legibly.

Angela shuffled the pages into a neat pile. 'I never let anyone perform the music again. I thought it had some sort of a curse on it. You know, because Geoff died. I can see now, I was being silly. We're going to have a wonderful concert, and we'll play this piece for Geoff.'

The mornings seemed very empty now the bakery was closed. Libby perched on a kitchen stool, breakfast mug in hand, while Mandy rotated marmalade, chocolate spread and peanut butter, munching one slice of toast after another.

'It's weird,' she said. 'It was such a pain, having to wake up at the crack of dawn to get into the bakery. I thought I hated it, but now I kind of, like, miss it.'

Libby swirled boiling water, added a drop of vinegar and lowered eggs into the pan. 'I know what you mean. Sometimes, I had to put the alarm clock on the other side of the room, so I'd have to get out of bed. Otherwise, I'd have gone back to sleep again.'

She rescued a slice of toast from Mandy's chocolate spread and centred a poached egg on top. 'Here, get some protein down you.'

Mandy gulped it down. 'Mmm. Trouble is, now I don't have to get up, I seem to wake even earlier and I can't get back to sleep because I'm worrying about getting another job.'

Libby ground salt on her egg. 'It must be even worse for

Frank. I don't think he ever missed a morning at the shop. Did he even go on holiday?'

'Not so far as I know.' Mandy licked her fingers. 'I suppose his wife will look after him. At least he won't be lonely.'

'I've a feeling Frank's happiest in the shop. He likes a bit of peace and quiet.'

Mandy laughed and a mouthful of tea went down the wrong way. She mopped streaming eyes. 'Are you and Max going to investigate the murders, like last time?'

Libby tapped one finger on the side of her cup. How much should she involve Mandy? She'd hate to drag the girl into any sort of danger, but Mandy had a sharp brain and she'd grown up in Exham. She could be useful.

Mandy interrupted Libby's train of thought. 'I know that look. It means you're already on the trail and it's not fair to leave me out. Anyway, there's nothing else for me to do all day.' She pointed at the kitchen clock. 'It's not even nine o'clock yet. I suppose I'll have to sign on, but what will I do the rest of the time?'

'I'm sure the shop will open again...' Libby sounded unconvincing, even to herself.

Mandy blew a puff of air through her mouth. 'No chance. Pritchards will muscle in on the bakery.'

Libby wrinkled her brow. She'd heard that name somewhere. 'The chain of grocery shops and bakeries?'

'They're all over the West Country.'

'How do you know they're interested in Brown's?'

'Per-lease.' Mandy tapped her nose. 'I have my sources.'

'Which are?'

'My friend Steve's got a mate who works at Pritchards. They're buying up all the empty shops, as cheap as possible. He says they'd do anything to get hold of a thriving business, like Brown's. It's meant to be secret, but...'

'I know, nothing stays secret for long in Exham.'

'See, I can help.'

'How does that help, exactly?'

Mandy banged a triumphant hand on the work surface. 'What if they're poisoning people deliberately, to get Frank's bakery blamed so they can buy him out?'

Libby spluttered. 'That's crazy, Mandy. They're a perfectly respectable business. They won't kill people just to open a shop.'

'Maybe they're backed by the Mafia.'

'In Exham? I doubt it, somehow. By the way, who's this Steve? Do I know him?'

'Oh, just someone I know from that club I go to on Fridays.' Mandy jumped down and busied herself tidying the kitchen.

'The Goth club? I suppose he listens to that music you like?'

'You mean Katatonia?'

'Er, possibly.' If they were responsible for the screeching from Mandy's bedroom. 'Anyway, I'd like to hear what he has to say. Your idea's crazy, but maybe we should eliminate it.'

'Come to the club.'

'You're joking. I'm far too old and I value my hearing. Could we talk to Steve at home, instead?'

Mandy beamed and Libby realised she'd been played. 'I'll ring him. I think his mum's away at the moment.'

Libby wiped down the kitchen counters. 'He lives at home, then?'

'Can't afford a flat, can he? No one can, these days.'

'Then that's what we'll do this evening. But meanwhile, if you really want to help?'

'Course I do.'

'Make me a list of the people in the cycle club and anything you know about them. Especially Vince and Kevin. I'm wondering why those two died, but no one else did.'

Mandy narrowed her eyes. 'Kevin's lived around here for ever, but Vince is new. Don't know much about him but maybe I can find out.'

Libby folded the cloth and placed it neatly over the edge of the sink. She'd need to make sure Mandy didn't run into danger. 'Take it easy. We're looking for a poisoner. A killer. I don't want to have to tell your mother I put you in harm's way while you're living with me. Just write down everything you know.'

Mandy nodded, but there was something about the determined angle of her chin that worried Libby. She'd never forgive herself if Mandy ended up in trouble. 'I mean it, Mandy. Take care.'

'I can look after myself.'

There wasn't much more Libby could say. Mandy was stubborn, and Libby, her landlady, couldn't lock her lodger in the house. She left matters there and set off in search of Marina. She was certain her friend had more information to give, if only Libby could pin her down for long enough to drag it out.

At least she knew where to find her. Marina had recently watched a Panorama programme and decided she needed to get fit.

'Don't want to die of high blood pressure, or heart disease, darling.' The difficulty seemed to be finding a regime that involved a minimum of exertion. Dismissing dieting, dog walking and running as undignified and exhausting, Marina turned back to an old passion. She'd learned to ride horses at her expensive boarding school, alongside minor royalty.

'At least I can ride sitting down,' she announced. 'Far more comfortable.'

Today, she'd be out at the stables, taking a quiet hack around the lanes.

* * *

The drive took Libby over an hour. Why Marina travelled all the way to a tiny village near Shepton Mallet for her lessons, Libby had no idea, unless it was in the hope of meeting celebrity jockeys riding out on the gallops.

A string of well fed, mild mannered horses puffed up a hill in the distance. Libby slowed. That had to be Marina bringing up the rear, in a fluorescent orange jacket. Libby drove round the corner, parked in sight of the stables, and settled down to wait. The open window let the country perfumes of hay and horse manure fill the car. Libby sniffed, trying to decide whether she loved or hated the smells.

The single file of horses clattered into the yard. They were huge — much bigger than Libby had expected. She'd never been within a hundred yards of a horse. She wasn't letting those hooves anywhere near her feet.

Plucking up courage, she left the safety of the Land Rover, hovering out of range, as stable hands led the horses into nearby stalls and the riders, chatting, drifted away. Marina remained, her back turned to Libby, deep in conversation.

Libby touched her friend's shoulder. 'Hello.'

Marina swung round, mouth open. 'Libby. What the — whatever are you doing here?' A crimson stain crept up her cheeks.

Her companion was new to Libby. Heavily built, immaculately dressed in full riding kit, he had a weather beaten, fleshy face crowned by a shock of snow-white hair. He flicked a riding whip lightly against mud splashed leather boots.

Libby flashed her warmest smile. 'Sorry to interrupt. I hoped I'd find you out here.'

Marina swallowed, neck tendons working. Her eyes flickered to her companion and back. 'Here I am. Taking riding lessons.'

'It looks like fun.'

The stranger turned full beam on Libby. 'I don't believe we've met.' His voice rumbled deep in his chest. 'My name's Wendlebury. Chesterton Wendlebury.'

Chesterton Wendlebury secured the best table in the Monmouth Arms, near the wood fire, ushered Libby and Marina into their seats, explained he had urgent business, and left.

Marina had regained her dignity. 'It's not what you think.'

Libby took a sip of orange juice and lemonade. 'I wondered what brought on your sudden enthusiasm for horse-riding. Where did you meet superman?'

Marina blushed. 'We're just friends. I bumped into him at one of the Round Table dinners.'

'Which you were attending with Henry?'

Marina swallowed a large mouthful of red wine. 'My husband and Chester are friends, and Henry does Chester's legal work. He has business interests in the area.'

'Looks like his interests extend beyond business.'

'Don't be crude, darling.' Marina pouted. 'Chester just happens to ride at the same place. Henry knows all about it, of course.'

'Of course he does.' Henry, a slight, balding solicitor with an air of perpetual worry, had never been heard to disagree with his wife about anything.

Marina pulled out a selection of the pins that had secured her hair under her riding hat. 'That's better. Anyway, you didn't come all the way out here by accident, did you? I know you, Libby Forest. You're on the trail of the poisoner.' She shook her hair loose, raking her hands through the apricot waves. 'I do hope it doesn't turn out to be that teenager lodging with you. She's such a pathetic little thing. So pale and gloomy looking. She might have forgotten to wash her hands after taking drugs, or something, and poisoned the sandwiches.'

Libby jumped to Mandy's defence. 'Mandy doesn't take drugs. Well, not in my house, anyway, and Frank's meticulous about health and safety in the bakery. We wear gloves whenever we touch the food.'

Marina sighed, theatrically, took a pair of silver earrings from her bag and slipped them with ease into pierced ears. 'You'll be getting a reputation as a collector of lame dogs, if you're not careful. Like Bear, and Max Ramshore.'

'Max is no lame dog.'

'Well, not exactly I suppose. Still, he'll let you down, believe me. Don't trust him, or his son, Joe. Mark my words.'

If Libby wasn't careful, Marina would be spreading gossip about her. 'Max is hardly more than an acquaintance of mine, I promise you.'

'Exactly.' Marina beamed, triumphant. 'Just like Chester and me.'

Libby gave up. The food arrived and she took a deep breath of garlic and parmesan cheese. 'Mmm. This pasta smells good. Do you often come here?'

'Sometimes.' Libby would be willing to bet Chesterton Wendlebury had intended to join Marina for lunch today. What

was really going on between them? Not that it was any of Libby's
business.

She swallowed a delicious mouthful. 'You told me something
about Kevin Batty.'

Marina tucked into ham, egg and chips with enthusiasm. So
much for trying to get fit. 'He was a frightful man.'

'You said he was a client of Henry's.'

'Did I? Oops.' Marina touched a finger to her lips. 'Silly me.
I'm not supposed to talk about Henry's work, but it's so difficult to
remember what I'm not supposed to know. It's very confusing.'

'Tell me about Kevin, anyway. It could be important. The
poor man's dead, so I don't think client privilege counts any
more.'

Was that true? Libby had no idea, but Marina was satisfied.
'Henry deals with corporate law, mostly. Firms who want to
merge or take each other over. Utterly boring.' She waved a fork
in the air.

'He was writing contracts for a London company planning to
buy land in Bridgwater. The land they wanted belonged to
Kevin's father. He used it for plant nurseries, but they were hope-
lessly full of weeds.'

Marina's eyes glinted. 'Kevin's father used to drink.' She
drained her own glass and poured another from the bottle, not
seeing the irony. 'Six large bottles of cider a day, that's what I
heard. No wonder he let the land go to ruin.'

'Kevin didn't run the business?'

'Not then. He was just his dad's messenger boy, lounging
around, drinking, and spending all night in the clubs in Bristol.
Until he found the company was offering mega cash for the land.
Kevin jumped at it and tried to persuade his dad to sell. They had
a flaming argument and Kevin's father had a stroke.'

Marina lined up her knife and fork on the empty plate and

looked round. 'Where's the waitress? I think I deserve pudding, don't you?' A harassed girl with a pony tail scurried across the room, eager to please.

Marina scanned the laminated list, ordered spotted dick, and turned back to Libby. 'Now, where was I?'

'Mr Batty's stroke.'

'Oh, yes. It wasn't Kevin's fault, but it gave him a shock. He inherited the business, cleaned up his act, refused to sell any of the Batty land and started making money by subletting to local farmers. He was worth a fortune, in the end. A very astute man, despite his ratty appearance.'

'What happened to the London company? Did they buy land somewhere else?'

'Disappeared back to London, I believe. Henry said they'd expected the yokels down in Somerset to be a pushover and thought they'd get the land for half what it was worth.'

Libby kept her voice casual. 'Do you remember the name of the company?'

Marina tapped manicured nails on the table. 'Let me see. It was a string of letters. 'ACT Ltd., or PMQ, or something.'

The initials meant nothing to Libby. 'So, Kevin turned out to be something of an entrepreneur.'

Marina chased the last spoonful of custard round her plate. 'Can't see that it has anything to do with poison in the sandwiches.'

'No, me neither. Anything else you know about Kevin?'

'Nothing interesting. He was a bit of an old car fanatic, but so are half the men round here. He's a regular at the American classic car convention. It's part of the country fair. Full of Chevrolets and Pontiacs.' Marina emptied her glass. 'The fair's only a couple of weeks away. You should get your friend, Max, to take you.'

'Maybe we could meet you there — with your friend, Chesterton.'

Before Marina could answer, the door of the pub crashed open.

'You!'

In the sudden silence, a tiny, red-haired woman, wearing an anorak and wellingtons, wove through the tables towards Libby. Every head in the room followed her progress. Libby froze.

To Libby's relief, the woman ignored her and pointed her bony finger at Marina. 'I saw your car parked down the road, Mrs Busybody. What have you been saying?'

Marina raised a dignified eyebrow. 'I have absolutely no idea what you mean, Mrs Wellow, and I'll thank you to stop shouting.'

The newcomer jabbed a scarlet painted fingernail in Marina's face, leaned closer and hissed. 'You told the vicar's wife my Theodore is no pure bred. It's a filthy lie, and he'll beat your Shipley into a cocked hat, come the show.'

Marina, purple in the face, looked ready to explode. She rose to her feet, towering inches above her opponent. 'Mrs Wellow, I'll have you know Shipley, whose Kennel name is Wellington Ship-shape, by the way, is a pure bred, registered springer spaniel.'

She gathered up her bag, lifted the orange jacket from its nearby hook, and tossed her head. 'I will see you and your unfortunate mutt at the show.' She swept regally out of the pub.

Libby resisted the temptation to applaud. Nothing would make her miss the county show, now. She paid the bill and drove home.

11

TRUFFLES

On Libby's return home, she found a neat list on the kitchen table, with the heading, 'Cycling club weirdos.' Mandy had been busy.

She'd scribbled a note at the bottom of the page.

Round at Steve's. See you there, later.

She'd even remembered to leave the address.

Fuzzy sat on the windowsill, two white front paws together. His gaze was unwavering, fixed on the garden where Bear was digging up any plant that had survived his last visit.

The dog looked up, noticed the cat and burst through the back door. Fuzzy stepped elegantly from her perch and drifted past, as though by mistake, heading for her bowl.

'You're a tease, Fuzzy.' Libby said.

Bear followed, gulping down a pound of beef while the cat nibbled gracefully on a few morsels of fish.

Libby snapped the door shut, restricting the animals to the garden and utility room. They weren't getting anywhere near her prized kitchen. She'd applied for a hygiene certificate and the inspector would arrive in a day or two. Animal hairs were not welcome on premises where food was prepared for sale.

Libby found it easiest to think in her beloved kitchen, surrounded by grinders, mixers and racks of saucepans, the tools of her trade. As she weighed and measured, chopped and tasted, her brain busied itself with the poisoning of Kevin Batty and Vince Lane.

She knew a little about Kevin, thanks to Marina, but nothing about Vince. She'd no idea what linked him with Kevin, apart from the cycling club. In any case, how could the killer be sure he'd targeted the right people? So many had been poisoned, but only two had died. Not everyone in the cycling club would have eaten the same things. There were plenty of different sandwiches. There was cheese and pickle, tuna, egg and cress, and ham salad, as well as Libby's cakes. The poisoner surely couldn't have poisoned all the sandwiches.

Libby poured chocolate into moulds, moving mechanically as her brain worked on the problem. If everything was equally infected, why had only Kevin and Vince died? Were they specially targeted? And if so, how was that trick managed?

Libby pulled containers from the new, dedicated fridge that had taken the last of her savings. She tore down a 'Poison' sign on the door. She'd laughed when Mandy stuck it on last week, as a joke. It wasn't funny any more.

Squirting coconut cream, lemon mousse, and champagne truffle fillings into chocolate cases took all Libby's concentration. With a defiant swirl, she finished the final confection, loaded up the dishwasher, and checked on Bear and Fuzzy. They were snoring, limbs entangled, in their favourite apple crate.

Libby took Mandy's list of cyclists up to her study. Most of the names were familiar. She found an Eddie Batty. Was he some cousin or uncle of Kevin's? Marina had said the area teemed with Battys.

There was Henry, Marina's husband. Libby paused. How much did he know about Marina and Chesterton Wendlebury? *Don't be nosy.* It was none of her business, really. Further down the list she found Vince Lane, Joe Ramshore, Simon Logan and Alan Jenkins, the garage owner who nurtured Libby's treasured Citroen.

Mandy had scribbled notes in the margins. Apparently, Eddie Batty was divorced from someone called Sarah, who'd remarried and was now Sarah Smith. Eddie's new wife was Christine, previously married to Vince Lane. That was the first link Libby had found between the two men, but it was remote. She dropped the paper on her desk. Almost everyone in Exham seemed to be related to everyone else, by birth, marriage or divorce.

A list of new emails popped up on the computer. Max's name leapt out at her and Libby clicked.

Just to let you know I might be off the grid for a few days.

She snorted. It sounded like an episode of Spooks. Max seemed to enjoy keeping her in the dark about his work.

Her eyes slid down the email.

Hope you're being careful. I've been in touch with Joe and he tells me the bakery's closed. Let me know if you need anything.
I met someone today who used to know your husband. He asked if you were living in Trevor's house in Leeds. You didn't mention you had a house up there?

Libby bit her thumb nail. Trevor's house in Leeds. A familiar, Trevor related ache pounded the side of Libby's head. She closed the laptop, fished aspirins from a desk drawer and washed them down with a handful of lukewarm tap water. She hoped she'd find out more in Leeds, but first, it was time to visit Mandy's friend, Steve.

* * *

Loud music told Libby she was at the right place. It drowned out the bell, so she banged on the door with her fist. The next door in the terrace opened and an elderly woman peered out, spectacles on the end of her nose. 'They'll never hear you with that racket going on.' She stumbled down the path, through Steve's gate and up to the door, hammered on it like thunder, leaned down and bellowed through the letter box.

'Oi. Steve. You've got a visitor.' Without another word or a glance at Libby, she shuffled back the way she'd come.

Mandy, cheeks flushed, hair in spikes and mascara smudged, opened the door. Libby stepped inside, straight into a small living room. She recognised the sweetish smell that hung in the air and sniffed ostentatiously.

'Are you high, Mandy?' The girl just giggled. If Steve was in the same state, Libby wasn't going to get much sense out of him.

A tall, thin teenager leaned, swaying slightly, against the door. Black hair, back-combed into stiff points, topped a face even paler than Mandy's. That must be Steve. A dragon tattoo climbed from a sleeveless black t-shirt and twisted itself around his neck. The boy's exposed arms were scrawny, his eyes half closed as though he were in a trance.

Libby took her time, letting her gaze roam round the room, waiting. The boy shifted from one foot to the other, growing more uncomfortable by the second. When she thought he was embarrassed enough, Libby said, 'I suppose your mother's out. I can't imagine she lets you smoke pot at home.'

The boy stared at the ground as he muttered, 'She's at the Bingo.'

'Then I suggest you get rid of the evidence.' Libby pointed at a jumble of cigarette papers, matches, and tins that she guessed contained something more exotic than tobacco. 'You'd better make yourself a cup of strong coffee, as well.'

Mandy giggled. Libby would have something to say to her when they got home. For now, she kept her attention on Steve.

'I thought Goths were supposed to be depressed.' The boy mumbled something she couldn't catch. 'I beg your pardon?'

He sighed. 'I said, not real ones. Just the posers and losers who do Goth 'cos they don't have any friends. They're the ones all over the internet.'

'So, where do real Goths hang out?' Interested, despite herself.

'Clubs, mostly. And record shops.' Steve pushed himself away from the wall. 'I'll get the coffee, I s'pose.'

Libby glared at her lodger and Mandy stopped giggling. 'You won't tell Mum, will you?'

'Not if you calm down and stop being so stupid. What were you thinking?'

Mandy tossed her head. 'It doesn't do any harm.'

'Well, we need to get some sense out of Steve.' The boy returned, balancing mugs, and handed them round with all the exaggerated care of a Victorian footman. Maybe he hadn't been as high as he'd pretended.

Libby said, 'Where did you go to school?'

The boy hesitated. 'Wells.'

'Wells? You mean, Wells Cathedral School? Do they let Goths study there?'

Steve blushed. 'I had a scholarship. Music.'

'He plays the saxophone,' Mandy chimed in. 'He's in a band.'

Libby ignored her. 'Do you have a job?'

'I'm on a gap year, before Uni.'

'Oh? Where are you going?'

'Royal College of Music,' he muttered.

A few pieces of information clicked into place in Libby's brain. Angela's husband was a musician. Exham was a close-knit community.

'Steve, are you by any chance related to Angela Miles?'

'She's my aunt. She was married to Uncle Geoff.'

'That's Geoff Miles, the composer?' Steve nodded, suddenly enthusiastic. 'I'm playing in her gig in a week or two. You can come, if you like.'

'It's a deal. Now, I want you to tell me what you know about this company that's trying to muscle in on the bakery.'

The atmosphere froze. Steve fixed his gaze on the floor and mumbled. 'What did you say?'

He heaved a heavy sigh and plucked at the frayed hole in the knee of his black jeans. 'They're called Pritchards. My mate says the top man lives in some manor house in the Cotswolds and gets around in a helicopter, but he started out as a barrow boy in the East End of London.'

'He's done well for himself, then?'

'My mate says he's crooked.'

'Does he? Any evidence?'

Steve licked his lips. 'He uses loopholes in the law to get businesses shut down, and then he moves on to their patch. Like when that tea shop in Riversmead had to close because it couldn't get a health and safety certificate. Pritchards bought up the premises and they're making a fortune. My mate says they paid off the inspector.'

Libby murmured, thinking aloud. 'Bribery's a long way from murder, though.'

Mandy joined in. 'What if they didn't mean to actually kill anyone, just make everyone in the cycle club sick. Then, the bakery would be shut down and Pritchards could move in.'

'It's a bit extreme, don't you think? Exham's just a small place, not big enough for a huge concern like Pritchards to care about.' Libby drained her mug. 'How could they have poisoned the food?'

She shook her head, dismissing the idea. 'No, I can't believe Pritchards would risk killing people just to get a foot in the door in Exham.'

Mandy looked disappointed. 'But you never know.'

Libby smiled. 'No, you never do.'

* * *

Libby left Mandy and Steve behind to tidy up before his mother returned. She took Bear for a final walk round the roads, promised him a trip out into the fields tomorrow, and returned home. She clattered ice into a glass, poured a hefty slug of gin and waved a few drops of tonic water over the surface, finished with a slice of lime and curled up on the sofa to think about Vince Lane.

He was almost as new to the area as Libby, and no one had much to say about him. Mandy said he'd sometimes worked at Alan Jenkins' garage. That was handy. Libby wanted to snoop around and ask questions. With the Citroen, suitably serviced, waiting for collection from the same garage, she had the perfect excuse.

Meanwhile, the thought of that house in Leeds nagged like an itch Libby couldn't reach. Max had mentioned it in the email.

Maybe he could help. She reached for her phone and dialled. Bear heaved himself up from the rug and rested his head on her lap. Libby scratched his ears.

'Are you busy?'

'No, actually I'm about to head back home. Business transacted; job done. What about you?' Bear's tail waved. He could hear his master's voice.

Libby swished gin round her glass. What exactly was Max doing at the moment? Had he just come from a shower, a towel round his waist, hair wet? Libby blinked to erase the thought and made herself listen.

Max said, 'I found out a bit about Kevin and his family firm. Seems he might have upset a few people over the land deal, but it was years ago.' 'Max's phone clunked as he set it down. 'Yes.' He was back. 'I'm looking at some of the paperwork.'

Libby's mouthful of gin found its way to her windpipe. It was almost as though Max had known what she was about to ask. 'Already? You've got it there?'

'On my laptop. Are you OK?'

'Gin went down the wrong way.' She finished coughing. Now, he'd think she sat around drinking on her own every evening. She could have kicked herself. She put the glass down. 'Go on.'

'The company he dealt with is called AJP Associates. They're still around.'

That was a blow. 'I was hoping it would be Pritchards.'

Max said, 'What do you think the P stands for?'

'No. Seriously?'

'Seriously. Pritchards, known to be moving in on properties in the West Country, is part of the group that tried to buy Kevin Batty's land. I'll see what else I can find out about them. I should be back tomorrow.'

Libby tried to ignore her stomach's tiny flip, not wanting to analyse her feelings about Max's imminent return. Would they quarrel again, or would their truce hold?

She dragged herself back to the reason she'd phoned him. 'Listen, about that house in Leeds. Have you heard any more?'

'No, sorry, but I'll see what I can do. I'm sure it's nothing to worry about.' Max's voice sounded odd, as if there was something he wasn't telling her. He changed the subject. 'How's Bear?'

'Listening to your every word.' It was true. The dog's mouth gaped. Libby could swear he was smiling.

'Give him a treat from me.' The tenderness in Max's voice took her by surprise. He sounded homesick, which was ridiculous – he was about to come back anyway.

Libby found she was smiling as broadly as Bear. 'I will. Come on over when you get here.'

'Will you feed me?'

'Beans on toast?'

'Perfect.' He was still laughing as the call ended.

As Libby yawned her way downstairs the next morning, keen to retrieve her beloved Citroen from the garage and, at the same time, winkle titbits of information about Kevin and Vince out of Alan Jenkins' brain, she caught the whiff of fish. Mandy, in the tiny back room beyond the kitchen, emptied a tin of dog food into Bear's bowl. 'And you've already fed Fuzzy,' Libby approved. 'I can smell it. You're trying to steal their affections.' She'd meant to tell Mandy what she thought about yesterday's pot-smoking, but she hesitated. Mandy was obviously on her best behaviour.

'Just one thing,' she said, as a compromise. 'No weed in this house.'

Mandy's face burned bright red. 'Yeah. Sorry about that, Mrs F. I'll be good.'

Bear finished his breakfast in three gulps and turned his attention to Fuzzy's. In the kitchen, toast popped up from the toaster. A pan on the cooker held scrambled eggs.

Libby smiled. Mandy really did feel bad. 'You've made breakfast for me, too?'

'I found a recipe online.'

Libby sniffed the air, catching an enticing whiff of herbs. 'Oregano?' Mandy nodded. 'Smells good.'

Mandy pushed across a piled plate; her face still pink. She watched, anxious, as Libby took a mouthful, chewed and pronounced her verdict. 'Perfect. Well done. Apart from – you know – did you have a nice evening with Steve?'

'Yes, thanks.' Mandy blushed again. 'I've said I'll go with him to his Aunt Angela's place today. The quintet are meeting to practice, though Steve says I have to call it a rehearsal. I don't know the difference.' She shrugged.

'They're playing Geoff Miles's long-lost work, I believe. Angela told me about it. Are you getting a taste for classical music?'

Mandy just giggled.

'Is Steve playing the saxophone. Is there a part for it in that piece?'

'No, just the clarinet. He plays that too.'

'Talented young man.' Libby began to rethink her first impressions of Steve. 'I'm going over to the garage later to see if the Citroen's ready.'

While Libby tidied the kitchen, for Mandy seemed to have used every pan in the room, her lodger spent an hour in the bathroom. She poked her head round the door before leaving the house.

'Nice jacket,' Libby said with a smile. The faux leather coat was a size or two on the big side. Libby was sure she'd seen it on the back of a chair in Steve's house.

* * *

Alan Jenkins' garage appeared quite empty, except for a single Cadillac with pointed wings, painted an especially glaring shade of pink. Seeing no sign of Alan, Libby was about to leave when a spanner clattered on the floor, accompanied by loud and heart-felt curses. A grimy arm reached out from under the car, groped around but failed to find the offending tool. Alan Jenkins slid out, blowing on his left hand and cursing.

He caught sight of Libby. 'Oops. Didn't see you. Sorry about the language there. Scraped my hand.'

'Do you want me to clean it up?'

He grinned. 'Nah. Happens all the time when you're around cars. Reckon the grease stops any infections.' His hand, filthy with oil, was a mess of old scabs. A new cut slowly oozed blood.

'Shouldn't you have one of those pits so you can get underneath the car more easily?' Libby asked.

Alan grinned. 'Where's the fun in that? There's one in the workshop, of course.' He jerked his head towards an adjoining building. 'That's where I work on everyday cars – like your little Citroen.'

He stroked the Cadillac's garish paint. 'When I'm tending to this old lady, I like to do it here. It feels a bit more hands on, you might say.'

Libby struggled to find something complimentary to say about the car. 'It's very — um — American. Isn't it?' What did people see in these old wrecks?

Alan patted the wing. 'Made in 1969. She'll be at the show next week, if I can get her on the road by then.'

'Is it, I mean, she, your only old car?'

He wiped a greasy hand over his face, leaving a trail of oil, his face screwed up as though in pain.

'She's not an 'old car', Mrs Forest, she's a classic.'

'Sorry. She's lovely, of course. I just wondered if you'd had time to look at mine?'

The frown deepened. 'Course I did. First thing after I brought it in, I gave it the once over.'

Libby enjoyed special treatment at the garage because Alan owed Max a debt from the past. Alan had been drawn into a gang ringing cars. Max's intervention had enabled the police to drop any charges in return for information and Alan's gratitude extended to Libby.

'What's Max up to at the moment, then?' He rubbed his hands with an old rag and stuffed it back in the pocket of his overalls.

'He's away. He'll be back tonight.'

'Planning something special, are we? Going out for a meal?' Alan's idea of a night out was a few jars in the pub and a kebab from the Greek take-away on the High Street.

'Home-cooked, I expect.'

Alan sucked his teeth. 'Lucky man, Max. And, how's that second book of yours coming on?'

'Slowly.' Libby groaned. 'The publisher's losing patience.'

'You tell me if he needs a word,' Alan said, wagging a finger. 'I'll sort him out.'

'I don't think that's necessary,' Libby gasped, imagining city boy, Mr Fortescue, in Alan's hands.

Alan let out a guffaw. 'Got you worried there, didn't I. Don't worry. I hate violence.'

Over in the workshop, the Citroen was buffed to a shine. 'I can see my face in the bonnet.' Libby admired the finish, detecting the smell of polish. 'But is the engine OK?'

'She'll stagger on for a bit, yet. A good goer, that's what she is.'

'Thank you for looking after her so well, and this time, I want a proper bill. No discounts. OK?'

He shrugged. 'If that's what you want.'

'It is.' She held out her credit card. 'First, though, I want to ask you a few questions about the cycle club picnic.'

Alan gazed at his feet; arms folded. 'Yeah. Thought you might start on that. Bit of a private eye, aren't you?'

She used the ploy she'd tried on Steve and let the silence build. Alan weakened. 'I was there when it happened.'

'Were you? I didn't see you. Were you ill, too?'

'Nah, not me. Took my own grub, didn't I? The wife made up some cheese and pickle sarnis and a piece of pork pie.'

'I never thought of pork pie as healthy eating before.'

Alan's brow furrowed. 'Healthy eating?'

'Never mind. It was a joke. I'm glad you were OK, but I was really wondering about Vince. He'd not been around Exham long, had he?'

'He was new. Arrived about ten years ago when they opened that new business park affair.'

'You mean the place by the M5 with the hideous green warehouses?'

He grinned. 'That's right. Vince drove a fork-lift truck.' Libby bit her lip. This was no time for jokes about lifting forks. 'He used to come down here of a weekend and work on the old girl with me.' Libby deduced he meant the Cadillac. 'Kevin came over, too.'

'So, the three of you were friends?'

The mechanic frowned, looking perplexed at the thought. 'Suppose so. Used to do a day on the car, clean up and have a few drinks in the Lighthouse Inn of a Saturday. Vince used to keep on about visiting a club, but my wife wouldn't have that. Kevin went, once or twice, I think.'

'Kevin and Vince were both single, then?'

'Kevin used to be married, until Sheila ran off with the window-cleaner. Good riddance, he reckoned.' He screwed his face in thought. 'Don't know about Vince. He might have had a wife once, but not living with him any more, if you know what I mean.'

'You'll miss the two of them, won't you?'

'Ah. Reckon I will, at that. We had some good times.'

Libby handed over her credit card. Alan grunted. 'Yep, gonna miss old Vince and Kevin around here.'

As an epitaph for his friends, it didn't sound too bad.

The doorbell rang, but this time, Libby's visitors were solemn faced police officers.

'Mrs Forest?'

Her mood plummeted. 'You'd better come in.' She offered tea. 'Milk, two sugars?' She recognised the older of the pair as Police Constable Ian Smith.

Arms folded across a round paunch, he eased himself on to a stool. 'We've met before.'

He'd been one of Joe Ramshore's team when Susie Bennett died. Libby forced a smile. 'We have.'

'Made fools of us all, didn't you?'

She swallowed. He clearly didn't mean to make this easy. 'I like to help the police whenever I can.'

A brief smile flickered across the face of the younger officer, a slim blonde woman. 'I'm Constable Sykes. Emily Sykes. We've just come from Sergeant Ramshore.'

'He's home, then?'

No one answered her question. Constable Smith bit into a hob nob. 'This is a very serious matter, you know.'

'Of course. Two people have died. It's a dreadful affair, but it's nothing to do with me or the bakery.'

'Now, I never said it was, did I?'

Libby looked from one officer to the other. Neither was smiling now. 'Am I some sort of suspect?'

'We're just making inquiries.' Constable Smith eyed up the kitchen, a pair of small, shrewd eyes noting every item. 'Make cakes and chocolates in here, Mrs Forest?'

'Yes.'

'Does your kitchen comply with health and safety regulations?'

She gulped. 'The things I make here aren't for sale yet. The inspector's due to come soon.'

He scribbled in his notebook. Constable Sykes nodded. 'It's a beautiful kitchen. Did you design it?'

So, this was 'good cop, bad cop.' 'Yes.'

PC Smith smiled, revealing a set of large, tombstone shaped teeth with a gap between the front pair. 'But there were chocolates at the bakery.' Libby's heartbeat raced. 'Were they yours?'

'They weren't for sale.'

'The cycling club came into the shop that morning, I believe.' Libby nodded. 'Did they eat any of the chocolates?'

'Well, yes. I mean, we were trying them out – Frank, Mandy and me – when people came in to the shop, and I think a couple of people had a taste...' Libby's voice trailed off, her mouth suddenly dry.

'I see.'

Forgetting her intention to answer questions as briefly as possible, Libby added, 'There wasn't anything wrong with the chocolates. I'm sure of it. I made them myself. They were samples. I'm starting a business...' She heard herself babbling and bit her lip.

'Does Mandy live here?'

'She's my lodger.'

'Does she come in the kitchen?'

'Of course. We often eat in here, and I've been showing her...'
Be quiet, can't you?

It was too late. 'Go on. What have you been showing her?'

'Just some recipes.' Libby felt sick. She'd dropped herself and Mandy in a hole and she was still digging. They'd now think Mandy might have poisoned the cyclists. 'Do I need a solicitor?'

'Now then, we're just trying to cover all the angles. Nothing to be worried about, but we might need to talk to you again.' Constable Smith's suddenly avuncular tone did nothing to calm Libby's nerves.

Her hands were shaking when the police left. Could the poisoning possibly have anything to do with her chocolates? She closed her eyes and tried to think back to the moment when the cyclists arrived in the bakery.

They'd been talking about Libby and Frank's new partnership. Mandy had a champagne truffle in each hand. 'Champagne to celebrate,' she'd said.

Frank bit the top layer of chocolate neatly from a coffee cream. 'You either love a coffee cream, or hate it,' he remarked. 'Me now, I love 'em.' It was one of the longest speeches Libby had ever heard from the baker.

Kevin had been first to poke a head round the door. His little round eyes lit up. 'Chocolates?' Mandy told him at length about the plans for the shop. Kevin leaned on the counter, much too close to Libby. Uncomfortable, she offered him a free sample.

Next thing she knew, the shop was full of cyclists.

But who had eaten the free samples? If only she could remember.

Wait a minute.

Her spirits rose. Mandy and Frank hadn't been sick, had they? It couldn't be the chocolates.

But then... She groaned. What if it was just one flavour that caused the problem? The lemon meringue, perhaps? She'd eaten one of those and Kevin ate several. Head thumping, Libby sank on to a stool. She tried to concentrate through rising panic.

Come on, you're supposed to be an investigator. Think.

Trying to stay calm, she breathed deeply, in and out, until her heart stopped thudding.

There were no chocolates left, so how could she work out whether they'd been poisoned?

She stayed quite still, thinking, and at last had an idea. All she had to do was remember who'd eaten which flavour.

Her heart began to thump again. She had to act fast, to find out before the police decided the chocolates were to blame.

One part of Libby's brain was shouting at her, telling her not to be irrational, but it was too late. She was sweating again, her heart hammering.

It wasn't just about the police finding out, any more, or what might happen to her. She had to know it wasn't her fault. She needed to be sure she hadn't killed those two men.

If only Max was here, she could talk to him. It would be all right. He'd find a way to prove the deaths of Kevin and Vince were not her fault. But Max was away. There was no one else.

Wait.

Simon Logan had been in the shop, had eaten chocolates, and hadn't died. That was a fact. She'd seen it with her own eyes. Libby could ask him which ones he'd sampled. He was so calm and in control. Even the thought of speaking to him made Libby feel better. He'd know what to do. Why hadn't she thought of him before? He'd made it clear he liked her, and she'd liked him.

How could she get in touch? Mandy would know. Mandy

knew everybody. It took Libby three attempts to dial the numbers on the phone, her fingers shook so much.

As Mandy answered, Libby gabbled, 'Simon Logan, he was in the bakery with the cycle club. Do you know where he lives?'

'Ooh, Mrs F. You do fancy him, after all. I knew it. I said he was perfect for you.'

'No, I don't fancy him.' Was that strictly true? 'Stop giggling, Mandy, this is important. I need to speak to him.'

'Well, that's easy. He's here.'

'Here? Where are you?'

'I told you. I'm with Steve at his aunt's house, rehearsing for the concert. Her room's got good acoustics, apparently, whatever that means. Simon's here too. He plays the violin.'

'I'm on my way.'

* * *

Angela lived in a small village just outside Exham. The Citroen crunched up the gravel drive and Angela waved from the window.

'So glad you've come. Yes, let Bear come in. He's very well-behaved.' She took off her spectacles and peered at Libby's face. 'You're rather pale.'

'I'm fine, thanks. Still tired, that's all.'

Angela patted her hand. 'We wanted to get on with our rehearsal as soon as we could. Let me introduce you to everyone. You know Mandy and my nephew, Steve, don't you?' Steve winked, as though Libby were a fellow conspirator.

'Marina's here, of course, although she doesn't play an instrument.' Marina never missed a social occasion. 'And here's Chesterton Wendlebury. Have you met?'

Chesterton Wendlebury engulfed Libby's hand in a warm grasp. 'Delighted to meet you again, dear lady.'

Angela explained, 'Chester plays the cello. And here's Alice Ackerman, a friend of Steve's from Wells, who's helping us out on the viola.'

Alice wore a very low-cut red T-shirt, skin-tight jeans and a winsome expression, and Steve stood very close by her. Libby glanced at Mandy. Arms folded across her chest, eyes narrowed, she held Steve's friend, Alice, in a steely glare.

Libby extracted her hand from Chesterton Wendlebury's, 'I'm sorry to interrupt you all.'

His voice boomed. 'Quite all right, my dear. We needed a breather.'

Angela steered Libby to the back of the room. 'Have a cup of tea while we finish, then we'll all have a glass of wine.'

Libby whispered. 'I had a visit from the police earlier.'

'No wonder you're looking pale. Was it Ian Smith? He's always been a bully. No wonder he's still only a constable.' She handed Libby a cup. 'Just relax and enjoy the music for a while. I hope you like it.'

Desperate to talk to Simon, Libby had no option but to wait and listen to the rehearsal. Unable to play an instrument herself, she loved to watch and listen to those who could.

The players stopped from time to time to repeat a phrase or correct a mistake. At one point, Chesterton called for a complete halt. 'I've lost my place, sorry to say. Afraid I'm getting old.' He scrabbled at his music, knocking a sheet off the stand. Patiently, the other performers waited while he picked it up and began again.

Libby had no opportunity to speak to Simon while the rehearsal continued, so she sat back, Bear at her feet, and told herself to relax.

CHAMPAGNE

For what seemed like hours, the musicians played. Libby began to think they'd never stop. She ached with tension. At last, Chesterton declared himself too exhausted to continue, and offered everyone a glass of the ice-cold champagne he'd slipped into the fridge earlier.

Angela dispensed cheese and biscuits while Bear woke and squatted, alert for fragments of food to fall, ready to snaffle every titbit before it hit the carpet.

Simon handed a full glass to Libby. 'Did you enjoy listening to our mistakes? I'm afraid age and lack of practice takes its toll. Chester and I are a bit past it, really. Most of the time I only teach, these days.' His smile was modest. 'Young Steve's very talented, though, don't you think? He'll go far.'

Libby couldn't wait any longer and abandoned any pretence at small talk. 'I have to ask you about that morning in the bakery. You know, the day of the cycling club picnic?'

'I'll never forget it.' Simon shook his head. 'Two good people killed on a trip intended to be no more than a happy day out in the sunshine. I was one of the lucky ones. I hardly felt ill at all.

Whatever it was that poisoned Vince and Kevin, I hadn't swallowed much.'

Libby blurted out, 'That's the trouble. I think it might all be my fault.'

'You?' Simon's eyes widened. 'What nonsense. What could you have done?'

'The chocolates.' It was almost a whisper. 'I'm afraid there might have been something wrong with them.' She shivered. 'I need to know which one you had. You see, I was ill as well, and so was Joe. Kevin had been in the shop with us, and he ate my chocolates. I'm not sure about Vince, because I never met him, but Kevin might have given him one.' Libby's voice squeaked. She slowed down. 'What if everyone who was ill had the same kind of chocolate? There were some chili flavoured ones, some with parma violet and a batch of lemon meringue.'

'And which did you have?' Simon's voice was very gentle.

'Violets and lemon meringue.'

Simon frowned. Libby's heart thumped. He looked so serious. 'Do you know,' he said, 'I think you're suffering from some sort of guilt complex. Survivor guilt, I think they call it. I had one of those parma violet chocolates and I was fine. Of course there was nothing wrong with them. They were wonderful, by the way. You're a very talented lady.'

Nothing wrong with the chocolates.

For a few seconds, Libby was silent, stunned. Then relief swept over her, leaving her weak and trembly. The lump in her chest disappeared.

It wasn't her fault. She hadn't poisoned anyone.

Simon was smiling now. His teeth were very white and even, and the smile lit up his face. He was a most attractive man. Libby felt a delicious glow start in the pit of her stomach and spread through her body until she knew her cheeks were flam-

ing. It was a good job she was sitting down for her knees felt
wobbly.

Simon leaned in. 'Libby Forest, I'd like to get to know you
better.'

Libby bit her lips to keep from grinning like an idiot. Deliberately, she sat back and looked around. No need to seem too keen.
Nearby, Alice Ackerman flicked a strand of hair behind one ear,
smiled and turned her back on Mandy, speaking exclusively to
Angela.

'Steve gets his talent from his Uncle Geoff, I expect?'

Steve shook his head. He looked very young and earnest.
He'd dispensed with the earrings and nose piercings today.

'I wish I had half his ability,' Alice went on as, behind her,
Mandy's eyes narrowed.

Simon murmured in Libby's ear. 'Look at that young chap.
Talented, young, not a care in the world. He's the spitting image
of his uncle. I'm not surprised that Alice girl is keen on him.'

Libby whispered, 'Mandy's furious.'

He laughed; his voice musical. 'All's fair in love.'

Was Simon flirting? If so, she was enjoying it. She felt a
twinge of guilt, quickly suppressed. Max wasn't here, was he? In
any case, they were friends, nothing more. She could talk to
anyone she wanted to.

Still, maybe she should change the subject. 'Did you know
Geoff Miles, then?'

'Oh, yes, we were old friends – at university together. That's
where he met the lovely Angela, of course, and cut me out as a
matter of fact. I'd had hopes of her for myself.' Simon grimaced.

He pointed towards the window. 'Look. The sun's shining.
Shall we take our glasses outside and make the most of it?'

Why not? Weak with relief that she wasn't the poisoner, with
a glass of champagne acting powerfully on her empty stomach,

Libby was in the mood to enjoy a bit of flattery from an amusing, intelligent man.

She stood up. 'It's certainly very hot in here.'

Bear followed them out, velvety brown eyes never leaving Libby's back. She ignored another hit of guilt. She was tired of Max's on-off approach to their odd, arms-length relationship. She owed him no loyalty. If only Bear wouldn't look at her like that.

They sat at a picnic table on the patio, surrounded by the scent of rosemary and lavender bushes. Libby raised her face to the sun's rays. Bubbles of champagne flooded her bloodstream, adding to the warm glow.

Simon raised his glass. 'Chesterton always has good taste, in wine as well as women. Have you noticed the way he looks at Marina?'

Libby giggled. 'They go riding together.' She bit the inside of her lip. The wine was loosening her tongue.

Mandy had come outside, too. She leaned on the garden wall, watching Libby and Simon. 'Are you all right, Mrs F?'

The child was smirking. 'I'm fine, thank you.'

Simon held out a bottle to Mandy. 'Can I pour you a glass of Mr Wendlebury's champagne?'

She shook her head. 'I don't drink.' Libby opened her mouth, about to protest, for that certainly wasn't true, but she closed it and said nothing. She wasn't Mandy's mother.

Mandy refused to meet her eye and suspicion kicked in. The young Goth was up to something.

The patio door slid silently open and Steve ushered Alice through. As she crossed the threshold, she tripped on the step and giggled. Steve raised an eyebrow.

Bear paced back and forth across the patio as Simon watched. 'Is there something the matter with your dog?'

'He's not mine. I'm looking after him for a friend.' Bear whined. Libby called the dog over. 'What's the matter? It's not like you to make a fuss.'

She scratched his head, he curled round her feet and she laughed. 'Did you feel left out?'

Alice stumbled to a patio chair and flopped into it.

'How much did she have?' Libby murmured to Steve.

'Just a couple of glasses.' He shrugged. 'Empty stomach, I suppose.'

Libby lost interest in Alice, for Simon's arm had touched her own, warm through his wool jacket. 'You played well, today, Steve,' Simon said. 'A chip off your uncle's old block, I reckon.'

'Oh.' Steve rubbed his chin. 'Right. Thank you. My uncle used to talk about you. He said the two of you used to be a team.'

'We were, but Geoff was the one destined for great things.' Simon smiled. 'We can't all be legends.'

'Uncle Geoff said you were more talented than him, but—' Steve stopped in mid-sentence, blushing.

'But he said I wasted my ability on advertising jingles.' Simon laughed. 'It's all right. Geoff called it selling my soul, but I made a good living from advertising for quite a few years before I went into lecturing. Geoff stuck to his guns – he had music in his soul. He wasn't rich, at first, but he wrote well. You should be very proud of him.'

'I am.' Steve's eyes shone.

'It a tragedy he died so young, just as his work was gaining popularity.'

Steve said, 'I was going to go to his concert. You know, the one that was cancelled the day he had his accident. Mum was taking me as a treat because I passed my Grade Six saxophone. I remember everything about it.'

'You were only young at the time. It must be ten years ago now. What were you – nine? A bit of a prodigy, weren't you?'

'Mum said Uncle Geoff was driving too fast...'

Simon touched Libby's hand. 'I don't expect you know the story.' He glanced into the house and dropped his voice. 'We don't talk about it much in front of Angela, because the accident was Geoff's own fault. He had a sports car. A Porsche. He'd had some sort of quarrel with Angela after the morning rehearsal and he drove away in a huff, without her. He was going much too fast, as he always did, and drove clean off the road.'

No wonder Angela hadn't told Libby. It must have been terrible for her. Imagine quarrelling, then watching your husband drive away and never come back. Angela would have felt it was all her fault. 'How dreadful. Poor Angela.'

'Yes, she never forgave herself. Don't mention it in front of her, will you?'

Libby remembered the manuscript. 'She told me about Geoff's last work: the one you're all rehearsing. She said he was writing it when he sprained his wrist, and he could hardly finish it. I saw the manuscript: you could tell there was something wrong with his hand at the end – the handwriting changed. It became almost unrecognisable.'

She broke off as Angela came through the doors, heading for Alice. The girl had left her chair and was swaying on her feet, humming quietly. Angela took her arm. 'I'm afraid Alice has had too much champagne. Would someone please take her home?'

'Mandy, were you topping up Alice's drink?' Libby tackled her lodger as soon as they were home. She folded her arms, blocking the girl's route to the stairs.

Mandy didn't look in the least abashed. 'She'll be fine, Mrs F. She didn't have that much champagne. She just can't take her drink.'

'Don't look so smug,' Libby scolded. Secretly, she was pleased. Mandy knew how to stand up for herself.

The girl giggled and shot a sideways glance at Libby. 'I could see you were having fun with Simon.'

'Don't change the subject. Anyway, it's none of your business.'

'So, you don't mind if I tell Max that Simon was all over you in the garden?'

'Tell him whatever you like.' It wouldn't do any harm for Max to know he wasn't the only fish in the pond. 'By the way, Max is joining us for dinner.'

'Oh, sorry. I meant to tell you. I'm going out.'

'Steve?' No wonder Mandy was full of beans. 'You really like him, don't you?'

Mandy's face was alight. She'd never looked so elated. 'We're going to the club.'

She disappeared upstairs, humming something tuneless and fiddling with her phone. Libby pounded herbs into a paste and stirred coconut milk, lemon grass and lime juice in a frying pan for a Thai curry. Its fragrance filled the kitchen.

The shower spluttered in the bathroom, reminding Libby she still couldn't afford to renovate it. *You can get used to anything.* She hardly noticed the orange bathroom tiles these days.

Drawers opened and closed and hangers rattled. There'd be a mountain of discarded clothes on the chair in Mandy's room. She was a lodger, so there'd be no need for Libby to nag about tidying the bedroom.

Libby remembered when Robert was at home, leaving over-sized trainers everywhere. He'd never have fitted into this tiny cottage, but still, Libby missed him. London, where he lived, seemed a long way away.

Both her children, leading their own lives.

Suddenly lonely, she re-read the email Ali had sent when she arrived in South America and her anxiety drained away. Ali sounded so happy, so full of life. The email had sparkled with excitement over the people she'd met and the job she was doing. Libby had printed it out and kept it in her pocket.

Libby felt a rush of pride. Ali and Robert had grown up, that was what had happened. They were independent, determined to stand on their own feet and she admired that. Of course they wouldn't tell her everything. She should trust them and stop worrying.

She hummed as she worked. The curry was almost ready and she was starving.

She enjoyed talking to Simon today and he'd seemed to enjoy their conversation. In fact, she'd been sure he was about to suggest they meet up somewhere, when Angela interrupted them.

She allowed herself to daydream a little. Where would Simon take someone on a first date? A restaurant? Maybe that expensive French place that just reopened in Exham?

The wooden spoon dripped sauce on the worktop. Libby wiped up the mess with one hand. Was she seriously thinking about going on a date with Simon? Hadn't she given up all that sort of thing? Time with Max didn't count – they'd always talked about Susie's death, or Mrs Thomson, or Bear. Their partnership was business only – if it was anything at all.

A phone rang and she jumped. *Don't be silly.* It wouldn't be Simon just because she was thinking about him, like ridiculous telepathy.

She wiped her hands and ran to the sitting room to find the mobile. If it was Simon, though, and he asked her out, would she go?

She found her phone but the screen was blank. Simon wasn't ringing then. Disappointed, she thrust the annoying object in a pocket.

It was Mandy's phone.

A shrill scream filled the cottage. The hairs on the back of Libby's neck rose as she took the stairs two at a time.

'Mandy? Whatever is it?'

The teenager sat bolt upright on her bed, tights round her ankles, leather skirt still unzipped. One shaking hand held her mobile phone to her ear, the other grasped the front of her t-shirt, fingers working, screwing the cotton into a ball.

'I – I'm coming,' Mandy stammered into the phone. 'I'm on my way.'

She dropped the phone on the bed and stared at Libby, eyes huge and black. 'It's Steve.'

'What's wrong?'

Mandy's thin frame shook so hard she could barely speak. Her mouth worked. 'The motor bike,' she whispered.

Libby took a long, trembling breath, determined to keep calm for Mandy's sake. 'Is he – is he...' She couldn't put the worst into words.

'He's in a coma. In Mountview Park Hospital.' Mandy stuffed a fist into her mouth but there was no holding back the sobs that shuddered through her whole body. Libby squeezed her shoulder, feeling helpless.

She could get Mandy to the hospital. 'I'll take you. Put some jeans on. Oh!' The champagne. Libby couldn't drive all that way after all that wine. 'Wait, I'll ring for a taxi.'

With the phone at her ear, she had a better idea. She glanced at her watch. Max might be home by now. She punched in his number. *Hurry up and answer, can't you?*

The phone clicked. 'Libby, how did you guess? I just walked in the door.'

Her shoulders sagged, tension draining away. 'I need you to take us to the hospital, right now.'

'What? Why?' Instantly alert.

'It's Mandy's boyfriend. He's been in an accident. We're at home and I've been drinking so I can't drive—'

Max cut her off. 'On my way. Hold tight.'

The phone went dead.

Libby helped Mandy, shocked and trembling, to shrug on the leather jacket – Steve's jacket. She poured boiling water on a teabag, blessing her speedy hot water dispenser, added milk, and stirred in plenty of sugar. 'Drink this while we're waiting and fill me in on what happened. Who rang you?'

'Aunt Angela. Steve was on his bike, on his way home. A car must have hit him, out near Middleton on the Levels.'

'Must have?'

'They didn't stop.'

'Didn't stop? But that's...' Libby bit back the words. No point in upsetting Mandy even more. But why hadn't the car stopped? It was unforgivable. The driver would surely know if he'd hit Steve's motor bike.

The catlike purr of an expensive engine took them outside. Libby hadn't seen the Jaguar before. Max must have used a hire car from the airport. She felt a twinge of guilt. His Land Rover was still parked where she'd left it, at Alan's garage.

'You stay here, Bear,' Libby ordered. 'We'll be back soon.'

The journey to hospital was a blur. Mandy sat in silence on the back seat, kneading tissues into damp balls. Libby filled Max in on the sketchy details she knew. 'Who'd leave the scene without stopping?'

The hospital smelled of disinfectant. Libby's stomach contracted. No wonder people hated these places, chilling worlds full of strange noises, preoccupied nurses and weary doctors. They threaded through the corridors. A cheerful, buxom lady with round glasses and a volunteer's badge pointed them towards the Intensive Care Unit.

Angela had already arrived with her sister-in-law, Steve's mother. Angela wrapped Mandy in a hug. 'He's just come out of surgery. His leg's broken, and he's concussed.'

Mandy whispered. 'Will he be OK?'

'We hope so.'

Mandy sank on to a seat next to Angela and blew her nose. 'I want to know who did it. I'll stay here for a bit, but you go, Mrs F. Find who almost killed Steve. The police will take months, if you leave it to them, but you and Max can do it – I know you can.'

If only Libby could feel so confident.

Angela said, 'Mandy's right. I'll look after her. Just do what you can, both of you.'

Unsure, Libby glanced at Max. He raised an eyebrow and his head jerked, infinitesimally, towards the door. He was right, of course. There was nothing more to do here.

16

COFFEE

The Thai curry was none the worse for waiting, but Libby could hardly taste it. Max laid down his fork. 'I phoned Joe while you were banging around in the kitchen. He's home, now, and none the worse for wear.'

'And are you two talking now?'

He looked thoughtful. 'Strangely enough, we are.'

'Maybe his near-death experience made Joe think about the things that really matter. You know, family and so on.'

Max stared at Libby with an odd expression on his face, as though he was trying to see what she was thinking. 'There's something wrong, isn't there, apart from Steve's accident? What is it, Libby? Is it your kids?'

Libby stopped pretending to eat. 'Not exactly. You remember that house in Leeds? You asked if I knew anything about it?"

' She put her thoughts in order. 'The truth is, I only discovered Trevor owned a second house after he died and I came across the deeds. I don't know where he found the money. He certainly didn't have much cash – remember, I wanted to redesign the bathroom when I first arrived here, but I couldn't afford to because I was broke? It's very mysterious.'

Max said, 'If there's a property you didn't know about, your money worries could be over.'

'I suppose that's true. It's just – well, who did he buy it for? A mistress?'

'Would you mind if he did?'

She swung round. 'Of course, I would,' she snapped. 'Except...'

She started to collect up the plates from the table. 'Except, apart from being angry, I don't think I would care. Trevor was a horrid man and I wish I hadn't married him, but I did, I can't change that, and I have two lovely children as a result. That's enough for me. Who cares what he got up to when he was away on business?'

Libby considered pouring out her worries about Ali and the crazy dash to South America, but this wasn't the moment. She'd leave it for another time. Her daughter could look after herself, safely out of the way of the Exham poisoner, and she didn't want to rely on Max for everything. That was one of the mistakes she'd made with Trevor.

'It's Steve's accident that worries me. It didn't happen by chance, did it?'

Max walked to the window, looking out into the night. 'Sometimes, good people get mixed up in bad stuff.' He sounded worried. Libby frowned. What did he mean? Which bad people?

'You think the accident was deliberate?' she said.

'I'm sure of it. The bike was hit hard enough to tip it off the road and into the rhyne. Steve was lucky to be found. He could have been in the ditch all night. Whoever did it must have felt the crash.'

Max shook his head. 'He could easily have died. I'm afraid

that might have been the intention, and the police are suspicious, too. Joe knew about it before I rang him. Ian Smith told him; I think.' That was the constable who'd interviewed Libby. 'They found paint on Steve's motor bike. They might be able to trace the car that hit him.'

He smiled, but only his mouth moved. His eyes glittered. 'You can relax, Libby, and leave this one to the police.'

She wasn't going to let that go. 'I can't leave it to them. You're frightening me, Max. Don't you think it's time you told me everything you know? What's really been going on? Kevin, Vince, Joe, Frank's business, and now Steve. What's the link that binds it all together? I thought we were a team, but I get the feeling you're hiding things from me. What happened to Forest and Ramshore?'

Max's eyes were bleak. 'I shouldn't have encouraged you. Stay out of it, Libby. People are getting hurt.'

Libby breathed hard, thumping her mug down with such force the coffee splashed onto the wood. 'They're the people I care about. I want to help, and I get the feeling you know far more about what's going on than you're saying.'

Max tapped his spoon on one hand, brow furrowed. 'Very well. I'll tell you what I know. You already heard about Pritchards, the subsidiary of AJP Associates. I've been tracking them for a client and I came across their interest in Exham. All I can tell you at the moment is that they're big, rich and very powerful.' He shot a glance at Libby, as if weighing up how much to say.

'Is that why you went away?'

'Partly.'

'Where to?' He dropped the spoon into his mug and stirred. The coffee must be cold by now. He was giving himself time to think. *Can't you be honest, just for once?*

'I can't tell you.' Max heaved himself to his feet. 'Sometimes, my work's very confidential.'

He wasn't just talking about solving the murders, or Steve's mysterious road accident. He was talking about their strange, unspoken relationship. Libby pressed her lips together, biting the flesh with her teeth, her anger fading and giving way to a cloud of depression, like damp fog. She felt her body slump. She couldn't bear lies and secrets. Trevor's betrayal had been more than enough for one lifetime. Libby needed, above all, to trust people.

It was her own fault. She could see, now, that she'd been expecting too much of Max. Deep down, despite all the denials, she'd been hoping something more would come of their odd friendship. Well, more fool her. She pulled her shoulders back and thrust out her chin. She was perfectly capable of solving the puzzle of Exham's poisoning and the attack on Steve, without Max's help.

'If you won't be honest with me, or tell me what's going on, you might as well leave now. And don't come back.'

Max's face was suddenly pale under the tan. A lump formed in Libby's throat and she opened her mouth, but it was too late. She couldn't take the words back.

He put his mug aside, neatly, on a coaster. 'I'm sorry I can't tell you everything. I wish I could.' He stood up. 'Maybe this wasn't such a good idea. Come on, Bear. Let's get home.' The dog leapt to his feet and Libby felt abandoned. Even Bear seemed happy to leave her alone.

Seconds later, both Max and Bear had gone.

Determined not to cry, Libby wandered round the suddenly quiet house, fiddling with cushions and curtains. She tried to stoke up the ashes of her anger. How dare he? She'd show Max Ramshore. Frank was in trouble, Steve was at death's door, her own business was in jeopardy and her husband had double-crossed her. If Max thought she was going to stay meekly at home, he had another think coming. She could put the jigsaw pieces together without his help.

With Trevor's house in mind, she made more strong, black coffee, pulled out an orange file that contained the solicitor's paperwork, sent after the estate was wound up, and flicked through it all for the hundredth time. Surely there must be some evidence of the house in Leeds.

Despite an hour's careful reading, Libby failed to find a single clue to explain what Trevor had been up to. She sat straight. There was one sure way to find out what was going on.

Her phone dinged. It was Mandy, texting to say Steve was in a medically induced coma, the doctors were hopeful, and she was staying with Angela that night. Libby flicked the chain on the door and, alone and miserable, fell into bed.

17

LEEDS

It was still dark the next morning as Libby left home. The sun rose behind the Mendip hills, bathing the motorway in shades of salmon and peach. A flock of birds rose, briefly blotting out the sky and the newly serviced Citroen purred happily.

Four hours later, Libby's satnav led her to a detached, Victorian house on the outskirts of Leeds. She drove past, assessing. The paintwork was neat, the windows clean, with bright curtains tied back at the side.

She checked the house number and, suddenly nervous, made her way up a short flight of steps to the dark blue front door. A column of four bell buttons ran up the side, a name slotted next to each one. The house was divided into flats.

Libby held her finger on the lowest bell, belonging to an A. Grant. No one came. She tried the next, J. Brown, and drew another blank. The occupants must be at work. Or maybe they were students, still asleep. No, not students. The curtains were too tidy.

The top bell brought footsteps, faint at first, then louder. At last, the lock rattled, and the door opened. A young woman cradled a baby on her shoulder. Almost as young as Ali, she was beautiful. Free of makeup, her perfect, English rose skin gleamed with health. Her eyes were enormous, deep brown, in contrast to the pale blonde of her long hair. Her delicate, elf-like face, creased against the light, peered from the darkness of the passageway.

Libby glanced again at the name beside the bell. 'Ms – er – James?'

'Yes. Do I know you?' The young woman frowned and shifted the child to her other hip.

'I'm Libby Forest.' Libby watched the woman's face, expecting guilt or embarrassment. It betrayed only mild surprise. If this woman was Trevor's secret mistress, she was also a brilliant actress.

'I'm so sorry for your loss,' she said. 'Please come in. I'm Tina, and this is Kyle.' Libby followed her up the stairs. 'I'm afraid my husband's at work at the moment.'

Libby felt a weight lift from her shoulders. She could easily deal with one woman and her child. Tina went on, 'We were wondering what would happen about the house. Were you wanting to go through the accounts?'

Libby shrugged and cleared her throat. 'Yes, please. It's taken a while to sort things out. Once I've dealt with the house, I'll be able to wind up my husband's affairs.'

Tina glanced back. 'Your husband?' Her voice lifted at the end of every sentence, so Libby wasn't sure if that was a question.

'Mr Forest, my husband.'

The woman's brow cleared. 'Oh, really?' She looked far from worried, as Libby had expected, but turned and led the way upstairs.

Tina reached the top of the house. Libby let her do the talking while she caught her breath and vowed to get fitter.

'We keep everything in the study.' Tina led them through a green painted door into a wide and sunny apartment, simply furnished.

Tina set Kyle, a round mini-me with his mother's hair and eyes, into a complicated stand that allowed him to sit in the middle of a carousel of toys, where he fiddled, banged and gurgled happily.

Tina left the room, returning in seconds with her arms full of files. 'Do you want to look at these while I feed Kyle? Cal, my husband, deals with all the properties.'

Libby smiled, hiding the shock that made her hands shake. All the properties? How many houses had Trevor owned? She took a deep, steadying breath. 'How old is Kyle?'

'Just six months.' The baby could be Trevor's, the voice in Libby's head whispered. The missing husband could be imaginary. *Don't trust this woman.* She seemed to know more about Trevor's affairs than Libby had ever done.

Tina put a stack of files on the dining table at the far end of the room, near the bay window. Silently, Libby spread them over the surface, wondering what she should look for. *AJP Associates.* The name jumped out. Pritchards was part of AJP. Pritchards, the company that tried to buy Kevin's land, that wanted more shops in Somerset. The company Max was investigating.

Libby flipped a glance back towards the woman and her baby, just in time to see Tina slip a phone into her jeans pocket. Suddenly wary, she gathered up the files. 'I'll take these away, if I may, Mrs James.'

'Oh,' the woman's face coloured. She looked round the room, distracted, seeming to search for a reason to object. 'Why don't you have something to drink first? I don't think—'

The door flew open, saving her from thinking.

A burly man, huge hands held close to his sides like a gun

fighter in a western, burst into the room. Libby jumped up, files clattering to the table, gripping the back of a chair, as two more, bigger, meaner looking men followed. 'What's going on 'ere, then?'

Tina nodded towards Libby. 'This is Mrs Forest.'

The man sneered. 'Well, I never. And what brought you here?'

Libby licked dry lips, using every ounce of will power to stay calm. 'I – er – I gather this is my husband's house.'

'Do you now?'

A familiar voice sounded from the doorway. 'That's right.'

Libby spun round. 'Max?'

Max ignored Libby and held out a hand to Tina's husband. 'Mr James, I presume?'

The man's eyes narrowed.

He covered the floor in two strides to shove his face close to Max's. Max smiled, not moving an inch. 'Good to meet you, although I fear you've been drinking. A bit early, don't you think?'

He wrinkled his nose and stepped sideways, closer to Libby, his eyes on Cal James. 'I haven't met your buddies, I'm afraid.'

James looked Max up and down, sneered, and waved his hands at the two heavies by the door. 'All right, boys, he won't give us much trouble.'

Max took Libby's arm. She let him lead her back to the table as he spoke to Cal James, 'We need to talk about these files your wife has very kindly produced. I see you've met Mrs Forest, by the way. Trevor Forest's wife. As you can see, she's a little surprised. She didn't know of your existence, or anything about the work you've been doing for her husband. I think it's time we let her into some of his secrets, don't you?'

18

TEA

'Before we begin, Cal,' Max said, 'and in case you had any thoughts of getting rid of me or Mrs Forest, I'll just warn you my friends are outside. I only have to press one button on my phone, and they'll be with us.' His head jerked towards the window. 'At the moment, they're enjoying a McDonald's in that blue BMW on the other side of the road.'

Cal James reached the window in two strides. He swore. Libby wracked her brains, trying to remember if she'd seen the BMW on the motorway. No. She hadn't noticed a thing. So much for her skills as an investigator.

James grunted. 'Me and the wife, we don't know nothing about anything. We just take the rents. For a fee.'

'And a nice, fat fee, I expect.' Max leaned back, the picture of relaxation. The two goons stood squarely in front of the door.

Max patted a chair. 'Sit down and get comfortable. This might take a while. Maybe your wife, or girlfriend, or whatever, will offer us a nice, soothing cup of tea. And we won't be needing your two friends.'

His voice was as smooth as silk but steel lay just beneath the surface.

Cal James dismissed the men with a shrug and a wave. Their footsteps clattered down the stairs and the front door banged.

'I suggest you show me what's been going on before I send for my colleagues. You'll get credit in court if you tell me what I need to know.'

Max took his phone out of his pocket and laid it on the table, switching it to record. 'Start talking, Cal. Things might not even get as far as a charge if you're helpful enough. Who knows?'

Libby sat on both hands to keep them from trembling. She hardly recognised Max. For a second, face rigid, he looked directly at Libby and one of his eyes twitched. The wink came and went so fast, Libby could hardly believe she'd seen it. She sat up straighter and squared her shoulders. She could play it cool, too. Her hand was steady as she sipped strong orange tea.

Max settled at the table, opening one file after another. 'Libby,' he said. 'I know a little more about Trevor than I mentioned..' She squirmed; their quarrel burning bright in her memory.

Max went on, 'I've been looking into his affairs for a while now. He owns several properties.'

'That's right.' Cal James grinned, showcasing a missing front tooth. Libby managed not to flinch.

Tina played with the baby, her lovely face betraying no interest in her husband's business. Behind that beautiful exterior there seemed to be very little brain. Libby smiled at Kyle. Poor baby, with these two for parents.

'Now, to business.' Max slipped off his jacket, hung it on a chair and rolled up his sleeves. 'All we need from you, Cal, is a run-down of the properties, plus the names and addresses of anyone involved in buying and managing them. Easy enough, isn't it? Start by showing Mrs Forest where the rent goes.'

An hour later, Libby's head reeled. Her husband had owned more than a dozen properties. They were rented out, with hundreds of thousands of pounds of rent money tucked away in a succession of different bank accounts.

Max locked the files in his briefcase and shrugged into his jacket 'Right, we'll be in touch.'

'Wait a minute. You can't take everything. What do I tell—?'

Max's face was grim. 'What do you tell your contacts when they find themselves locked out of the accounts? Not my problem, Cal. You'd better start thinking. Now, shall I call my friends and get them to take you to a nice, safe police cell?'

Cal rose.

Max took Libby's arm. 'Come on, let's go,' he drawled. 'Thanks for the tea.'

His fingers bit into her skin. He hissed in her ear, 'Have you got your car keys?'

Stumbling down the stairs, Libby fumbled in her bag, feeling through tissues, lipsticks, pens and loose coins with trembling fingers. She finally located the bunch of keys. 'Here they are.'

She almost expected the Citroen to have vanished, but it was waiting where she left it, fifty yards down the road as though nothing unusual had happened at all. They climbed in.

Max snapped. 'Get going. Fast.'

Libby turned the key in the ignition, foot on the accelerator, over-revving the engine. It spluttered. Her heart pounded. She tried again and it sprung to life. Libby caught sight of James' two minders in a dirty, unmarked van on the corner. 'Won't your friends stop them following us?'

'What friends?'

'The ones in the—' Libby broke off, her insides sinking. 'You mean, you were bluffing? You don't have any back-up?'

'Sorry. None.'

The Citroen's wheels squealed as Libby pumped the pedal. They were getting out of there as fast as the car could take them. 'Max, we could have been killed.'

'It's OK,' Max twisted to look behind, 'Here, don't forget your seatbelt.'

Relief tingled in Libby's fingertips. 'I think you'd better explain.' A thought struck. 'Where's your car? I take it you followed me up here.'

'I hired one. I'll courier the keys to the agency and they'll pick it up. I had a feeling we'd be leaving in this very charming old tin can.'

Libby's hands on the wheel had stopped trembling, but her voice squeaked. 'Do I take it Trevor wasn't the nine-to-five insurance salesman I thought?'

Max shook his head. 'I'm sorry, Libby. This has been a shock for you. I found Trevor's name on some of the Pritchards invoices, talked to one of my colleagues and discovered he owned that place in Leeds, but when I mentioned it to you, you couldn't explain it. I was stuck – I couldn't give you the details, not while there was an investigation going on'

Libby drew a sharp breath. 'Pritchards?' The company she suspected of being behind the poisonings had links to Trevor.

Max was still talking. 'We both knew Trevor owned a house in Leeds, but you had no idea how he could afford to buy it. When I found you'd gone, this morning, I put two and two together. I had a hunch you'd take matters into your own hands.'

'You mean, you didn't trust me enough to tell me about my own husband?'

'I thought—'

'Oh, I bet I know what you thought. 'Poor little woman; mustn't upset her or let her in on my very important investigations into Pritchards.' So much for our so-called partnership.'

Furious, Libby crunched the gears. Max looked straight ahead.

After a few miles of silence, Libby gave in. She needed to know the whole truth. 'Are you going to tell me what's been going on, or not? Was Trevor some kind of Mr Big?'

Max gave a short laugh. 'No, but he was part of a large-scale fraud.'

Libby forced herself to sound cold and calm. 'You mean, he was a criminal.'

She drove in silence, digesting the news, piecing together all the little clues. All those years together, and she'd had no idea. She'd ignored Trevor's long days, supposedly in the office, the strict rule that his wife and children keep out of his study, his refusal to let her take any part in the family finances. All the time, he'd been a petty criminal.

She was glad she'd stopped loving him years ago, but she would never forgive him. She thought of another angle. 'Am I about to be in trouble? Will I lose my home?'

'No, of course not, but you won't receive any of the ill-gotten gains. You see, Trevor was laundering money for a gang. It went through several hands, including his, on its way to becoming legitimate. It started with the gang's ill-gotten gains from a variety of crimes. Stolen cars, for example.'

Libby had a light-bulb moment. 'Wasn't that what Alan Jenkins at the garage was involved in?'

Max had helped his old school friend, Alan, out of that mess.

'That's right. Through a series of intermediaries, the gang paid your husband, Trevor, an innocent-seeming insurance sales-man, to buy houses. He'd rent them out for a while, then sell them on and buy some more. The money, almost untraceable, eventually found its way to drug cartels in Colombia.'

'And Pritchards are involved?' Libby tried hard to understand.

'Pritchards, or AJP Associates, the parent company, have moved on to buying up business premises as well as rental houses, but we don't have nearly enough evidence to convict them of fraud. We'll be working on it for a while longer before the police move in.'

Libby's mouth hung open. 'The money ends up paying for drugs?' Exotic drug barons seemed a million miles away from Trevor, her self-righteous husband.

'Drugs which are then imported to the UK, among other places. It's the biggest business on the planet.'

Libby thought it all over as she drove. She could understand Max's refusal to tell her what was going on. He was worried she wouldn't keep it to herself. But they were partners; he should at least have told her everything he knew about her husband.

She glanced sideways. Max's face was blank, attention fixed on the road ahead. She was glad they were nearly home. His voice was polite and formal as he unfolded his body from the car.

'I'll need to keep the files but I'll get back to you if I find anything legitimate you can access. Maybe there'll be a little to fund your new business, but most of it is laundered money.'

Safely home, Libby poured a large glass of red wine and drank it down in one draught. The truth was, she could trust nobody. Trevor and Max had each taken her for a fool in their different ways. She'd thought she was the one doing the detecting, but all the time she was missing clues about her own husband. A dark pall of failure had settled over her and the ground she walked on seemed suddenly to have shifted, like sand on a beach. Nothing was as it seemed.

At least the kitchen was her own. She ran her hand over the small pile of her books on the countertop. She'd been so proud of them, but the excitement of becoming a real, published author had long drained away. She clutched the wine glass until the stem was in danger of snapping. Men always spoiled things. She'd had it with men.

She picked up the bottle, about to refill her glass.

She stopped, the bottle held aloft. How was Steve? She'd hardly spared a thought for the boy all day and her phone had been turned off. She dragged it from her bag and pushed the switch.

There was a message waiting from Mandy. 'Steve still in coma but no worse. Frank in jail.'

Sleep was impossible that night. Alone in the house, tossing and turning in bed, Libby listened to the first drops of rain tapping on the roof and clinking against the windows.

At last, she gave up the unequal struggle with sleep and wandered downstairs, made a cup of hot chocolate and, wrapped in a duvet, watched old films until daylight.

At last, the clock hands scrolled around to a sensible time for visiting the police station. Libby fed Fuzzy, showered in the ugly green and orange bathroom, dabbed mascara on her eyelashes, swiped lipstick across her mouth and shrugged on her old parka. She wished Bear was with her. Her eyes filled. She'd made up her mind to have nothing further to do with Max Ramshore, and that meant no more contact with the dog she'd grown to love.

The police station was unwelcoming, the seats in the entrance covered in cold terracotta tiles. Libby finally diverted the civilian receptionist's attention from sorting piles of paper, asked to see Constable Smith, and settled down for a long wait.

'Mrs Forest.'

She jumped. She'd been there less than five minutes. 'Joe? You're back at work already?'

'As you see. Have you come to confess?' Joe's pallor and the dark rings under his eyes gave him the look of a tired child. Libby was on the verge of offering to take him home and make him tomato soup.

'Or maybe you've seen the wrong side of my father.' Joe offered a tight smile.

Pulling herself together, Libby followed him meekly through doors that clanged, through an open plan office. Rows of police officers glanced up from computers, barely registering any interest as the pair passed through.

At last, they entered a tiny room at the back of the building. 'Your office?'

Joe blew air through his lips. 'I'm not nearly important enough for my own office. This is an interview room.'

Libby examined the room. 'No microphones or cameras?'

'Not here. Informal discussions only. You're not really under suspicion, Mrs Forest. No motive. Although,' he went on, 'plenty of means and opportunity. Working in the bakery, you could poison the whole town if you wanted.'

She ignored that. 'Then, if you don't suspect me, maybe you could call me Libby?'

He let the ghost of a smile pass over his face. It was gone in a fraction of a second. 'Well, then, Libby, how can I help you?'

'I hear you've arrested Frank Brown for murder, but I can't believe anyone would think he's a killer. He's such a lovely man.'

Joe leaned back, gazing at the dirty yellow ceiling, obviously undecorated since the days smoking was allowed. His gaze moved to Libby's face. 'I can't tell you much, Mrs – er – Libby, but since you helped us out over that last business, I'll give you what I can.'

A tiny grin tugged at Libby's mouth. This was the first time anyone from the police had admitted she'd helped solve last year's murder at the lighthouse. She bit her lip and made a solemn face. She didn't want to annoy Joe.

He was explaining. 'The thing is, unlike you, Frank does have an all-important motive, which means he has the full set; means, opportunity and motive. Easy enough to put digitalis or digitoxin, or whatever the men in white coats call it, in the sandwiches, or the cakes. Or even the chocolates.' Libby beat down a familiar twinge of guilt and had to remind herself it wasn't the chocolates.

He's just tormenting me.

Joe's barely there, enigmatic smile reminded Libby of his father. She felt a pang of loss.

'Anyone can get hold of the stuff, on the internet or from prescription medicines for heart problems. Frank's old mother's taken Digoxin, one of the proprietary brands, for years.'

He tipped his chair forward, leaning both elbows on the table so he could look straight into Libby's face. 'Frank has a ready-made source of the poison and every opportunity to toss it in the bread or cake mix.'

He was enjoying this a little too much, in Libby's opinion.

He went on, 'Kevin Batty did the dirty on Frank.'

'I know. They had a quarrel over the price of flour, but that was years ago.'

Joe's face fell. She'd managed to steal his thunder. 'As it happens, you're right, but so far, it's the only motive we've got.'

Libby wouldn't leave it there. 'It's a pathetic motive. Why leave it so long to get revenge? You've decided Frank's guilty, and you're not even looking at other people. What about big business, for one thing? Pritchards are trying to take over premises across the West Country.'

Joe snorted. 'Seriously, do you think a multi-million pound company like Pritchards would kill two people just to get their hands on Brown's bakery? I mean, it's a nice shop, I grant you that, but I bet they could buy Frank out with their small change.'

He was right. A bakery in Exham on Sea would be almost beneath Pritchards' notice.

Libby kept a rein on her tongue. She couldn't share the information on the money laundering operation in Leeds. Max had probably told her more than he should yesterday. She could see, now, how difficult it was to keep secrets.

Had she possibly been just the tiniest bit unreasonable towards Max?

Joe seemed to have lost interest. 'Chief Inspector Arnold's satisfied we've got our man so we'll be bringing charges.'

The legs of Libby's chair scraped the floor as she jumped to her feet. 'Well, I never heard such nonsense in my life. Honestly, Joe, Frank's motive is no stronger than Pritchards'. What about Vince? Why would Frank want to kill him?'

Joe flapped a hand in the air. 'Maybe Vince and Frank had some sort of quarrel as well. We don't know, yet, but we'll find out soon enough, don't you worry.'

'Besides, why did only two of the cyclists die, while everyone else survived?'

'Maybe they both had a sweet tooth so they ate more of the Eccles cakes. Frank would know that sort of thing. He's been feeding cake to Exham for years.'

Libby raised her voice. 'That's absolute rubbish, Joe. Are you going to let a man like Frank rot in jail, without even bothering to look for the real culprit?'

Joe fixed his gaze on the ceiling once more. 'If you think you know better, Mrs Forest, by all means go ahead and prove us wrong.'

'That's exactly what I shall do.'

Arrogant man. Libby marched across the floor, ready to sweep out. One hand on the door, she turned. 'And another thing...'

Joe still sat at the desk, rocking back, watching, both eyebrows raised. The angry words died on Libby's lips. She suddenly understood what Joe was signalling.

He knows Frank isn't guilty, but his boss has tied his hands.

Without another word, she slammed the door and left.

* * *

She revved the Citroen's engine hard and drove home in record time, to find Angela on the doorstep with Mandy in tow. A glance told Libby that matters at the hospital were still bad.

'Mandy needs to sleep,' Angela said. Without a word, the teenager trailed upstairs.

Libby shrugged out of her coat and heaped coffee into cups. 'You don't look much better yourself.'

Angela cradled her cup. 'Steve's still in a coma. They're keeping him like that to let his brain recover.'

The words, *if it can*, hung unspoken in the air. 'Steve's mother is at the hospital now.'

'Then, maybe you should go home, too, and get some rest.'

Angela grunted. 'I wanted to talk to you first. I wondered if you and Max had got anywhere. You know, investigating?'

Libby finished her coffee, thinking hard. She couldn't ignore Angela's appeal for help, or Mandy's distress. If working with Max could help her find the murderer, Libby mustn't let pride get in the way, just because Max had kept things from her.

The truth was, the two of them made a decent team. He'd once said, 'People tell you things, Libby. You sit down with a slice of cake and start to chat, and before they know it, they've poured out all their secrets.'

She made a pact with herself. From now on, she'd try not to fly off the handle every time Max annoyed her, but she'd keep the relationship purely business. Nothing personal. No more cosy evenings drinking wine and flirting, and no more stupid arguments.

Mind made up, Libby brewed more coffee and produced a well-matured Dundee cake. 'Some of the things Steve told me might be important.'

Angela let her breath out in a loud sigh. 'I knew you were the right person to help, Libby.'

'Let's not get ahead of ourselves.' Libby couldn't share the information about Pritchards or money laundering gangs, but she needed to know why they might be interested in Angela's nephew. 'Maybe you can tell me more about Steve. What's he really like?'

20

ANGELA, STEVE AND GEOFF

Angela put on her reading glasses and then took them off again. 'Steve was musical from the day he was born. Geoff and I weren't able to have children, so Geoff was thrilled when his nephew started playing the recorder.'

Libby screwed up her nose. She'd been forced to play the instrument at school. She'd produced a regular series of high-pitched squeals like a dawn chorus of cats before her parents let her off the hook.

Angela went on, 'Steve was only four. His mother, Geoff's sister Grace, and Thomas, his dad, were musical as well. That's how we all met, taking music degrees at University. Geoff would have been pleased as Punch to know Steve was going off to the Royal College and making a career in the business.'

'Steve's quite a star, then.'

She nodded, seeming close to tears. 'We're going to postpone the concert, of course. It can wait a few months until he's better. But, what if – if things don't improve? What if Steve's brain is damaged, and it's permanent?'

Her hand covered her mouth, as if she wanted to take back

the words. 'You see, he's like his Uncle Geoff in so many ways. They both loved music more than anything, but they shared more than that. It's a touch of the devil, that's what my mother said when I married Geoff. Geoff could be wild.'

'Like Steve.' Libby thought of the drugs paraphernalia in Steve's house, the ripped t-shirts and the tattoos.

Angela frowned, making a strangled sound. She burst out, as if she couldn't hold the thought back any longer. 'It would be too cruel if they died in the same way as each other, on the road.'

Libby waited, as her friend gained control. Finally, Angela swallowed. 'To be honest, Geoff's accident was his own fault.'

'Go on.' This didn't seem to be leading anywhere. Geoff died ten years ago, and Libby already knew about the accident. She wanted to hear more about Steve. Still, she'd hold her tongue and let Angela get things off her chest.

'He loved music and fast cars, did Geoff. And, to be honest, sometimes he drank too much.' Angela was twisting a ring on her wedding finger. It flashed, mesmerising, as she turned it round and round. 'We were rehearsing for the concert. It was the same music we were playing the other day.'

Angela gave a sad little laugh, more like a hiccup. 'Geoff was angry with me that day, because there was a mistake in the printing of the posters. I hadn't proofread them properly and his name was spelt wrong. We only noticed during that last rehearsal. Geoff was furious. He called me all sorts of names. Still, I was used to that. It was just his way.'

A rueful smile crossed Libby's face. She knew about ranting husbands.

Angela went on talking. 'He said I was to get it fixed and meanwhile he'd go to the hotel for lunch on his own. He set off, in the Porsche, as fast as usual. The road was steep and twisty, and he was so mad, he must have been careless. Everyone else followed him, while I stayed behind, on the phone to the printers.'

She had to stop for a moment to gain control of her voice. 'The others saw his car upside down in the valley.'

She paused to blow her nose. Libby asked, 'Who found him?'

'Oh, didn't I say?' Angela counted them off on her fingers. 'Apart from Geoff and myself, there was Steve's father, Thomas, his mother, Grace, and Simon. We called ourselves the Circle of Fifths. They were all very kind to me. I don't know how I'd have survived without them.'

She gave a watery smile. 'That's one of the things about music. It brings people together. The members of the quintet were my closest friends.'

Her eyes filled. 'Not many of us left now. Steve's father died last year, from cancer. Grace and I both gave up performing regularly when Geoff died.'

'So, Steve and Alice were the newest members of the quintet.'

'That's right. Two very talented young people.'

Libby murmured, 'Have you known Alice long?'

'Steve met her at Wells. They're very competitive. Alice is rather brilliant, at her other studies as well as music. She's off to Cambridge this year.'

Libby breathed a small sigh of relief on Mandy's behalf. Her rival would soon be leaving the scene.

Angela rose and stretched. 'Look at the time. I must have been here ages. And I hardly talked about Steve at all.'

She looked around for her scarf. 'There is something I wanted to mention, though. When we talked about the manuscript, before, I said Geoff sprained his wrist while he was writing it. Do you remember?'

Libby thought back. 'The scruffy writing?'

'That's right. Then later, I thought about it, and realised it was the wrong year.'

'The wrong year? How do you mean?'

'He'd sprained his wrist the year before.'

'And it had healed by then?'

'It must have, if he was playing the clarinet again, mustn't it He was playing in the concert. I suppose he was over-tired, and that's why his writing was so careless. He often took on too much. Didn't know how to refuse work. It was nothing to do with the sprained wrist, at all.'

Angela tied the silk scarf round her neck. 'Anyway, I won't grumble, because he left me very well off.'

Halfway down the path she turned back. 'By the way, Marina rang me to remind me it's the county show tomorrow. Are you going?'

Libby had completely forgotten. 'Good job you reminded me. Marina told me about it, and I've taken on a stall.'

21

BISCUITS

A flicker of mixed excitement and terror woke Libby. Today was the spring show. It was a grand affair, apparently, the first she'd ever attended, with a wealth of competitions and exhibitions in the programme. The ploughing competition would take up three nearby fields, the year's best lambs would be on show in the main ring, and the American classic car rally would cover half the rest of the showground.

It was also Shipley's big day. The dog show was planned for the afternoon. No doubt Marina had risen early to shampoo her springer spaniel and primp him. Libby had no intention of missing Marina's show-down with Mrs Wellow.

She'd had to spend almost the whole night preparing for her stall. The health and safety inspector had visited late yesterday, peered through wire-rimmed glasses into every inch of the kitchen, pursed his lips at the array of separate sinks and fridges and, reluctantly, as though it pained him, let Libby have the prized certificate. She could offer her wares for sale at last.

Today she'd be letting children ice their own biscuits, hoping their parents would buy a copy of *Baking at the Beach* and maybe a bag of hand crafted chocolates.

She drew back the curtains to find rain blowing horizontally from a uniform grey sky. Not a single inch of blue broke the monotony. Crazy, holding an outdoor show so early in the year. Still, her granny had always said, 'Rain before seven, fine before eleven.' With a little luck, she'd turn out to be right.

Libby dug out her warmest waterproof jacket and a new pair of sheepskin-lined wellies. At least her stall was in a tent, not outside at the mercy of the weather.

She loaded the car with tins full of product, boxes so weighed down with books she could hardly lift them and piles of giveaway bookmarks. The Citroen coughed its way to the show site.

After three trips back and forth to the car, Libby spread clean white sheeting over her allotted table and unpacked her wares.

'Morning, Mrs F.' Alan Jenkins appeared at the door of the tent, almost unrecognisable in a clean waxed jacket and wide brimmed hat. 'How's the car?'

'Overworked, I'm afraid.'

'You been driving her hard, then?'

'Just up the motorway to Leeds, but I don't like the noise in the engine.'

He sucked his teeth. 'What did I tell you? She needs gentle treatment. She's a lady, that one.'

Bear appeared from nowhere, reared up to plant his paws on Libby's shoulders and licked her face. She scratched the rough fur on top of the animal's head. Max, close behind, hauled the animal down, clipping on a lead.

Libby glared. 'Keep Bear away from the food on the stall, won't you?' She winced. She'd meant to build bridges with Max and be business-like, but instead, she sounded plain bad tempered.

'I heard you'd be here.' He smiled, but the glint in his eye told Libby he was annoyed.

She flashed a synthetic smile. 'Sorry, I've got to set up.'

She bent down behind the table, unloading books. Alan, with surprising tact, had melted away.

Max joined her. 'I'm sorry I kept things from you – about the house in Leeds, I mean. Won't you forgive me? Look, the sun's coming out.'

Reluctant, she glanced through the tent's entrance. A tiny patch of sky had turned a slightly paler shade of grey. 'Call that sun?'

'You wait. The weather's already drying up. Look, I'll even buy one of your books.'

That was too much. Imagine Max, who ate takeaways or visited restaurants for his meals, attempting to bake a cake. Libby felt the corners of her mouth twitch. She offered an olive branch. 'Do you think I dare sell chocolates, after what happened? I've got a hygiene certificate.'

'Of course. If you don't, people will think there's something wrong with them. You know you didn't poison anyone. It's the bakery that's in trouble, not you.'

Libby straightened up and stretched. Her trestle table, neatly covered in white sheeting, decorated with red ribboned cellophane bags of chocolates in wicker baskets, was inviting.

The day wore on into an afternoon of watery sun. Mandy arrived, almost back to her old self after nearly twelve hours of sleep, and took over the stall for the afternoon.

She settled down in a huddle of children and biscuits and stuck her tongue out. 'Like my new stud?'

Libby shuddered.

The last few drops of rain had dried up as Libby wandered outside and the dog show was under way on the other side of the park. She caught sight of Marina leading Shipley into the ring. And, there was Mrs Wellow, on a collision course with her rival. It was too good to miss. She set off at a run towards the ring.

A voice cried, 'Look out!' just as something hit Libby hard in the chest. She fell, landing heavily on her back, every ounce of breath squeezed out of her body. Bear barked, paws on her chest, as with a flash of gleaming chrome, a car whizzed past just inches away.

Libby scrambled to her feet, gasping.

A hand on her arm steadied her. Max shouted, 'You idiot. Can't you look where you're going?' he sounded furiously angry.

Bear whined, mouth open, tongue lolling.

Libby shuddered. 'I think Bear just saved my life. Where on earth did that car come from?'

The car had juddered to a halt and Chesterton Wendlebury stepped out. 'You almost went under my wheels, dear lady. Are you all right?'

Libby cringed. 'That was stupid of me. I wasn't looking where I was going. Sorry. I'm perfectly OK. You didn't touch me.' She knew she was gabbling nonsense but she couldn't stop herself.

A crowd was collecting and Max still held her arm. 'I think you need a stiff drink,' he said.

She nodded. Anything to get away from all those eyes.

Wendlebury slapped Max on the back. 'Good idea, good idea. I'll park the old lady and join you.'

A half pint of locally brewed beer in hand, Libby found a space on a straw bale in the refreshment tent. Bear lay at her feet. She took a long gulp, glad of the warm, malty taste at the back of her throat. 'I feel such a fool.'

Max laughed. 'I'm surprised we don't have more accidents here, with such a lethal mix of people and cars.'

'What kind of car was that, anyway?'

'A Mustang Convertible. Made around 1965, I believe. It's one of Wendlebury's collection; he owns dozens of them. He takes them from one show to another. Alan's here somewhere as well, with one of his.'

He examined Libby's face, his eyes anxious. 'You're sure you're OK?'

Libby remembered the conversation she'd had with Alan a few days ago. 'Several people in the area have old cars – what Alan calls classics – don't they?

'Most of them are probably here today, at the show.'

'Did Kevin Batty own one?'

'Used to. He spent hours fiddling around with it, he and Vince. They were mates.'

Libby said nothing. Her mind was too busy. She opened her mouth, then closed it again. She wouldn't tell Max, yet, about the idea she'd had. He kept things from her and she could do the same to him.

22

'Are you sure you're all right?' Max still looked worried.

Libby forced a smile. 'Sorry. I'm just embarrassed at making such a fool of myself. I was on my way to watch Marina do battle with Mrs Wellow at the dog show, but I think I'd rather stay here for a while.'

Max's leg felt warm and strangely comforting against Libby's. He took a long draught of Butcombe Gold beer, taking a minute to roll it round his mouth.

'Good idea.' He frowned. 'Listen, Libby, I want to apologise. I should have told you what I knew about Leeds. I'd no idea you'd go rushing up there in your old tin can. You could have been in real danger, you know. Fraud is white-colour crime, but that doesn't mean the people involved aren't dangerous. Don't go running off on your own again, will you?'

Libby swallowed. 'If we're still partners, Ramshore and Forest, we need to talk more. And we need to stop arguing and tell each other about ourselves. You know, personal things.'

Max leaned over to pat Bear. 'Hmm. I'm not good at sharing.'

'I've noticed. You've hardly told me anything.'

'Then I'll try to do better. What did you want to know? Ask me anything you like.' He swept an arm in a wide gesture.

'I don't want to be nosy,' Libby began.

Max snorted.

'No, seriously,' she insisted. She searched for the right words. 'Look, I'll tell you something about me, then you tell me something about you. Something personal. How about that?'

He nodded. 'Sounds fair.'

'Well, you know my daughter came to stay?' Libby told him about the row with Ali, and how devastated she felt when Ali told her she was leaving the country.

Tears started in her eyes. 'I never really understood Ali. She was Trevor's daughter much more than mine, and now, I'm afraid I've lost her.'

Max took her hand. 'None of us get parenting right, but I think you said just the right things to your daughter.'

Libby sniffed and blew her nose.

Max said, 'What about your son?'

'Robert? He's fine. He has a long-time girlfriend in London, and he rings me when he remembers. At least he hasn't gone to the other side of the world.'

'And now it's my turn, isn't it?' Max drew a long breath. 'While we're talking about children, I suppose I need to tell you more about mine. I'm surprised no one in town's given away my guilty secrets.'

Libby waited patiently, although she felt consumed by curiosity.

'I had a daughter, too. She was ten years younger than Joe.'

Was? Libby felt sick. 'What happened to her?'

He cleared his throat. 'When Debbie and Joe were growing up, I was in banking. Away in London for days at a time, working all the hours in the week, I hardly saw the kids or Stella, my wife.

I meant well. I had good intentions and we all know what happens to them.' He shrugged, looking suddenly unsure of himself.

'I thought I was doing the right thing, being a good husband. I made money. Plenty of it. We had a second home in Hampstead, not to mention a place in Italy, but I was never at home with the family. I didn't have time for holidays, or helping the kids with homework, or going to meetings or sports days at their schools.'

He emptied his pint glass. 'It's a common story. Nothing special. Stella didn't need to work, but she grew bored with nothing to do all day but go to lunch with her friends. I guess that's why she started drinking.'

He balanced his empty beer glass on the straw. 'I loved my kids, but I thought providing for them made me a good father. They had everything they wanted, except my attention.' He laughed, but it sounded harsh. 'Joe hardly wanted anything. He was on the way to being a scientist. He used to run experiments in the garage – I'm surprised he didn't blow it up. Debbie, though, liked having nice things. Clothes, toys, ice-skates. When she was twelve she wanted a pony and, like a fool, I bought one. She kept it at the riding school.'

'Gingernut, it was called. After a while, she stopped riding the poor animal. He was getting fat. I came home one weekend and the phone rang. It was the stables, to say they were worried about Gingernut's health. He needed more exercise. They even mentioned the RSPCA.'

He shrugged. 'I should have let Stella deal with it, but it was eleven in the morning and she was already well down her second gin and tonic. So, I became a hands-on dad and gave Debbie a good talking to.'

He shook his head. 'I don't think I'd ever punished her before. I said we'd sell the horse and sent her up to her room.'

He reached into his pocket and pulled out a wallet. 'Here she is. She was a lovely girl. It was my fault she was spoiled.'

Libby looked at the photo. Max's daughter had his eyes.

She wished he'd stop talking; it was leading somewhere she didn't want to go, but she knew he needed to finish the story.

She whispered. 'What happened?'

'I bet you can guess. Debbie took no notice of me, slammed out of the house, caught the bus to the stables and took the horse out for a ride. On the road...'

Libby put a hand on his arm. 'There was a crash?'

He nodded. 'A lorry sped past, too close. Gingernut reared. Debbie fell off and hit her head. She wasn't wearing her hard hat, and she died.'

Max kept his eyes on the photo. 'As you can imagine, the marriage didn't last long. I spent even less time at home, had an affair with a colleague, my wife found out, and so on. The usual story. We divorced. Joe wanted to stay with Stella, and I let him. I'm afraid I ran away from it all.'

Max glanced at Libby, then looked away, eyes bleak. 'I left the job and came back to Exham, where I'd grown up. I did nothing for a while but hit the bottle. It was Joe that saved me, oddly enough. One day, he arrived at the door with a degree, a girlfriend and a job with the police, and gave me a piece of his mind.'

He managed a grin at the memory.

Libby could imagine. She glanced round, making sure no one could hear. 'That's when you retired and started your second career in financial tracking?'

'That's right. If Joe could make something of himself, so could I. But it's shaming to know your son's a better person than you and I've been hard on him as a result. When he was poisoned, I thought I was going to lose him, too.'

No wonder Max had been short-tempered since that day.

Libby hung her head. If only she'd been less prickly, less worried about her own affairs, she'd have seen there was something seriously wrong. She opened her mouth, not sure what she was about to say.

Chesterton Wendlebury loomed above her head. 'Well, it looks like you're in fine fettle.'

Bear growled.

'I'll join you, if I may.' He smiled at Libby, showing his large teeth. 'Seems to me you're a bit accident prone, Mrs Forest. Only missed you by a whisker.'

Libby smiled, forcing herself to be polite, hiding a shiver. Chesterton Wendlebury made her uncomfortable. 'How did Marina get on in the dog show?'

'It's still going on. Thought you might like to go over there with me, cheer her on?'

Max stood. 'We'll all go. Should be fun.'

Libby slipped her arm through his and he gave her hand a small squeeze.

The judging was under way. Seven finalists paraded round the ring. Shipley had made it to the last few, alongside Mrs Wellow's Manchester Terrier, Theodore. Marina and her diminutive, red-headed rival ignored each other, their eyes fixed on the judge, a dapper man with a shooting stick.

Finally, after walking round each dog several times, and a spate of loud harrumphing, the judge made his decision, raised a hand, and beckoned Shipley to jump on to the winner's podium.

Mrs Wellow tugged on Theodore's lead, dragged him across to the front of the podium and jabbed a finger at Marina.

'I knew that would happen.' Her voice was shrill, reaching every ear round the ring. 'A cheat, that's what you are. You've bribed the judge.'

The audience gasped, thrilled. 'Oh, I say!'

The judge intervened. 'You can't say things like that, madam.'

'Can't I just? You watch me.'

Mrs Wellow spun round, to the audience. A camera whirred as the photographer from the local paper took a series of close-ups. 'I'm telling you all now, Marina Selworthy is nothing but a cheat. That dog of hers is no pure breed. He only won because she's sleeping with one of the local toffs, and that's a fact.'

Laughter rippled through the crowd. Marina gasped, one hand on her ample chest. 'How dare you!'

'Now then.' Constable Smith materialised from the audience and took Mrs Wellow's elbow. 'There's no need for that sort of talk, is there?'

The red-head shrugged free. 'You'd better watch out.' Her outstretched finger followed Marina as she left the judging ring, head high, Shipley dancing at her feet. 'I'll be getting my own back on you, just see if I don't.'

* * *

Back at the stall, Libby counted the proceeds. 'Do you know, I think we've actually made a profit.' She handed Mandy a pile of notes. 'Thanks for your help.'

'I had fun.' The teenager's face was flushed.

'You're very good with children. Much better than I am.' Libby put the last few biscuits back in their tin. 'How's Steve doing? Angela told me he woke up last night. Do you know when he'll be well enough to come home?'

'In a week or so, I believe. The doctors said this morning that they think he'll be all right.'

'He had a lucky escape.'

Libby chose her next words with care. She didn't want to

frighten Mandy. 'Have the police said anything more about the accident?'

Mandy shook her head and Libby let it go. Poisoned cyclists, Steve's motor bike, classic cars, road accidents. She shrugged and picked up a pile of empty boxes. There was a visit she had to make.

23

IN THE RHYNE

Libby dropped Mandy at home and then climbed back in the car. 'I won't be long.'

She knew plenty about Kevin Batty and his old feud with Frank, but Kevin wasn't the only victim of the poison attack. She still didn't know enough about Vince, Kevin's friend, the other cyclist who died. Why had he been killed as well?

She pulled Mandy's list of local people out of her pocket. There he was; Vince Lane, with an address in a village out on the Levels. Mucklington. The name rang a bell. Libby concentrated until she remembered. Ah, yes, the great floods had cut the place off from civilisation. Boats, floating up the main road, had head-lined the national news for days. Had Vince lived with anyone out in the countryside? Libby was consumed with curiosity. Even if he lived alone, his neighbours would be able to tell her about him, and she was longing to take some action. A trip across the Levels was just what she needed.

She fiddled with the satnav, turned the car and set off, soon rewarded by miles of green fields stretching out as far as she could see, criss-crossed by drainage rhynes. No wonder the cycling club loved their days out here. Libby wished she had Bear with her today. He adored the freedom of the Levels.

She had a feeling she was getting closer to the truth of Steve's accident, but she couldn't grasp any clear link with the death of the cyclists. Maybe they were two separate events? She pondered that thought for a moment, then shook her head. She felt sure there was a connection, if only she could figure it out.

She glanced at the satnav. Mucklington was only half a mile away. She put her foot down on the accelerator, watching out for more treacherous bends hidden by withy, and soon found herself on the single road to the village. The surface was smooth, newly laid, the road recently raised several inches to combat any future flooding. The fields of pasture nearby were bright with spring green and grazed by contented cows.

Libby drew to a halt outside a short row of terraced cottages, left the car and tapped on the door of number three, but no one answered. She tapped again, stepped back and squinted at the windows on the first floor. A single curtain dangled limply. She dropped her glance to the ground floor. There were no curtains, blinds, nor other sign of life down there. She stepped closer, shaded her eyes with one hand and peeped through the window. A cooking hob and a sink were visible, but otherwise, the room was empty.

'They're gone.'

Libby jumped, startled, at the voice in her ear.

An elderly man wearing a flat cap and brown overalls nodded. 'Vince's wife left years ago and now, he's gone too.' The man laughed, and the laugh turned into a cough. Recovering, he looked Libby over and pulled off his cap. 'I always thought his heart would kill him off, but someone got there first.'

'His heart?'

The old man nodded. 'Vince used to work on the farm over

yonder, along with me.' He jerked his head towards the field of cattle. 'Farmer had to let him go on account of the heart failure.' He sniffed. 'On a mountain of tablets, he was. Only a young man, half my age. I used to come in of an evening. 'Vince,' I'd say, 'Vince, you need to give up the cider,' but would he ever? Not Vince. 'I'll go when it's my time,' he'd say. 'The cycling keeps me fit."

The man shook his head as though puzzled by Vince's stupidity, advanced closer, and peered over Libby's shoulder into the house. 'Your Vince was chairman of the cycling club, you see. Had been for years. When his heart first played up, they used to come around here often, to see how he was going. Every single member of the club must have tramped up and down this path at some time.'

He scratched his head, lost in memories. 'Then, when Vince got better, they let him pootle along at the back on his old bike. I thought the cycling might give him a heart attack, but he wouldn't give up. It took a dose of poison to finish young Vince.'

'Ah well.' The old man put his cap back on. 'Vince's time came quicker than he thought, didn't it? None of us know when we'll be going. Look at me – passed my threescore years and ten a while ago, but I'm still here.'

He jerked a thumb at the house. 'This place'll go up for auction, I suppose, though who'll want to buy anything here since them floods I don't know. No value in houses, here, these days.'

He sketched a vague salute in Libby's direction and shambled off. Libby, perplexed, wondered whether to knock on any of the other doors. It was quiet out here. No one else was in sight and there was no sound of children playing. Everyone was at work, or shopping, or about their own business.

She shivered, suddenly nervous as though someone stood

close behind, watching. She spun round to check, but she was quite alone. She was letting the quiet of the Levels spook her.

Giving in to temptation, she climbed back in the car and began the drive home.

She slipped a CD into the car's ancient player. One of the benefits of independence was listening to music she chose herself, without husband or family rolling their eyes at her choices. Spirits suddenly high as Vince's row of deserted cottages disappeared from her rear view mirror, she turned up the volume on the Eagles, singing along at the top of her voice to *Hotel California*.

She drove past a small outcrop of trees and stamped on the brake. The road bent sharply, and the front end of a Range Rover roared into sight just feet away. Libby wrenched the steering wheel to the left, skidded on a patch of mud, tried to correct and felt the car slide sideways, seemingly in slow motion. Hands clenched to the wheel, she hung on tight as her front wheels lurched off the road and slid over a patch of grass into the accompanying rhyne. The engine stalled, but The Eagles still sang, unbearably loud now.

Libby flicked off the radio and restarted the engine, revving hard. The front wheels spun, failed to gain traction, and the car remained stuck, the front end hanging over the ditch.

She gave up, turned off the engine, unclipped the seat belt and leaned awkwardly against the door.

Someone tapped on the window. Libby groaned under her breath. Not Chesterton Wendlebury. This was the second time he'd almost run her over.

He threw the door wide. 'Good gracious, m'dear. What a way to meet again. Are you hurt?'

'Not at all. But I'm stuck.' Chesterton, his vast bulk straining against his riding kit, leaned over to squint at the front of the car. 'We'll soon have her out of there,' he pronounced.

He strode across to the rear of the Range Rover, threw up the boot and fumbled inside, emerging with a length of rope. He fastened one end round the tow bar.

Libby stepped forward, hands outstretched, hoping to regain a little dignity. 'Here, I'll fix it on to the car.'

'Good heavens, no, m'dear. Let me do it. You must be shaken.' She had no alternative but to watch in impotent silence as he fastened the tow rope to the Citroen's bumper, climbed back into the Range Rover and revved the engine. Slowly, smoothly, he heaved the Citroen on to dry land. 'There we are.' Beaming all over his ruddy face, he untied the rope. 'No damage done; I think. You'll be right as rain.'

It was too late for indignation. She'd missed her chance. Complaining that the Range Rover had been speeding seemed petty now its owner had rescued her. Libby forced a grateful smile and fluttered her eyelashes. Men like Chesterton Wendlebury liked women to be helpless and weak.

'Now, no need to thank me,' he went on, condescendingly. 'Just be careful in future. These roads can be tricky when you're not used to them.' He was standing very close. Libby found herself backing away.

His smile was warm, his teeth very large and slightly yellow. 'Look what happened to that unfortunate boy, Steven. I hear he's still very poorly.'

Libby swallowed. 'The doctors are hopeful he'll be fine.'

'Good, good.' The smile hardly altered. 'Let's hope he's on the road to recovery, shall we? That little girl lodging with you, what's her name, Amanda, is it? She'll be relieved when he's back on form.'

'Mandy. Yes, we all will.' Libby sidled closer to her car,

suddenly nervous. What was Chesterton Wendlebury doing out here? 'Were you on your way back from the riding stables?'

He stared back along the road, as though he could see something out of Libby's sight. She leaned against the door of the Citroen, gripping the handle, the cold metal solid and comforting in her hand.

Chesterton went on, 'That's right, m'dear, had a charming ride with your friend, Marina.' His gaze returned to Libby's face, as if he were daring her to comment. 'I'm on my way home to change. Back to business, eh? No peace for the wicked. Now, what brings you all the way out here?'

She thought fast. Instinct told her to keep her council, not give away the reason for her journey to this man. She didn't trust him. Two near misses with his car were too big a coincidence for her liking.

'I came out for a spin to clear my head.'

His roar of laughter startled a flock of geese grazing on a nearby field. It sounded artificial to Libby's ears. 'And you landed in the ditch as a reward, did you? Stay closer to home next time, that's my advice.'

He laughed again. 'Oh well, must be getting on, as there's no harm done. If you're not hurt, my Board meeting awaits. I'll watch you start up, make sure your little car's still functioning.'

Libby's brain whirred into action at his mention of the Board. She had a hunch. Trying to sound casual, she said, 'Is that the Board of Pritchards?'

Wendlebury's brows came together. Her words had hit their target. 'Can't deny it. One of the irons I like to keep in the fire, you know.'

'I hear you're looking for premises around here.' Libby kept her voice light.

'Now, now, m'dear. Let's not worry about business. You should get home – make yourself a nice mug of hot chocolate. That's your speciality isn't it, chocolate?' The words were barbed. 'I'd offer to make you some myself, but this meeting's important.'

Ostentatiously, he consulted his expensive looking watch. 'Heavens, look at the time. Can't be late. Better get that car started.'

He stepped towards Libby. She snatched the door open and slipped into the driving seat in a single movement, and turned the key in the ignition. The car coughed, and Libby drew a sharp breath. *Please, please, start.* The prayer worked and the engine turned over. Giving silent thanks for Alan Jenkins' car maintenance skills, she wound down the window, smiled sweetly, waved and drove off.

As the car accelerated smoothly, she glanced in the rear view mirror. Chesterton Wendlebury stood for a long moment, watching, before climbing into his own vehicle. He continued on his way, driving in the opposite direction to her. As he disappeared around the corner, she took her foot off the accelerator and pulled in to the side of the road. She needed to stop and take a breath.

She glanced in the mirror once more and gasped, gripped by sudden terror. The Range Rover had turned round. Chesterton Wendlebury was approaching, fast.

Chesterton Wendlebury was following her. Libby had to get home. Every inch of her body on high alert, she stamped on the pedal. The car juddered, gathering speed.

Don't break down now.

The Citroen, small and nippy, perfect for the narrow roads along the rhynes, took hairpin bends in its stride. Libby held her breath, knuckles white with tension on the steering wheel, right foot glued to the accelerator.

The tyres screeched.

The engine whined.

Libby's eyes flicked to the rear view mirror and she exhaled, at last. The Range Rover had fallen back.

As her foot relaxed, the car slowed. Chesterton Wendlebury had let her go.

Relief flooding Libby's veins, she longed for home and the safety of Hope Cottage. She wouldn't be driving on the Levels again for a long time.

Her brain worked overtime. Was Chesterton Wendlebury trying to kill her? He'd come near to it, twice. If so, it must mean

Libby's interest in Kevin and Vince's death threatened him in some way.

If he was behind those murders, there must be a reason.

It didn't take Libby long to work it out.

Land must be the answer. Land, ripe for development, waiting to make millions for a clever businessman like Chesterton Wendlebury.

He was on the Pritchards' board, and Kevin had prevented that company from acquiring the land they wanted. Wendlebury wasn't the kind of man to let the Kevins of this world stand in his way. He'd never let go of a grudge.

When Kevin Batty stood up to Chesterton Wendlebury, he signed his own death warrant.

Wendlebury, through Pritchards, had clearly been working for years towards his revenge. No doubt he'd soon approach Kevin's family, trying to buy the land cheaply now Kevin wasn't there to fight back.

Libby thought back over the conversation with him. They'd talked about Steve. She shuddered, hands shaking on the wheel, stealing snatched glances through the mirror as the Range Rover slipped further behind. Had her questions put her on the list of people standing in Wendlebury's way?

As she reached Exham, Libby shot one more glance in the mirror. The Range Rover had disappeared.

Tears of relief filled her eyes. He'd given up – for now.

She screeched to a halt outside Hope Cottage, leapt from the car and ran home. She was safe, for now. She was lucky. Wendlebury's meeting had been too important for him to waste more time chasing Libby.

Unfortunately, the danger remained. He knew where she lived. There was nowhere in Exham to hide. Shaking, Libby pulled out her phone, planning to dial the police. Her fingers began to tap the keys, hurriedly at first. Her heart thudded.

The police would protect her.

Her fingers stopped, hovering above the phone.

She hadn't thought this through. What was she going to tell them?

She tried to look at today's events through the eyes of the police. She'd skidded into a ditch. Chesterton Wendlebury, a pillar of the establishment, had chivalrously stopped on the way to his important meeting and pulled her out, but instead of showing gratitude, she was accusing him of trying to kill her?

She cut off the dial tone. Joe Ramshore would support her if he could, but she lacked hard evidence. Frank Brown was still the likeliest suspect for the murders.

She sighed, wondering what to do next, and the answer hit her between the eyes.

Only one person would listen.

She phoned Max.

'Hello, Libby. That was quite a day at the show.' The warmth in his voice sent a rush of emotion through Libby. A stomach jangle and a smile she couldn't quite shake off, along with a flicker of guilt.

Wendlebury, she recalled, had interrupted Max's confidences. She hadn't been able to respond properly, but there was no time for that, now.

She took a shuddering breath. 'Max. I need your help, again.'

His tone changed, sounded urgent. 'What's wrong.'

'He's after me. Can you come?'

'Calm down. Is someone there with you?'

'No. But he's on his way.'

'Who is? And, where are you?'

'Wendlebury.' She could hardly say the name through her

chattering teeth. 'Chesterton Wendlebury. He's coming after me. I'm at home.'

'Wendlebury? Libby, what are you talking about?'

'Stop arguing. Just get here, Max. I need you.'

'Okay, lock the doors and stay inside. I'm on my way.'

Libby, forcing herself to stay calm, checked the locks on the doors and windows, and then checked them again.

She held the phone in one hand, counting the bars that registered the strength of the signal, sick with fear. How long would it take Max to arrive? Twenty minutes? Trembling, she watched the hand on the kitchen clock tick round.

Six minutes, then seven. Maybe, if Max drove fast, he could do it in fifteen...

The doorbell rang. Libby almost dropped the phone, weak with relief. He'd arrived already. Max must have really put his foot down.

Libby staggered to the front door and flung it wide open. 'Thank you for coming so quickly—'

She stopped talking.

Simon Logan stood outside; a broad smile etched across his handsome face.

Libby breathed out. He wasn't Max, but he'd do very well for the moment.

25

IN THE KITCHEN

With Simon here, Libby was safe from Chesterton Wendlebury.

'Simon? Did Max send you?'

'Max? No, I wanted to ask you something. Can I come in?'

Libby breathed deeply, in and out, to control her pounding heart as she ushered him into the kitchen.

'Are you OK?'

He was taking her arm, looking into her face.

Libby smiled. She couldn't help it. Simon was tall, strong and handsome, and those warm brown eyes seemed to draw her in.

'You've saved me.' She muttered. 'Someone's after me.'

'After you? Who?'

'Chesterton Wendlebury. He killed Kevin Batty and tried to kill Steve, and I'm next.'

At the bewilderment on Simon's face, Libby gulped hard. Of course, he must be confused, hearing this for the first time. She should explain. Before she could say another word, Simon took a long step, threw his arms round Libby and hugged her.

'You're shaking. You must be imagining things. I mean, Chesterton? Everyone knows him.'

Libby leaned into his body. His voice, deep and gentle, sounded very comforting.

'Why don't you tell me all about it?'

She swallowed. 'I'm sure Wendlebury killed Kevin and Vince and poisoned everyone in the cycling club. He's the killer. He was driving after me, following me through the Levels – I only just managed to get away.'

'You mean he chased you in that enormous Range Rover and you lost him in your little Citroen? I don't think so.' Simon laughed, his voice loud in the tiny cottage.

Libby stepped backwards, away from him. Something was wrong.

Simon stood inches away, smiling, one hand out of sight behind his back.

Libby, suddenly nervous, took another step back, banged her elbow on the breakfast bar and stumbled across the room, Simon following.

He purred in her ear, his voice no longer comforting. 'If he'd wanted to catch you, he would have managed it easily.'

Libby looked into the man's eyes.

They glinted, ice in their depths, and he took another step.

She whispered through dry lips. 'I've got it all wrong, haven't I? It's not Wendlebury, is it?'

The past flashed through her mind, like a video, and the jigsaw pieces fell into place.

Simon had been at the picnic. He'd offered to help, and she'd handed over the sandwiches.

Alan Jenkins had described Kevin Batty and his love of cars.

Vince had a long-standing heart condition.

Angela's husband, Simon's friend, had died in an accident...

Libby's back pressed against the sink; Simon so close she could feel his breath on her face.

'It's not Wendlebury, no.'

Libby stammered, 'It was you, all the time.'

Simon's left arm remained hidden behind his back. His right hand shot out and grabbed the neck of Libby's sweater, pulling her face even closer.

'You've been interfering a little too much, Mrs Forest. All that talk of manuscripts and sprained wrists – you're too clever for your own good. You knew I'd written that music, not Geoff, didn't you?'

'N-no. I didn't realise...' Music? What was the man talking about?

'All those questions you've been asking at the garage, about Kevin Batty. You've been after me for days.'

'What do you mean? I wasn't—'

'Don't pretend. You've talked to them all. Alan Jenkins, Steve, Angela Miles. You've been snooping around, finding a fact here, a snippet there...'

She must keep him talking while Max was on the way. He'd be here any second. He'd save her from this madman – for there was madness in those stony eyes.

'Angela?' she repeated. 'What does she have to do with it?'

He sneered. 'Don't pretend you don't know about Geoff and me. You've been getting friendly with the Miles woman – she told you about Geoff, and you put two and two together, to make five. Or possibly six.' He sniggered. Libby shuddered at the sound.

'Geoff's death was over and done with. Forgotten. Water under the bridge. I felt safe in Exham – until Kevin opened his big mouth.'

'How? What did he say? What happened?' *Hurry, Max, hurry.*

Simon's grip on Libby's sweater relaxed a little.

'We drank in the Lighthouse Inn. The three of us; Alan, Kevin and me. Kevin was a bore. A silly little man who deserved what he got.' He chuckled.

For a second, Libby thought he might let her go. She pulled away an inch, but he yanked her back, his knuckles digging painfully into her neck while he talked.

'One night, after a few pints, Kevin started on about the old days when they used to fix cars. Alan remembered Geoff Miles's Porsche, and the crash. One of the steering tie rod nuts on Geoff's Porsche had been loose. He'd been afraid he'd get the blame for Geoff's death, but the inquest dismissed it. Luckily for me, Geoff was a terrible driver, always speeding round the bends... It was his own fault.'

'But you'd loosened the nut?'

'You're such a clever woman,' Simon sneered.

Unable to move her head, Libby peered from the corners of her eyes, searching for something to grab, anything she could use to disable this madman.

He thrust his face closer, spit flying from his lips. 'Kevin was cleverer than people thought. He had his eyes on me all the time Alan was talking. I saw the light dawn in that ugly rat face, and sure enough, the next day he phoned, offering to forget all about it for half a million quid.'

Simon's lip twisted. 'The fool. Always after money. He found out he was messing with the wrong man. No one blackmails me.'

Where was Max? He should be here by now.

Simon's hand gripped tight round Libby's throat, crushing her windpipe, his body pushing her hard against the sink.

She croaked, keeping him talking, 'Why would you kill Geoff?'

Simon bared his teeth in a grin. 'He double-crossed me – stole my work. We were supposed to be friends, colleagues, both of us struggling to make a living in music. I did twice as well as him, back then, writing advertising jingles while he messed about with 'serious music'.'

Fury distorted Simon Logan's face.

'Then, he had a mental block. He was stuck. Couldn't write a note more of his quintet, the one intended to take the music world by storm. Like a fool, I helped him out. He was a mate, you see, and he swore he'd share the credit.'

His hand gripped until Libby's head swam. Her breath came in short gasps. If Max didn't appear soon, it would be too late.

Simon's eyes turned glassy. 'No one cared about Geoff's work for years until, suddenly, he was offered a job writing a film score. It made him famous. Before long you heard his stuff everywhere. He toured Europe and America, and then, like a magician, he produced that long-lost quintet. The critics loved it and he lapped up the praise.'

He whimpered suddenly, like a self-pitying animal. The sound chilled Libby's bones.

'He never mentioned my name. Not once. I couldn't prove I'd written it. Who would have believed me? He was the maestro, the famous composer. The worst of it was, he employed me to perform it. As a favour to me.'

Tears streaked down Simon's face. His voice shook. 'We were friends and he cheated me. He'd already stolen Angela from me, tempted her away and married her. I had nothing left and he had everything. He deserved to die.'

He smiled into Libby's face, 'And so do you.'

The doorbell rang.

Libby screamed. 'Max!'

'He's too late.'

The doorbell kept on ringing. Max hammered on the door.

Simon laughed. 'The door's too solid. He'll never break it down.

Still throttling Libby with one hand, he brought his other arm round from behind his back. Something glinted in the light.

'Stop!'

The shriek came from the door to the hall.

From the corner of her eye, Libby saw Mandy.

'Stay there,' she gasped, but Mandy ran, screaming like a banshee, grabbed Simon's arm and twisted it round behind his back.

With one hand still at Libby's throat, he couldn't throw Mandy off. The syringe fell from his fingers and shattered on the floor.

Simon swore, his grip on Libby's throat loosening a touch.

She grabbed the sleeve of his jacket and with all her strength, held on.

He raised his free arm to strike her, but Mandy was back, the chocolate grinder in her hands.

With a crash, she brought it down hard on Simon's head.

He fell heavily, awkwardly, cracking his face against Libby's cherished marble floor tiles, and lay still.

Mandy and Libby looked into each other's faces, aghast.

Mandy whispered, 'Is he dead?'

At that moment, the glass in the kitchen door shattered and Max's face appeared.

Hysteria bubbled up. 'You're too late,' Libby croaked, and slid to the floor.

Mandy ran to the shattered kitchen door and let Max in.

'It looks as though you've managed perfectly well without me,' Max complained, as Libby sat with her back propped against the wall, grinning like an idiot.

Max checked Simon's pulse, found he was still breathing and rang 999. 'You two are no good for my ego. You didn't need me at all. We should restrain him, though, just in case he wakes up.'

Libby searched in the drawers and pulled out a handful of plastic ties.

Max took them. 'Perfect.' He clipped Simon's wrists together behind his back.

'Not too tight,' Libby said. Max looked from her to Simon, smiled and pulled the plastic tie a notch tighter.

Libby scrambled to her feet and hugged Mandy. 'I'd forgotten you were even in the house.'

'I was fast asleep for hours. I never heard a thing. Then Aunt Angela sent me a text and woke me up. I was about to ring for a taxi when I heard your kerfuffle in the kitchen, so I ran downstairs—'

'And saved my life.'

Mandy blushed. 'Always happy to help, Mrs F. Now, look.' She tilted her phone so Libby could see the screen.

Steve awake. On the mend. He'd love to see you.

Mandy's smile threatened to split her face in two. 'But why was Simon Logan attacking you?'

'He wanted to kill me, like he killed Kevin and Vince.'

Max pointed to the broken syringe on the floor. 'I imagine the police will find that's full of digitalis.'

26

ORANGE DRIZZLE CAKE

Joe arrived with Constable Ian Smith in tow, as Simon began to rouse, twitching and cursing. Ian Smith rammed a pair of handcuffs on the man's wrists. 'Though, to be honest, Mrs Forest, your plastic ties work just as well.'

Simon squirmed, face twisted with fury, lips curled in a snarl. Every sign of the courteous gentleman had vanished. PC Smith dragged him to his feet and shoved him into the police car.

'We'll need statements from each of you,' Joe said, 'but they can wait. I want to hear what Mr Logan has to say for himself first.'

Max had an arm round Libby. She didn't object for her legs felt distinctly wobbly.

Max still seemed confused. 'I don't understand much of this. Why did Simon Logan poison Kevin and Vince and try to kill Steve and Libby? None of it makes sense.'

Libby leaned against his shoulder. 'I think I understand most of it,' she said, 'but we need to talk to Angela. She's involved.'

Mandy's hand flew to her mouth. 'I forgot. She sent another

text. She's going to the local history society meeting and she told me to ask you to bring the cakes.'

Libby laughed. 'Cakes. Just what we all need. Max, I bet you've never set foot in a local history meeting.'

'I'm game for anything. Let's go.'

* * *

The meeting was in full swing as they arrived at Marina's house.

'Darling,' she cried, 'thank goodness you've arrived. We're all dying for cake. We'd given up on you and I was just about to break out some old custard creams, instead. You've saved us.'

They trooped into the beautifully elegant drawing room. Chesterton Wendlebury's bulk spread over both seats of a two seater chesterfield. 'Mrs Forest,' he said, 'I'm so glad to see you. After our little incident, I realised I had my days confused. My meeting isn't until tomorrow. So, I turned around and followed you into town.'

He chortled loudly. 'I must say, dear lady, you're impossible to catch on the road. I never knew a little Citroen like that could travel so fast.'

Libby's cheeks burned. Did the man realise she'd been racing to get away from him? That twinkle in his eyes made her wonder.

She let Marina take the orange drizzle cake, slide it onto the waiting plate and hand it round, neatly sliced. Marina wriggled into the space next to Chesterton. Libby glanced at Angela, who raised an eyebrow. Had no one else noticed how much time those two spent together?

In the corner of the room, the society's longest-serving member, Beryl, flicked through a sheaf of papers. Libby's heart sank. Was Beryl about to give her long-anticipated talk on the history of the post office?

There was only one way to escape it. 'We thought you'd want to know we've discovered who poisoned Kevin Batty and Vince Lane and tried to kill Angela's nephew, Steve.'

In the hubbub of gasps, guesses and questions that greeted the announcement, Beryl gave a weary sigh, folded her notes and slid them into a battered brown handbag, snapping the catch shut with a click.

Marina raised her vigorous contralto above the rest. 'Come on, Libby. Stop milking it and tell us.'

'It was Simon Logan.'

As the noise died down, she explained. 'I was very stupid. You see, because two members of the cycle club died and several others were taken ill, it was easy to think the poison was meant for everyone. In fact, Kevin Batty was the only intended victim.'

Libby watched her audience. Each face betrayed surprise, excitement, confusion, or a mix of all three.

'Simon was very clever. He'd brought digitoxin, ready for Kevin, to the picnic, but when I delivered the sandwiches that day, he saw a chance to cover his tracks. He took them all from me.'

It was embarrassing. Annoyed with Max for keeping secrets, for not trusting her, she'd been easily flattered by Simon's attention. He'd rushed over as soon as she arrived, but he hadn't been at all interested in Libby. He was just keen to get his hands on the food.

Libby kept her face turned away from Max. 'Simon had plenty of time to add poison to the food. Just a little from his syringe in a sandwich here, or a cake there, so that most people swallowed some.'

She thought back to the scene at the water's edge. It had looked so innocent. 'He wanted to make sure Kevin died, and poisoning the food wasn't enough. It was just a cover. Simon injected a huge dose of poison straight into Kevin.'

Someone asked. 'Wouldn't the pathologist find marks from the syringe?'

'I puzzled over that, too, until I realised Alan Jenkins had given me the answer, quite by chance. When I was in the garage, Alan grazed his hand. He told me it happened all the time and he showed me his hands – they were covered with cuts and scrapes. Kevin loved tinkering with classic cars, like Alan, and his hands would be just as battered.'

Libby was thinking aloud. 'All Simon had to do was wait until the first effects of the digitoxin in the food made Kevin ill. While he was nauseous and woozy, Simon injected him with a full dose, positioning the needle on the site of an old graze. One little needle mark would be almost impossible to find among the scratches on Kevin's hand. Simon was a cool customer.'

Marina frowned. 'I suppose he had a mouthful or two of the poisoned food. Just enough to make himself ill. No one suspected him at all. I can understand how he made sure Kevin died, but why Vince?'

'Later, I met Vince's neighbour. He told me Vince had a heart condition and took medication. I bet Vince's medical records show the doctor prescribed a form of digitalis to keep his heart regular. The dose from the sandwiches, combined with his regular tablets, gave him a fatal overdose. Vince's death was unintended – an accident.'

Libby suddenly remembered something else Vince's neighbour had said. 'Members of the club used to visit Vince when he first had trouble with his heart. Simon was in the club – he'll have been in the house. He could have gone to the bathroom, found Vince's medication and helped himself to some. He didn't need to go to the trouble of collecting foxglove leaves. All he had to do was crush Vince's tablets and dissolve them.'

Angela shivered. 'You've told us how he managed it but not the reason. Why on earth did Simon Logan kill Kevin Batty?'

'It goes back ten years, I'm afraid, to the day your husband died.'

Angela gasped; her face suddenly pale.

'I'm sorry,' Libby said. 'No one suspected foul play when Geoff crashed his car, because he was driving far too fast.'

'That's true,' Angela whispered.

'Simon Logan had loosened a steering tie rod nut on Geoff's car, making it steer erratically, knowing Geoff would eventually go too fast and crash off the road. He could have tampered with the car any time – maybe several days before the crash. All he had to do was wait. No wonder he was certain he'd got away with it.'

Angela's knuckles were pressed to her face.

Libby swept on, keen to finish the story. 'One day, Simon was in the Lighthouse Inn with Kevin and Alan, and they got talking about the old days and their favourite subject, cars. Alan mentioned the loose steering tie rod nut on Geoff's Porsche. Simon Logan was shocked. He'd got away with murder for years, and assumed he was safe. Kevin saw his face and jumped to the right conclusion. Unfortunately for Kevin, he then tried a spot of blackmail. I imagine Simon played along, maybe even made a payment or two, all the while plotting to kill him.'

Max put in, 'We all know Kevin was brighter than people gave him credit for and he certainly loved money.'

Angela was shaking her head slowly, dazed. 'I don't understand. Why would Simon want to kill Geoff? They were friends. At one time, I thought they'd be partners, but then Simon went off to make money from his jingles. Why did Simon hate my husband?'

27

BACK IN BUSINESS

If only Libby didn't have to tell the whole tale. She'd give anything to leave matters there, but Angela deserved the truth.

She sighed and let the words tumble out. 'Simon killed Geoff out of jealousy, partly because you married him instead of Simon.'

Angela flushed scarlet.

Libby braced herself to deliver the final blow that was going to break her friend's heart. 'Simon did nothing about it at first, and they stayed friends. After all, Simon's career was solid, while Geoff had yet to make his mark in the world. He even helped his old friend out. But then Geoff double-crossed Simon and stole his work. It was the last straw.'

All the colour drained from Angela's face. 'Stole his work? What do you mean?'

'You remember the different style of writing on the last few pages of Geoff's manuscript? It was nothing to do with a sprained wrist, or tiredness, or anything like that. It was Simon's writing. He composed the music. Geoff had a block and he couldn't finish the quintet, so his friend did it for him.'

Angela walked over to the window to gaze out towards the smooth green knoll behind the house. Her words were strangled when she spoke, as though her throat had constricted.

'It's true Geoff was having a few problems. He told me once he thought his creativity was drying up, but then he seemed to get over it. If only I'd known he was struggling.' She twisted the cord of her glasses, tying it in knots. 'I never realised. Oh, Geoff, why didn't you tell me?'

Libby said, 'He asked his old friend to help him out. Then, by the time he was famous, he'd convinced himself it didn't matter that the work was Simon's.'

Angela scrubbed at her eyes; the ball of tissue close to disintegration. 'I knew Geoff could be selfish. His work always came first, but I would never have believed he'd let his friend down like that. How could he be so dishonest?'

Marina heaved herself off the sofa to offer Angela an expensive, scented handkerchief.

'And the attempt on Steve?' she reminded Libby.

Libby thought back to the scene at the rehearsal:

Friends, enjoying the sun on the patio,

Mandy getting her rival drunk,

Simon explaining how Geoff always drove too fast.

'Steve was there when we talked about the manuscript. How the writing was different from Geoff's. Simon told me about Geoff's accident. He must have been trying to put me off the scent. I was getting too close, asking about Kevin, then talking about the manuscript.'

Her shoulders sagged. 'That was when he decided he had to get rid of me. First, he tried to deal with Steve, who remembered Geoff's accident so clearly. Simon knew that one day Steve would put two and two together, as Kevin had. It must have been easy, driving up close behind Steve, forcing his motor bike off the road.'

Angela blew her nose.

Libby continued, 'The police will discover a match between the scrapings of paint on Steve's bike and Simon's car. After that, Simon came to finish the job and kill me. He would have succeeded, too, but for Mandy. She's the real hero of the day.'

Angela's damp smile wavered but she said, 'Mandy's quite a girl, even if she does her best to put everyone off with those awful tattoos.'

Libby opened her mouth, then closed it again. No need to tell anyone of her suspicion that Mandy's tattoos were fake. The girl was entitled to a little deception.

Libby's phone rang. She slid it out of her pocket and pressed the green button. 'Mandy? Is everything OK?'

'More than that. Frank's no longer under suspicion and the bakery's opening again tomorrow. Frank says, please bring plenty of chocolates because he's contacted the press and they'll all be there in the morning. Oh, one more thing," Mandy coughed. I'm sorry I pointed you in Simon's direction. I got him all wrong. Maybe I'll stay out of the dating business for now."

* * *

Ali rang that evening. She gave a blow by blow account of the journey to South America, complete with love-struck declarations of Andy's kindness, cleverness and street-wisdom.

As her phone battery was dying, she asked, 'Anything exciting happened in Exham, Mum? Did you solve the great food poisoning mystery?'

Libby took a deep breath. No point getting Ali in a flap, not when she was on the other side of the world. 'It's all sorted out. Fuzzy and I are having a quiet evening. Enjoy yourself.'

With Simon safely in police custody, charged with at least one murder, and the bakery due to open tomorrow, the future looked suddenly bright. Only Angela was left saddened by the revelations about her dead husband. Libby would call round to see her, soon.

It was late by the time Libby put the finishing touches to the batch of chocolates. Proud, she counted the trays and the pile of cardboard ballotins. Tomorrow, they'd be on sale at the bakery.

Every single member of the local history society had put in a huge advance order.

Max had brought her home after the meeting, trying to persuade her to get an early night and promising to meet next morning to walk Shipley and Bear on the beach.

Libby waved him off, glad they were friends again. No matter how maddening the man could be, she knew she could turn to him when she needed help.

Friendship was quite enough, for now. She was ashamed to think how quickly she'd succumbed to Simon Logan's false charms. So much for her proud boast of independence. Her powers of intuition obviously needed a reboot if she wasn't to fall for every attractive killer she met.

The cat stretched out on the sofa, catching the last rays of sun. Libby poured a glass of wine, curled up beside Fuzzy and stroked the soft head.

Who knew what would become of Max and Libby in the months to come? He was still investigating AJP Associates. Pritchards were innocent of Kevin's murder, but they were still in Max's sights for fraud and money laundering, and he'd be off on his travels again soon, gathering evidence. At least he'd promised to leave Bear with Libby in future.

Libby still had to get to the bottom of Trevor's involvement. Maybe tomorrow she'd think about it. There were still loose ends to be tied up.

Tonight, it didn't seem to matter. Libby sighed, contented, pleased that Mandy would be back soon from a visit to Steve. For the first time, Libby felt at home in this funny little seaside town.

She buried her face in the cat's warm fur. 'I think we'll stay in Exham on Sea a while longer, Fuzzy.'

ACKNOWLEDGMENTS

I count myself lucky to live in Burnham on Sea in Somerset, a hidden secret in England's glorious West Country.

When I set out to write the Exham-on-Sea mystery series, I used the lighthouse in Burnham as the first location.

I changed the name of the town as I would hate any of my neighbours to imagine I'm writing about them. Not all the characters in the Exham-on-Sea books are as lovable as Bear, the enormous sheepdog.

Just as it takes a village to raise a child, so it takes many people to publish a book. I've been helped by many friends and family, especially my long-suffering husband.

My publishers, Boldwood Books, have done a great job with the recent make-over for the series, so I'd like to thank all of them for their help and support.

Most of all, I'd like to thank my readers, whose enthusiastic support has been wonderful.

MORE FROM FRANCES EVESHAM

We hope you enjoyed reading *Murder at the Lighthouse* and *Murder on the Levels*. If you did, please leave a review.

Sign up to become a Frances Evesham VIP and receive a free copy of the Lazy Gardener's Cheat Sheet. You will also receive news, competitions and updates on future books:

https://bit.ly/FrancesEveshamSignUp

ALSO BY FRANCES EVESHAM

The Exham-On-Sea Murder Mysteries

Murder at the Lighthouse

Murder on the Levels

Murder on the Tor

Murder at the Cathedral

Murder at the Bridge

Murder at the Castle

Murder at the Gorge

The Ham Hill Murder Mysteries

A Village Murder

ABOUT THE AUTHOR

Frances Evesham is the author of the hugely successful Exham-on-Sea Murder Mysteries set in her home county of Somerset. In her spare time, she collects poison recipes and other ways of dispatching her unfortunate victims. She likes to cook with a glass of wine in one hand and a bunch of chillies in the other, her head full of murder—fictional only.

Visit Frances' website: https://francesevesham.com/

Follow Frances on social media:

twitter.com/francesevesham
facebook.com/frances.evesham.writer
bookbub.com/authors/frances-evesham
instagram.com/francesevesham

ABOUT BOLDWOOD BOOKS

Boldwood Books is a fiction publishing company seeking out the best stories from around the world.

Find out more at www.boldwoodbooks.com

Sign up to the Book and Tonic newsletter for news, offers and competitions from Boldwood Books!

http://www.bit.ly/bookandtonic

We'd love to hear from you, follow us on social media:

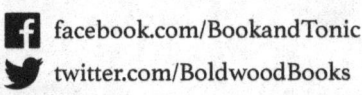

facebook.com/BookandTonic

twitter.com/BoldwoodBooks

instagram.com/BookandTonic